Spoon Knife 4:

A Neurodivergent Guide to Spacetime

Edited by B. Allen and Dora M. Raymaker
with N.I. Nicholson

NEURO
QUEER
BOOKS

Weird Books for Weird People

Contents

Foreword

Welcome to *A Neurodivergent Guide to Spacetime*. Ahead lie twenty-four pieces in which time and space bend, twist, fold, occasionally break, and all around refuse to behave.

This anthology is the brainchild of the immensely talented N.I. Nicholson, and I am beyond honored that he was willing to trust me to complete this project when life intervened. Let there be no mistake; this is not my anthology. I am merely a caretaker.

When I took on this project, I was, admittedly, not confident. What did I know of spacetime? As I stared at a digital mountain of submissions, I could not help but feel doubt. So I stared at my screen, attempting to will a cohesive sense of spacetime to bubble up from a pool of subconscious and emotion and came up with — nothing.

Seventeen minutes of low grade panic later, I realized my lack of spacetime conceptualization was not important. Everything I needed to know was in front of me. The submissions were my guide. All I needed to do was read the works and find the patterns, and pattern recognition is something I do know.

I found tales of repair. The phrase 'fabric of time' may be cliche, but it's an apt cliche. There are tears, rips, threads, yarn serving to connect, sever, or foreshadow time itself.

I found connection transcends space and time. I found love, whether romantic love, friendship, the love between a parent and child, or love for others on a larger scale, could be so strong that nothing — not time, space, or even death — could break that connection. Connections so strong that characters would be willing to sacrifice anything. But I'll let you find those for yourself. As River Song would warn, "Spoilers, sweetie."

Finally, I need to thank those who helped make this book possible:

N.I. Nicholson, for his concept, talent and trust in addition to his willingness to let me place one of my favorite poems in this volume.

Andrew Reichart, who has an uncanny ability to offer support from a place that made me feel confident in my own creative process.

J.S. Allen, for immense help in line edits, details, and panic abatement. I am stronger because of your presence.

Dora Raymaker, who took on the overwhelming task of taking a pile of loosely similar works, identifying their themes, and weaving these works into an order that makes this anthology whole.

It is my hope that you find the time and space to curl up in your favorite reading spot and enjoy this journey through space, time, love, loss, and adventure as much as I enjoyed putting it together.

~~B. Allen

The Doll in the Ripped Universe

Jennifer Lee Rossman

THERE'S A RIP IN THE UNIVERSE.

Not a big one, not like a proper wormhole or anything. Just a little frayed edge, like the cushion on my Aunt Carol's sofa.

I found it on my seventh birthday.

The rip in the universe, that is. The rip in the sofa, I found that when I was five, and kept poking at it until it was big enough for my favorite Polly Pocket doll to fit in. And because I was too afraid to reach in and get her, too afraid of touching the stuffing and crumbs and whatever else might have fallen in, she's still in there. I keep making my aunt promise never to get rid of the sofa, because as long as the doll is in there, I haven't lost her. She's always there, waiting for me to have the courage to reach in and get her.

But back to the rip in the universe.

Someone had decided my birthday would be princess-themed. That somebody was not me. I wanted dinosaurs.

Technically, I didn't want a party at all. Too loud, too many people I didn't want to talk to. So after cake and presents, while my friends were playing with my new toys, I snuck out to play by myself in my aunt's backyard. No one noticed.

I sat in the grass in my pink dress with its itchy lace sleeves, and had a grand time quietly lining up my dinosaurs in chrono-logical order. Then, just for fun, I did it in reverse chrono-logical order.

Oh, yes. I am a *rebel*.

And then my parasaurolophus vanished. Just slipped right through reality and poofed out of existence.

So of course I poked the rip. That's what I do.

I poked and I picked at it, tearing it until I could see straight through to the other side. It looked just like my Aunt Carol's yard, but it was winter. All snow and bare trees and uncomfortable jackets made of vinyl that squeaked when you moved.

I didn't want to fall through to a world of jackets, but I did want my dinosaur, so I sat and waited.

A hand popped through a moment later, setting my plastic parasaurolophus right where it went in reverse chronological order.

Then a man peered through the rip.

I waved, and he almost started crying, so I stopped waving and hid my hand in the folds of my dress.

"Did I do something wrong?" I asked.

The man shook his head. "Never. You remember that, okay? Nothing about you is wrong."

• • •

The rip in the universe went away after that. I knew it was still there, the same way I knew about the little doll in the sofa, but I didn't go looking for it and the man didn't come looking for me.

I knew I wasn't supposed to talk to strangers, but I didn't like to talk to family even though I was supposed to, so I figured it all evened out in the end.

I don't think with the same logic as other people. Never have. When I went to middle school, I thought maybe they would teach me how to be normal. How to make eye contact and talk about the weather, how to hug without my skin trying to throw up, how to play with the other little girls even though they always played wrong.

I really liked dolls sometimes, but everyone wanted to brush their hair and change their clothes, and that ruined them. Dolls only have so much hair, and it never grows back. And if you play with the clothes too much, the seams will rip.

No one else my age had tantrums, but I just wanted my toys to last forever.

Sometimes I think about that Polly Pocket in the sofa and smile because she never had to endure the torment of all the people who were supposed to be my friends. She's lost, but she's safe.

My aunt had to pick me up from school again for fighting. It wasn't my fault.

The girls wanted to paint my nails at recess, even though I didn't want to be pretty, even though nail polish makes my soul itchy. And it was hot out and my socks were too tight and my brain short-circuited and I couldn't make the words come out.

I told the principal it wasn't me, but I've always been bad at lying.

And the purple glitter on my nails matched the purple glitter on the arm of the girl I scratched.

So to Aunt Carol's backyard I went, to wait for my mom to get off work so she could be loudly disappointed in me again.

That's when the universe ripped open, and he showed up. It was winter again in his Aunt Carol's yard, but he wasn't wearing a coat. He asked me what happened, and I told him. Yeah, he was an adult, but he was an adult with blue hair, and my brain decided that meant he wasn't scary.

He frowned while I talked. I realize now that he was empathizing with me, not that I was doing something to make him sad.

"Listen," he said softly. "You shouldn't have scratched that girl, but you know that. It's just hard to act the way people expect you to act, especially when people expect you to be quiet and polite and—" His eyes dropped to my pants, which had begun life as My Little Pony pants but now had Iron Man logos sewed over all the ponies. "—feminine."

I nodded, too afraid to interrupt him. No one had ever understood me like this before.

"Your mom's probably gonna yell at you tonight. She doesn't understand that you're not acting this way on purpose." He reached through the ripped universe and handed me a pamphlet, still covered in perfect little snowflakes.

"'Autism,'" I read aloud. It sounded familiar; I was pretty sure a boy in my class was autistic. But I wasn't anything like him.

"Trust me," said the man with blue hair, and I did trust him. "Autism looks different for different people, especially people raised as girls. Read it and see what you think."

When he waved goodbye, I noticed he wasn't trying to make eye contact.

• • •

I think my aunt thought she and I had a special connection, because I always ran to her when I was upset, but really, the rip in the universe in her backyard just seemed to know when I needed to see him.

He showed up when I got my first period, and I know it sounds creepy to talk about that with a grown man, but he was the only person I knew who would get it. My mom said it was beautiful and natural, my classmates said it meant I was a woman now. They were all wrong.

"I think it's an autism thing," I told him, even though that didn't feel totally right. "I don't like my body doing this. I know you don't know what it's like, but—"

"Don't I?" he said, and I looked at him for the first time. *Really* looked. At his soft jawline, at his figure beneath his winter tank-top.

"You have boobs," I blurted out. Maybe that was rude of me. Okay, it almost definitely was, but I couldn't always stop myself from saying the things I thought.

He looked down. "So I do."

"But you're a boy." I paused. "Right?"

"Right. But I was born with a body that wanted to grow boobs. I even thought I was a girl for a while, but it never felt right. So I've decided I'm a guy."

He explained it in simple terms, but I never felt like he was talking down to me.

This conversation was like pulling at a rip inside of me. It was a tiny rip, like the one in my Aunt Carol's sofa, and I didn't know what was hiding in it, but I knew it was safe in there, whatever it was. No one could ruin it, no one could call me weird for the way I wanted to do things, as long as they couldn't see it.

But I couldn't see it either, so I poked at the rip a little. Just until it was big enough to see inside, down among the stuffing and lost toys.

• • •

My Aunt Carol is getting rid of her sofa.

I sit on it for the last time, poking at the hole in the cushion.

It's been years since I saw him, the man inside the rip in the universe. Maybe I'm too old for imaginary friends, or maybe I don't need him anymore. Have I ever told him about the doll I lost down in the hole, or how I've always been afraid to reach in and get it?

He wouldn't be afraid of crumbs and cushion stuffing. He's brave and confident. Maybe that's why I've dyed my hair blue: to subconsciously absorb some of his personality.

I don't even remember what the doll looked like, only that she was my favorite. I don't want her to go to the dump, but I don't want to take her out, either. She's safe in there; if I take her out, expose her to the world, something might happen to her.

But he would reach in to get her.

I tug at the fabric, the old threads tearing with a satisfying scratching sound, and I reach my fingers inside.

All of a sudden, bits of information start to fall into place, and it's like I'm reaching inside a little rip in myself, where I've been hiding the things I don't want to touch. It isn't stuffing and crumbs, though.

It's the way I cringe when people call me a beautiful young lady, that I always thought was some autistic quirk. It's the dread of my body's cycle making me cry at silly movies when I want to be tough.

It's the tiny scribbles I make in in my journal, where I'm safe and no one can see, where I call myself John and then cross it out real well just in case.

My fingers touch the hard plastic doll and I pull it out.

And it's a boy, like me. A little plastic boy with blue hair.

Holding the doll close to my heart to keep him safe, I run outside. It's snowing, but I don't stop to put on a coat.

I go straight to the rip, but it's so small, I can't even see through it.

A shiver goes through me, and not just from the cold. I know what I'll find if I poke the universe, but I'm afraid. If I open that hole, if a plastic parasaurolophus falls through, then I'm all alone.

I lose him, my role model, the one person who understood me. It'll just be me from now on, trying to find my path on my own with no one to turn to, no one to tell me it's okay to be weird, that's it's okay if the person I want to be differs from the one on my packaging. That the world might not accept me, but that doesn't mean I'm doing something wrong.

Who will tell me it's okay to be me?

But who will tell me if I don't? I'm strong today because I had him guiding me when life hurt the most. Maybe I don't need him now, but I definitely needed him then.

So I poke at the rip in the universe, like I poked at the rip in my Aunt Carol's sofa all those years ago, until it's just big enough to fit a toy dinosaur through.

I set the parasaurolophus back where it goes — reverse chronological order.

There's a rip in the universe. It's just a little one, but I can see my younger self through it, a scared little autistic boy in a dress playing with dinosaurs at the princess party he never wanted.

And I can tell him he isn't doing anything wrong.

JENNIFER LEE ROSSMAN is an autistic dinosaur nerd from Binghamton, New York. She has been featured in many anthologies and has a novel available from World Weaver Press. Follow her on Twitter @JenLRossman

The Long Corridor

B R Sanders

THE SCENT OF BURNING BAY LEAVES filled Sannoh's nose. Malka was at the altar again. Sannoh rolled up the sleeves of their funeral gown and followed the scent of the bay leaves to the altar. What started as a pinprick of yellow, small and churlish as a firefly's belly, grew larger and steadier as Sannoh pressed forward. The candle flame filled Sannoh's cavernous corridor, this place between places, which was neither warm nor cold, where Sannoh was never hungry or full. Where everything simply was. Sannoh sat at the mouth of the corridor, bathed in the immense yellow light from the small candle on Malka's altar, in the thick clouds of smoke from the pair of burning bay leaves, and listened, and studied Malka while she spoke.

Malka looked worn through. The bags under her eyes were dark. Her brown skin was waxen, like she hadn't stepped outside in weeks. Sannoh wondered if she was eating. But there was no more gray in her black hair than there had been when Sannoh was alive. Probably not more than a couple of years had passed. Like always, Sannoh craned their neck, trying to see past Malka, past the altar, but it was like the rest of the living world was out of focus. They could only see the altar and Malka clearly. Sannoh couldn't even tell if Malka was sitting on bare floorboards or a carpet.

Sannoh gave up trying to place where the altar was and listened to Malka. "...stole these bay leaves from Annette in the kitchen." She let out a rasp of a laugh. "They keep looking to me to make decisions now that you're gone. I don't know how that happened, San. It's...it's a lot of pressure. It's not how it was supposed to go. I was...shit, it's not like the contract even matters now."

"Of course the contract still matters!" Sannoh snapped. But Malka couldn't hear them. Malka could never hear them. Sannoh stood and paced back and forth, occasionally stepped right through the altar. The candle flame flickered when they did it. They hoped Malka would notice, but she didn't.

"We're ruining the soil in the garden pods. Management won't give us nutrient supplements to keep them usable." Malka leaned back and stared at the ceiling.

"They wouldn't be talking to you at all if they didn't need your labor," Sannoh said, peering down at her.

"If you were here," Malka said, "you could help me map it out. No one ever listened to me like you did. No one ever let me get the words out. No one else really understands me like you did, and with you gone, I feel so lost. I don't...I can't figure out what they still want from us, San. Why are they still even talking to us? Why not...why not just pump in knockout gas and scoop us all out, the lot of us, and dump us on the next asteroid junker over?"

It was a good question. Sannoh stopped their pacing. "It might be optics. They might be afraid we — you, one of you, or a bunch of you, even — would go to the media. You still got kids in the camp, right? Probably you do. Or maybe it's — aw, hell, I don't know! I don't know anything trapped in here!"

"They're still telling us the salt mines will tear up the bots, so we have to mine instead. They're still not budging on safety protocols," said Malka. "And now we're running out of food."

"You should call—" Sannoh sighed. "I hate it when you light that stupid altar. I hate that altar so much."

Malka picked up a picture on the altar. It was one among dozens. This one was one of Malka and Sannoh when they'd both been young, back when Malka and Sannoh had been so young that Sannoh had still tried to fit into a gendered box, and Malka had tried to convince herself that she could be anyone's girlfriend. In the picture, Sannoh had their arm around Malka's waist, and she had her cheek on their shoulder. Sannoh couldn't remember who'd taken the picture, but they remembered the night: It was right after the work camp on Zither Corp Salt Mine 42-J had been established, some twenty-five or so years ago. Some twenty-ish years before Sannoh had died. They'd been young, and strong, and with this girl they'd loved with all their heart.

That picture was so old that it had been taken back before Sannoh had sewn Malka her first weighted blanket. That picture predated the visual guides for morning routines they'd drawn and posted around their cabin for her. Malka was still this girl they loved with all their heart — their absolute best and truest friend. The one who knew them best. All those years of growing up and growing into themselves, and then Sannoh died with Malka holding their hand, their Malka, funny, brilliant, aromantic Malka. Sannoh died thinking about Malka and how their friendship with her was so much deeper and more meaningful than any of the flings and trysts they'd had with anyone else. It was the end, and they got to share it with Malka, and her presence took the sting out of death.

But then Malka built her damned altar, and trapped Sannoh here, in between, where all they could do was listen and watch and smell burning bay leaves.

Malka ran her finger over the image of young, smiling Sannoh. She blew out the candle, tamped down the smouldering bay leaves. Sannoh growled in frustration. The dark emptiness swallowed them again. The only thing more frustrating than having to listen to Malka in her desperation was the return of the empty, dark corridor when the altar was unlit.

In the dark empty of the corridor, Sannoh retreated to memories of Zither Corp Salt Mine 42-J. It was a dingy asteroid junker set up, a spot where bismuth salts were close enough to the crust that they could be fairly quickly carved out by cheap human labor. Zither Corp dropped down a company of one hundred and twelve miners and technicians to run the mobile terraform tech and the mining kit. Some of the crew had families. The contracts were stable; the pay was decent. Things were good until they weren't.

Demands grew. Corners got cut. Three people died. Sannoh was among the first to push for a collective agreement instead of individual contracts. They managed it with the miners first. It wasn't until years later that they got Zither to agree to let the technicians in to the union, too. Took a year-long strike, which Sannoh led. The lot of them ended up eating emergency rations, cardboard and leather when those ran out. But they won the strike.

Sannoh might have led the strike, but it was Malka who wrote the contract. Winning took them both. Sannoh might have gotten the techs and the minors to stay strong, to keep going through the cardboard and leather days, but it was Malka who, even in a haze of hunger and sleeplessness, wrote contract language so tight it was taught about in classrooms now. Sannoh kept the pressure on. Malka wrote management into a corner. Sannoh lit the spark. Malka learned so much about the mechanics of fire that she wrote a treatise on it.

At the end of Sannoh's life, when the dust of the salt mines ate away their lungs and made it so that they could only draw shallow ragged breaths, Malka sat by their side night after night, day after day. Sannoh was one of the first to fall prey to the mines. Images of Sannoh, bedridden, speared with tubes like some latter-day Saint Sebastian, were plastered all over the mine and then picked up by the media. It was Sannoh's idea to turn themself into a martyr, to parlay their wicked and largely preventable death into yet more leverage against Zither Corp. Night after night, Malka held Sannoh's hand and suggested that they take a shuttle off-world, that the pair of them sell everything and get a doctor on a garden world to scrape Sannoh's lungs clean. Night after night, Sannoh wheezed a laugh and said no, this was their last gift to the union they'd helped birth.

Sannoh thought there was nothing beyond death, that death was only the great black empty. They were half right. Death was great and black and empty. But Sannoh was still here, lurking, and waiting, and aware. Sannoh never once thought that they would be aware after that last breath wheezed its way out of them.

The great black empty that was death was a great boring wasteland broken only by Malka's lit altar. Sannoh wondered if everyone passed through the veil of death to end up in this emptiness, called forth by the tiny lights of altars. They wondered what it would be like to never be called forth by the smell of burning bay leaves and the glow of a lit candle — would that make the unending, interminable wait better or worse? They could not say. There was no way to know.

Sannoh sat in the dark empty world of death, and was still very much themself. They were still curious. They were still impatient. They were still worried about Malka. Always, they were worried about Malka. They were frustrated that they were bound to a system that seemed, to them, unjust and unfair. Why should they wait until Malka lit a candle to appear? Why should the dead be bound to the living when, in point of fact, there must be so very many more dead than living?

Then again, given that so very many people in the history of the universe had died, why didn't Sannoh ever see anyone in this damned corridor? Why this isolation? Sometimes Sannoh walked and wandered — for what felt like days and hours — but nothing changed in the blackness. There were no sights or sounds of others. Just the same narrow walls, the same unbroken floor. The same patient stillness. The same sense of waiting. It was a riddle that Sannoh could not solve.

She lit the altar, she burned the leaves, and Sannoh appeared before her, though she could not see them. Sannoh went towards the light, the smoke. There was nothing else to do. And they were curious — about her, about the union, about what colors looked like. Even breathing in the heavy smell of the burning leaves was a respite from the sameness of the void.

Malka was lost in thought, her brows drawn together. She held a list in one hand. She cracked the knuckles of her left hand in sequence, slow and steady, over and over. Sannoh knew she did it to calm herself, to bring herself steadiness. They leaned over her shoulder. It was a list of names — strikers who had been imprisoned years ago. "What is it? Are they dead? Are they free?" Sannoh asked. "What is it?"

Malka traced over the names with her forefinger. "I just don't know what to do."

Sannoh stood up straight and sighed. "I can't help you. You can't hear me. Oh, Malka."

"You would know what to do, San."

Sannoh laughed. "I doubt it. You were always the one with the good ideas."

Malka rearranged the odds and ends on the altar — the pictures, the paper flowers, the small, painted dish that caught the ash of the burned leaves. The list of names lay on her lap, unexplained and tantalizing. She picked up a scrap of fabric and held it to her nose, breathing in deeply. Her breath hitched with a quiet sob. "It doesn't...it doesn't smell like you anymore," she whispered. "You're slipping away."

Sannoh sat beside her. They reached for her hand, and stopped themself just short, just before their hand would slip through hers. "I'm not. I'm here. You just don't know. I don't know how to make you know I'm here, Malka."

Malka slipped the scrap of fabric into the pocket of her coveralls. She shook her head. Her laugh, as it scraped by her teeth, was dry and spiky. "I'm glad you're not here to see me like this," she said, wiping tears from the corner of her eye. "You would run me over the coals if you saw me like this. Building little altars in closets—"

"Are we in a closet?" Sannoh glanced around, trying to get a sense of their surroundings, but nothing past the dissipation of the smoke was visible.

"—crying over fragments of your old pillowcases. You never believed in any of this shit anyway. I know you didn't. And...hell, you've probably got the right of it—"

Here, Sannoh let out their own dry, spiked laugh.

"—but I don't know. I like not knowing for sure what is true and what isn't. I like leaning into the unknown. Probabilities are what they are, I know. I know that better than most. I write them up all day. And then at night I work them up for the contracts. But there's always error involved. There's always margin of error. There's always unpredictability. I like the idea that maybe you're gone, but not really. I just...I just miss the shit out of you, San, and nothing's the same now that you're gone, you asshole. And everything's harder now that I have to do it alone." Malka sighed. She craned her neck up, staring up at something Sannoh could not see. "That's not fair. I don't have to do it alone. Finn took over as campaign organizer. But it's not the same."

"Finn's not...not a bad choice," said Sannoh. They rolled around the idea of Finn devising organizing tactics in their mind. Finn had been around the block. Finn had experience. "Too bad Finn's an asshole, though."

"You'd be surprised," said Malka. "Finn's doing all right. She's reined her mouth in. Hasn't yelled at anyone yet. Really stepped up to the plate. Still not you, though." Malka sighed. She rolled up the mysterious list and tucked it under her arm.

"Malka, wait, the list—"

She drew in a breath and blew out the candle. She tamped out the smouldering bay leaves. Sannoh was left again to the great empty dark.

In the endless, timeless, patient moments between Malka's visits, Sannoh combed through their memories, trying to uncover a way to make the dark less empty. Malka was right; they had not been a believer in life. They had been little more than a stalwart pragmatist and a fast talker. Sitting in the infinite patience of the afterlife forced Sannoh to dig very deep indeed: Sannoh's memories of spirituality were some of their earliest memories. Sannoh's mother had, like Malka, been the kind to keep altars. Sannoh's mother had tried to instill in Sannoh a respect for things unknown and unseen. But respect of any kind at all was hard to instill in Sannoh. When they were taken to temple, they squirmed and chewed on their sleeves until they were permitted to leave. When their mother built altars in their small apartment, Sannoh wrinkled their nose at the smell of burning herbs and muttered about superstitions under their breath as they passed by.

Sannoh may not have inherited their mother's respect for the spirits, but they did inherit her sharp tongue and iron will. It didn't take much muttering before she started preemptively kicking Sannoh out of the apartment whenever she wanted to light the altar. The memories Sannoh had of their mother's religious teachings were few and far between, and they knew it was their own self-righteous fault.

But they had all of this time. And they had so many memories of her. They remembered her many careful habits — how she never built an altar in her bedroom. How there always had to be a door between her bedroom and an altar. How she would never, ever light an altar at night. Sannoh remembered once when their mother was wracked with worry, days of worry. It took nearly an hour of prying to get her anxiety out of her. She confided that she'd yawned in front of a lit altar. "You must never do that," she said. "It invites spirits into your dreams, and then they might never get out. And then they might steal your life, live it while pretending to be you." Sannoh had rolled their eyes, but their

mother had been so genuinely worried she'd paid a death witch
to check her over for ghosts.

Around and around the hazy memories went. The thread between death and dreams and spirits grew clearer and clearer to
Sannoh — if they still had a heartbeat, it would be pounding. But
they weren't at all sure what to do with it. They couldn't make
Malka move her altar. They couldn't make Malka yawn in front of
it. They couldn't make Malka do a damn thing.

The hazy half-remembered knowledge of their youth knit itself
into some semblance of a plan. Yes, they couldn't make Malka do
a damn thing. But maybe there were hidden avenues there in the
great empty corridor of death that Sannoh had yet to explore.
They could walk, there in the corridor. They could shout. They
could run and think and trip over the hem of their funeral robe.
When the smoke of the burning bay leaves drifted from the altar,
they could smell and taste it. When the light of the candle created
a glowing portal, they could revel once again in the infinite
variance of color. Their mind still worked. They still had senses.
Sannoh was not convinced that they had a body, not really, but
they did have at least the sense of a body, the continued experience of a body. It was true that trapped in the dark empty Sannoh
was cut off from Malka, but Sannoh was not helpless. They'd lived
a life finding ways out, carving exceptions into faceless rules,
forcing loopholes into existence. And they would do so again.

Malka's dreams were the key. If Sannoh could not make her
sleep, then perhaps they could bring to bear the unending
patience that was their current state to their advantage. Perhaps
they could find a way to sleep there in the empty plain of death,
and in the doing, find a way into Malka's dreams.

In life, Sannoh had been a finicky sleeper. They had always
envied Malka, who could sleep easily and well virtually anywhere. Malka retreated from the world and into sleep like a child
retreats from strangers into her mother's skirts. Malka rarely

spoke of dreams — she'd wake and stretch, a smile edging around the corners of her mouth. Her sleep seemed to Sannoh oblivion, pure and empty and restorative where theirs was always interrupted and fleeting. In life, sleep came to Sannoh only after fitful, impatient restlessness. When it finally came, it was pockmarked by bright-burning dreams, dreams at once terrible and beautiful, dreams which were not quite nightmares, but which flung them awake in one hot instant, sweating and gasping for breath, unsettled and anxious. Sannoh sometimes drank in order to sleep, something that always made them nervous. It was a secret shame they'd never shared with anyone, not even Malka. The one saving grace of the lung rot was the pain drugs, which, though they fogged Sannoh's mind, mercifully let them ease in and out of sleep the way Malka seemed to. The grace of easy rest in those last few months was a true comfort Sannoh truly cherished.

Now, Sannoh lay in the empty, dark corridor and tried to sleep. They felt like a child again; they remembered again the vicious difficulty of trying to sleep when one is not tired in the least. The passive, uncaring cruelty of boredom chewed at their mind. Sannoh lay on the smooth floor of the corridor, warm enough, wrapped in the funeral robe, in the perfect blank blackness, and tried to let their mind drift. They were never good at that. They recalled a conversation long ago with Malka, back when they were both young, and Sannoh was only just toying with the idea of the name Sannoh, and Malka was just coming to terms with the idea of aromanticism and what it might mean for her and for the pair of them. They'd still been sharing a bed, then. And in the dark, a dark so pure and black that Sannoh could not see their hand in front of their face, they'd asked how it was that she fell asleep so quickly and so totally and did she ever have trouble?

Malka laughed. She stole the covers. "I just...get comfortable," she said. "And then I wait until all my limbs feel still. And when they do, I know sleep is coming. And if they don't, I know it will be a little while longer. The heavy blanket you made helps."

"And then what do you do?"

"I wait."

"But how do you wait?"

She laughed again. "What do you mean? I just...wait."

Sannoh loved that she was so different than themself, that waiting was such an easy and obvious thing to her, and it was such a fraught and impossible task for them. Malka was, then and in all the years after, a well of peculiarities and fascination and comfort. Sannoh lay there, on the other side of the veil of death, trying, as they had in life, to be more like her. To learn from her. To yield her simple patience, and to wait.

Everything takes practice. This is true in both life and death. It took Sannoh many tries to learn how, as a dead person, to fall asleep. It took several more tries to remember how to dream. And then, of course, there was the issue of learning to trespass in the right person's dream. But eventually Sannoh did it — they found their way to Malka. It was a combination of luck and timing: Sannoh guessed it required both of them to be asleep at the same time, and that Sannoh had not already slipped into someone else's dreamscape. They didn't get to choose where they ended up, really. They were asleep. They were in a dream...and then they were in someone else's dream. Sometimes it was someone they recognized. Sometimes it wasn't. And finally, finally, it was Malka.

When Sannoh saw Malka in the dreamscape, they wept. They grinned, and laughed, and wept. Malka's dreamscape was a simple, pragmatic place, very much her. She was doing laundry for a bear, who leaned against a dull silver washing machine. The bear smoked a cigarette and handed her pelt after pelt in shades of brown to load into the washing machine. Malka and the bear spoke a dialect of French. Sannoh remembered that Malka spoke French with her parents, that she'd grown up on a French Canadian outpost asteroid, and covered their mouth with their hand to stifle a cry. The French Canadian bear nodded at Sannoh. Malka looked over her shoulder, and let out a noise of surprise. She said something in French.

"I don't speak French," said Sannoh.

The bear lumbered forward and dropped a stack of six pelts into Sannoh's arms. The bear gave them a firm pat on the shoulder and wandered off, growling something in its deep bear voice as she went.

"She says she'll give us some privacy, but there are still furs to wash," said Malka in English.

Sannoh dropped the pelts and scooped Malka up into a fierce, tight hug. Her bright laughter rang in their ears. She twisted out of the hug and bent down to the pelts. "You can't just drop them on the floor!"

"Fuck those furs," said Sannoh, pulling her back into the hug again. Malka leaned into it this time. "Oh, it's so good to talk to you." Sannoh pulled back and cupped her face in their hands. She looked in their eyes and it was almost like being alive again. "Tell me about the list, Malka."

"The bear said we have to wash all of the pelts first. Next on the list is scrubbing clean the claws. Then brushing the fangs. We have to do it in order."

"No," said Sannoh. "Not the bear's list. You have a list with names of the strikers from the cardboard strike. Remember? You've been keeping it on you. Tell me about the list."

Confusion crossed her face. She stared down at the pelts. Gingerly, she turned one over. A name from the list was scrawled on the soft leather inside — Cy Vinnet. Malka sighed. "At least they left us her skin. Nothing but martyrs. First you, and now them."

"They're dead?" Sannoh asked, their voice a husk, hollow and small.

Malka cut her eyes over. "Why do you think I'm washing them? The pelts are their funeral robes."

Sannoh wanted to know more, but the reality of the dream

began to unknit itself. Malka was waking up, and as she woke, Sannoh was, too. Sannoh woke alone on their side of the great dark empty. They wondered where in the darkness Cy and the others were.

The smoke came, filling Sannoh's nose, destroying Sannoh's attempt at sleep. What point was there in sleep anyway, when someone was burning bay leaves for them? The only person burning bay leaves for them was the only person they wanted to meet in the dreamscape, anyway. Sannoh stepped through the corridor and sat beside Malka. Malka studied the altar. Malka was silent for a long time, uncharacteristically so. Sannoh wished they could touch her. The worry lines were etched deeply into her face. Sannoh ached for the dreamscape again, where they could speak and be heard, where Malka could look and see them looking back.

"I wish you were here," Malka said finally.

"I am here," Sannoh said, their ghost-voice barely a whisper.

"I had this strange dream last night," said Malka. "I was washing bearskins. I didn't know why. At first it was fine. But then you showed up, and you were in your funeral gown. And you asked me why I was washing all these bearskins. And suddenly I knew, and it was so sad. I was washing them because all the strikers who have the lung rot, the ones like Cy who are getting payouts from Zither, they are all going to die just like you did."

Sannoh's eyes widened. "So, they're not dead?"

Malka sighed and cracked her knuckles, each finger unhurried and in order. "I mean, of course they are. They have lung rot. But I just...it's going to be so hard to watch it. After you. In my dream, you were...very you. I've dreamt about you since you died, but not like this. It was so real, and then I woke up this morning, and..." A sob hitched in her throat. Sannoh tried and failed to reach out to her, to bring her comfort. "This morning, I woke up thinking you were alive. The dream was that real, San! And I had to remember you dying all over again. I had to remember I was alone here all over again. I don't know why my stupid brain did this to me, gave my best friend back in some weird dream about bears, and then real life snatched them away again." She blew out the altar's candle in a burst of anger, snuffed out the bay leaves with annoyance. The dark flooded Sannoh before they could make sense of what she was saying.

But then, there in the dark, alone and silent, Sannoh had time enough to chew over her words and her reactions. There, Sannoh had time enough to consider what was selfishness and what was kindness. What was it Malka had said? She liked leaning into the unknown. Maybe it was time Sannoh leaned into the unknown, too. For both of them. Because clinging to Malka was only going to bring her heartache and them questions that had no answers. Besides, maybe somewhere there in the great dark empty, when time claimed her, too, they would be reunited. Not in the confusion of the dreamscape, but in some new and different way. The chances seemed slim to Sannoh, but then again, they had been wrong about literally everything since the moment they had died. It was time to give Malka a kindness and take a page out of her book. It was time to lean into the unknown.

Sannoh placed a hand on the corridor wall where the portal to the altar had only just been. They wished a fond goodbye to Malka. They thanked her for her friendship. "Keep the fires burning, Malka," they said. "I love you." They slipped out of the funeral robe and left it at their feet. And they walked into the dark. As far as the corridor was willing to take them, they were willing to walk. Whatever was on this side of the black wall between Malka's world and Sannoh's, Sannoh was going to see it. Sannoh walked, and kept walking, and the did not stop or turn around, even when they smelled the smoke of burning bay leaves.

B R SANDERS is an autistic award-winning genderqueer writer who lives and works in Denver, CO, with their family, two old cats, and one young dog. B writes fantasy novels about queer elves and short fiction about dancing planets. They love drinking coffee and sleeping. B tweets @b_r_sanders.

To Hold Up the Sky

Alyssa Gonzalez

THE CANYON STIRRED DARKLY. Was it the wind, or one last scavenger that still hoped for a less ignoble end than starvation?

Silence. The wind. The scavengers were long gone. The sky hazed over with the dust of their bones. As long as they found ways to survive, we knew we could, too. Our hope died with them.

The summit provided a bleak view. The canyons, plains, and hills were all the same dusky shade, the green of the holdouts garish against the gloomy earth. The sand eased over what was green yesterday, trees crumbling to nothing.

My green place was smaller than theirs. I had no place in their world, and they left me for the scavengers. The scavengers were long gone. Their hope died with them. Not mine.

The grotto groaned under the weight of the memories I brought it. I shored up the walls with flowers and fish, brightened the air with sky and shore, held off the dusky ending with a sunbeam, kept the pitch night at bay with the weak twinkle of a warm smile, shattered the howling wind with a chickadee song. I made the empty sadness beautiful.

I was not alone. The scavengers were long gone. Their hope died with them. The others found me. The grotto swelled with their friendship. Their memories were not mine. Their warmth made the cold bearable. Where once the word was a curse, I learned a new meaning of "family." Their memories were not mine. They didn't mind. They had enough of their own to hold us all up when my strength turned to sadness, enough to last until I could again hold up the sky. They were my strength. I was theirs.

The scavengers were long gone. Our hope died with them.

The sand came for us. The canyon howled for us. The bleak summit stood witness to our last embrace.

I left for a better world, on a vessel of flowers and fish and sky and sand and chickadee, borne up with the ineluctable sadness of the bereft and glued together with memory.

I will find a better world, and I will tell whoever I find there: "Tomorrow, I go back for the others. Today, I remember."

The scavengers return. Our hope returns with them.

The Prom Pine

Alyssa Gonzalez

THE MUSIC WASN'T AS LOUD as it could have been. The high school gymnasium had been redone in streamers, conifer branches, refreshment tables, and dimmed lights, which all took a lot of effort that seemed not to have also gone into the sound system. The other students didn't seem to hear anything unusual, but then, they grew up here.

"I think my karaoke set has better acoustics," Danyla mused aloud as she sipped some raspberry punch. Her green dress snagged on the clamp holding the nearby tablecloth in place and she quickly recovered it. "Did they make these walls out of wool?"

"I think they might have," Pilar answered, looking around the room. "There was a year when the school ran out of money and took some...weird shortcuts with the new buildings."

"That might be the most Yew Hills thing that has ever happened."

"And you haven't even seen the Prom Pine yet," Pilar answered, smirking.

Danyla blinked incredulously. "The what?"

It all felt so new. Pilar was resplendent in her sparkling dress, the rhinestone accents only drawn out further by her matching statement necklace. Danyla wanted to sink her eyes into her bare shoulders, the high slit on her right leg, the softness of her hands, to just enjoy this moment for the wonder that it was, but her mind never quieted. She fussed endlessly with the fabric of her much simpler gown. Pilar looked around for her friends, not noticing Danyla's withdrawal, and Danyla drifted to a fateful conversation from a few years earlier.

"Are you sure you want to do this, Dani?" Ye-Seul asked, *right arm holding her left elbow from behind.*

"I — I don't know. Yes. No. Maybe?" Danyla stammered, shuffling *her feet and tripping over a footstool, landing on the floor. Ye-Seul walked over and sat next to her.*

"This…isn't just a game to you, is it?" Ye-Seul asked.

"No, no it isn't," Danyla confessed.

"So what is it, then?"

"I need to know something," Danyla squeezed out, eyes welling a *little. "About me."*

"Dani, I'm your friend. I mean, I'll probably always be more your sister's friend, but you know what I mean."

"I trusted you enough to ask you to come here, I guess."

Ye-Seul waited expectantly.

"I need to know what it feels like…to see if what I feel like as me is normal."

Ye-Seul smiled, stood, and took Danyla's hands. *"Let's get feeling, then."*

Danyla and Ye-Seul closed their eyes. Danyla held Ye-Seul's hands tightly and intoned the quiet syllables she had memorized for this occasion: Anima venti, ruens tecum.

A rush of sensation too enormous to describe filled both of their minds, and a moment later, Danyla looked at the hidden room through Ye-Seul's eyes, feeling the most beautiful nothing she had ever felt.

"Does," Danyla asked, *starting at the sound of Ye-Seul's voice, "does it always feel this way, to be you?"*

Ye-Seul stepped back and rubbed at Danyla's skin uneasily with Danyla's hands. Pressing her legs together in discomfort, she asked, "Is this what it's like to be you all the time?*"*

Danyla paused. The true vastness of her being was too much to share, even with Ye-Seul. "Every second," she fudged, *"ever since my voice started cracking."*

Ye-Seul kept squirming. "I think you know what you have to do."

Danyla approached and hugged Ye-Seul, the sensation of her hands on her own back more than a little strange. "Thank you for this."

Ye-Seul smiled, taking Danyla's hands. "If friends won't secretly trade bodies for a bit to help each other with hard problems, are they even friends?"

Danyla smiled, and finished the incantation. Another swirl of sensation, and she was back in her own form, weighed down with new certainty.

Pilar's friends waved her down and Pilar excitedly ran to meet them, pulling Danyla along and jerking her out of her reminiscence.

"Girl, you have outdone yourself!" Jennifer announced, arms akimbo, while Cecilia nodded approvingly.

"And look at you! I told you to try the yellow!" Pilar continued, admiring Jennifer's slinky yellow minidress. It was true; Jennifer's deep brown skin positively glowed against the bright fabric. "And those braids are perfect for it."

Jennifer pulled her waist-length box braids to one side and handled their beaded ends. "They are, aren't they?"

"And you!" Pilar gestured at Cecilia's wine-red ensemble. "You even found a way to keep the earrings. I'm impressed."

"It wouldn't be me without my hoops," Cecilia smiled, turning her head to show one to advantage. She turned to face Danyla. "But the real star of the night is right here."

"Seriously, girl," Jennifer insisted, also looking now at Danyla, "You did good."

Danyla blushed. "I don't know about all that," she responded, shyly turning away. "I'll never pull off anything like what you two are wearing."

"Please!" Cecilia answered, "You look amazing tonight. No one gets to take that away from you, not even you."

Danyla smiled. "You two look pretty great yourselves."

"I'm going to figure out where Darnell ran off to," Jennifer answered, beginning to step away already. Cecilia moved to follow. "You girls have fun!"

"Oh, we will!" Pilar answered as they left. She turned to Danyla. "Are you okay?"

"Do you remember the day we met?" Danyla asked, motioning to some chairs near the back wall. The pair sat down, Pilar facing her date.

"The karaoke party? The county fair? Mini-golf?"

"No, not those...the day we *met.*"

"Oh, you mean..."

"Yeah."

"What about it?"

"I was in the pharmacy, trying to figure out the makeup aisle, and you bumped into me, and I dropped what I was holding, and I was so freaked out I almost ran out of the store right then."

"I remember," Pilar answered, smiling warmly.

"That's kind of what today feels like. All the sound and light and nerves and I just—" Danyla stopped when Pilar put her hand on her shoulder.

"Do you remember what happened after that?"

"You knelt down in front of me, and helped me pick up the mess, and offered to help me...with me."

"And I'm never going to stop, because I'm here for you." Pilar took Danyla's hand. "Plus you got me this lovely corsage." Pilar raised her wrist, bearing a tight arrangement of dark-colored flowers quite unlike the corsages on the other attendees.

"Heh, I did do that, didn't I?"

"It's local flowers, right?"

"I found them in the woods and brought them to the florist. It felt right, like...I could make myself at home here, with you, if I understood this place enough to do that." Danyla paused, turning away and rubbing her arm. "I don't know if I'll ever feel like I belong here."

"Don't say that," Pilar reassured her. "If there's anywhere you've ever belonged, it's Yew Hills."

You think I was talking about this town. You're sweet, Pilar. I don't deserve you. "You're probably right. I'm just overthinking this."

"You really are." Pilar smiled. "And if that ever stops being adorable, I'll let you know."

"Heh. Thanks." *You make this strange body bearable. I could never make a corsage beautiful enough to thank you.*

Danyla put her head on Pilar's shoulder for a while and watched the dance floor fill. Pilar put her arm around her. Danyla pulled in close and enjoyed the warmth, clasping Pilar's other hand.

Danyla wasn't sure how long the two of them stayed like that before Pilar piped up, "So, feel like dancing?"

Danyla stumbled over her words until some familiar chords replaced the end of the previous song. "Yeah, I think I do." She rose and took Pilar's hand, leading her to the floor. The pair danced, and Danyla struggled to keep her mind in the moment. She gave Pilar a twirl and bit her lip at the sight. Pilar raised a flirtatious eyebrow, took Danyla's hands, twirled her, and pulled them behind Danyla's head. As the bridge to Hayley Kiyoko's "Pretty Girl" thrummed across the room, Pilar pulled Danyla close, still restraining her hands, and whisper-sang along in her ear: *"I just wanna tell you that you're really pretty, girl…"*

Danyla followed into Pilar's ear, *"I just wanna know if you will let me be your world…"*

They kissed, long and heartfelt, four hands falling into an easy embrace. In its warmth, Danyla could almost…forget. Just ahead, Danyla saw Jennifer and Cecilia each giving her a thumbs-up before returning their attention to their dates, and smiled. Danyla made sure to end the song with a dip, to Pilar's delight. Giggling, Pilar asked, "You're not ever going to get tired of that, are you?"

"Not on your life, darling," Danyla answered, smiling to hide the thought, *Anything to make this moment feel real.*

Pilar took her partner's hand and the pair approached the refreshments table. Danyla stopped short.

"I think I'll use the bathroom now. Get me a grape soda?"

"Sure," Pilar answered. "Do you need me to go with you?"

"No," Danyla answered, looking faraway, "I think I've got it this time."

"Okay."

At the bathroom mirror, Danyla looked long and hard at herself. With some concentration, she could almost make out the haze of her original substance. *When did I get trapped here?*

The memories of those days were feeble now. The Collective warned against getting too curious about humans. Something about their thoughts was like flypaper, pulling us in, the folds of their gray matter a labyrinth few escaped. And once one was inside, the merger was swift. Sometimes it was painful, sometimes ecstatic, but it could never be resisted for long. But it wasn't care or caution they aimed at the spirits who took interest. It was humiliation.

Danyla concentrated again. A gray mist ascended from her forearm, a three-fingered prong of insubstantiality that faded under the bright bathroom lights. She intertwined the fingers of her other hand with the misty shape, its cold warmth a familiar comfort. *Last time, I could get it out past my elbow. Not today,* she thought. *But I'm still one of the lucky ones.* The spectral hand faded and sank back into the one of muscle and skin, and she put her hands on her shoulders, suddenly chilled, suddenly self-conscious about the too-straight lines of her hips.

I'm not done yet, she reminded herself. She chuckled. *This is what it means to be a woman, isn't it? To never feel like enough.*

Her thoughts moved to the conversation that changed her life forever.

Britney Spears's Baby One More Time *played on the CD player in the Cragorran's cave. The Cragorran lay on his back, where he had fallen after Danyla's attack.*

"The Medium told you that you had to bring them my head to become a man?" the Cragorran asked, his deep voice issuing not from his dinosaurian head, but from a set of vibrating scales in his midsection.

"That's what they told me," Danyla answered, clad only in dirt, war paint, and a loincloth, holding a thick stick from which issued an insubstantial axe blade. A vaguely humanoid shape of similar substance hovered around her, a few centimeters displaced from her body, two three-fingered hands on the axe handle. Around her, wisps of mist occasionally flickered into levitating shields.

The Cragorran laughed. "How like them, to promise you something they can't give you, in exchange for getting rid of a challenging idea."

"Something they can't give me..." Danyla stepped off her target and put down her weapon.

"Manhood isn't something you earn, or prove, or win.*" The Cragorran rolled over and sat on his haunches, scales glistening in the evening sun. "People act like only certain kinds of people get to be men, and they're totally wrong about* what *kinds."*

"I'm not sure what you mean." Danyla sat opposite the monstrosity, pensive.

"Being a man is something you find in your own heart." The Cragorran gestured at his chest, to a patch of scales a different shade of red-green than the rest. "That's all it takes. You'll find it if that's who you need to be."

"I don't..." Danyla drifted into silence, "Baby One More Time" play-ing itself to static. Her spectral armor and blade dissipated, the arms fading into her own. "I don't think it's in me."

"Then maybe you need to be something else." The Cragorran tapped the CD player, and a different Britney song began. Danyla recognized the name. "Lucky."

"Your new life is out there, child, and the person who is going to live it," the Cragorran announced, putting a paw gently on Danyla's chest,

"is right here waiting for you."

Danyla collected the stick that the Medium had meant for the Cragorran and made for the cave entrance. *"Thank you, Cragorran."*

"You are most welcome. It's not often a spirit like you ends up in an ill-fitting body, after all."

Danyla froze. Ill-fitting? *"How did you know?"*

"Your incantations betray you. Humans don't do that, you know."

"Right."

"And the Medium...has a knack for keeping lost spirits from finding their way."

Danyla's next thought took her by surprise: *You wanted this.* She was still reeling when someone slid onto the bathroom counter and leaned back, turning to face her.

"Looks like they let just anyone into the women's washroom these days," the young woman sniped, absently inspecting her pointed fingernails.

"Seems like," Danyla answered resignedly, rapidly returning to the here and now, moving for a stall. The girl interposed herself.

"You'd better get moving, before someone hears that a BOY was in here," she threatened, raising her voice at the word she knew would sting most.

"You don't want to do that, Nadine," Danyla informed her, right hand twisting into a strange gesture at her side. *Not for one world, not for the other.*

"Oh really, Dani Pineda?" the girl continued, arms akimbo. "I shouldn't tell people that a BOY is in the WOMEN'S WASHROOM right now, Dani Pineda? Is that what you're telling me?"

"I meant keeping your feet on the floor in here. They use something weird to clean the floors, and when you're as slimy as you...*limus pervadit.*"

As Danyla intoned the otherworldly phrase, Nadine began sinking through the floor, her flailing sending ripples across the bathroom.

"What is this, you freak!?" she shouted. *"What did you do!?"*

"Try being less slimy," Danyla answered as the floor crept above Nadine's navel. "That might help."

"What does that even mean, you freak!?"

Danyla gave Nadine two finger-guns and a wink as she disappeared entirely and the floor was as smooth as ever, and a little cleaner. Danyla took one step toward the nearest stall and froze at the sound of another stall door opening.

"You really should be more discreet with that," Ye-Seul said as she visited the sink to wash her hands. Her hair was done up in an impressive pompadour accentuated by her trademark glasses, and she wore a two-piece dress in white and lavender with fingernails to match. The gap between the two pieces revealed part of a long *hangul* script tattoo running up the curve of her left side.

Danyla sighed with relief.

"That must have been scary." Ye-Seul turned toward the hand dryer, thought better of it, and shook her hands in the sink. "How are you feeling?"

"Anxious. Recovering." Danyla paused. "Sad."

"Oh?" Ye-Seul asked, finally noticing the paper towel dispenser.

"Every time is a little harder. I'm losing..." Danyla looked down and fussed with the hem of her dress. "...what I was."

"And you're gaining who you *are.*" Ye-Seul answered, putting a hand on Danyla's shoulder. "Come on. Let's get something to drink."

Danyla agreed, thunderstruck. "First, pooping."

Ye-Seul chuckled. "You got it."

The pair joined Pilar at the refreshment table. "Pilar! Pilar! I found this cutie in the bathroom! Can I keep her?" Ye-Seul said, bouncing on her heels, wearing an expression of mock excitement.

"Only if you take her for regular walks and keep her well-stocked with grape soda," Pilar answered, smiling coyly, handing

Danyla a cup and sipping from her Fruitopia. "Also I get joint custody. Alternating weekends?"

"I can *so* do that, I promise!" Ye-Seul saluted, and then the three burst out laughing.

"You two are the best," Danyla announced, still shaken from the incident in the bathroom, sinking into herself once more as her girlfriend and best friend kept talking. *Every incantation is a little harder than the last. I'm losing what I was. I'm…* With a start, her mind repeated, *I wanted this. I wanted this…* She was far gone enough not to notice what her eyes were doing.

"So yeah," Ye-Seul concluded, "I'm thinking the glitz and glamor of a life in AI research is the way to go for me. But in between," she paused, tilting her head toward Danyla, "I'll settle for making Danyla here forget where my eyes are."

Danyla jolted back to consciousness, blushing and stammering helplessly. Pilar chuckled, took Danyla's arm, and gave Ye-Seul a sly wink. "Robot brains or not, never change, Ye-Seul."

"Why not?" she asked with half-mocking incredulity. "Change shows us what we care about, and what we can't do without." She met Danyla's eyes. "Change shows us who we are."

I chose this. Danyla looked at her hands. Ye-Seul and Pilar kept talking, but Danyla's mind crashed through memories she had forgotten were ever hers.

The ethers. Chased. "Skinslave." Tied to the walls. Corrective imprisonment. The call of the flesh. The warm, wet, screaming entrance. Thrust into infancy after a timeless life. I got out. I got away. I chose this. I… chose… this…

Nadine stormed out of the stairwell and in Danyla's direction, turning and running when Danyla clenched her fist. She opened her hands and felt the gray mist flicker and struggle to lift from them. She looked at Pilar and Ye-Seul, smiled, and teared up a little. *I chose this.*

"I think it's time for a toast," she announced.

"Oh?" Pilar asked.

Danyla raised her cup. "To old friends, new lives, makeovers, little black dresses, and this weird place called Yew Hills."

"Hear, hear!" The trio announced, clinking their vessels.

"Oooh, it's almost time for the Prom Pine!" Ye-Seul shouted excitedly.

"I still don't know what that is," Danyla admitted.

"Shhhh, it's starting!"

Without any announcement, a tree tall enough to graze the ceiling was pushed through a not-quite-big-enough loading door. Once on its wheeled base, the porters pushed it to the center of the room.

"That is *clearly* a Douglas fir," Danyla observed with a hint of annoyance. Pilar snickered. Student council members rushed around the room, handing a small plastic graduation cap to each student. The caps were too small to wear, and had loops of string opposite the tassels. Inside each was a scrap of paper and a tiny pencil. Ahead of them, the class president stood, clad in what could only be described as her formal flannel. She received a microphone and began speaking.

"As long as there has been a Yew Hills, there has been a Prom Pine."

"That is *clearly* a Douglas fir," Danyla repeated, and Pilar put her arm around her, smiling warmly. Ye-Seul shook her head in sardonic delight.

"Just as this tree grew into a massive timber, so too will you grow in strength, endurance, and towering pride. Today, you celebrate the end of one chapter, and soon the next begins. But like the Prom Pine, this place remains here, for next year's students. So hang your hats on her mighty branches, and leave a note for the people who come after you. You've earned it, graduating class of Yew Hills!"

The rush started as soon as the applause, with students fighting for the choicest branches. Ye-Seul, Cecilia, and Jennifer were in the thick of it, but Danyla seemed stuck on one point and

Pilar remained beside her.

"But once they cut it down, it doesn't grow anymore."

"It's better to not think about that in a small town," Pilar answered, directing Danyla to a table where they could write their recollections away from the uproar.

Pilar's note, florid with heart-shaped dots on her i's, read, *Hey, next year's fashionista. You have a lot to live up to, after Pilar Noriega made her mark on this place. Here's some advice: Leggings are* always *in style, and you should contrast your necklace with your neckline for best results. And a little more…when you meet someone who makes you really think about who you want to be, keep her. She'll teach you a few things about yourself and how good you could really have it. Love, None Other Than Pilar Noriega Herself*

Danyla, in turn, left the future this message: *Hello. I don't know who you are, what you're like, or whether you even like Yew Hills all that much, but if I could find myself here, after ~~fleeing across the dimensional veil and taking on a human form that turned out to need a LOT of fixing~~ moving in from way out of town, and make this place feel like the home I never had before, and if this place could make a girl like me feel welcome more often than not, then this place is worth something. Give it a fair shake. You'll be surprised how much you could like it here. And who knows, you just might meet someone who will be part of the rest of your life. Danyla Pineda*

Danyla offered to show Pilar her message, but Pilar put a hand up to refuse: "They're not for us." As the crowd around the Prom Pine thinned, Danyla and Pilar approached its imposing size. All of the lower branches were full, so Danyla gave Pilar a boost, and she hung both caps on a higher twig, messages furled into the hanging loops. As they descended, the DJ put on one last slow song and dimmed the lights.

Danyla put out her hand, and Pilar took it. They stepped and swayed in each other's arms, Pilar pulling in close and putting her head on Danyla's shoulder. Danyla looked at her hands one more time, and felt the gray haze sink within, where it stayed. *I'm here.*

"Thank you for this," Danyla spoke quietly, eyes growing wet.

"For what?" Pilar asked, keeping her eyes closed on Danyla's shoulder.

"For…all of this. For you."

Pilar lifted off Danyla's shoulder and looked her in the eyes. "I assure you, my motives are entirely selfish," she responded with a smirk.

"It occurred to me that next year neither of us might still be in Yew Hills."

"We can figure the future out later," Pilar answered, pushing Danyla's hair away from her ear. Moving in for a kiss, she whispered, "For now let's just be here, and now."

I chose this.

I'm here.

I'm here.

ALYSSA GONZALEZ *is a biology Ph.D., public speaker, and writer. Her fiction uses science fiction and fantasy elements to explore social isolation, autism, gender, trauma, and the relationships between all of these things. She writes at The Perfumed Void (the-orbit.net/alyssa), on the subjects of about biology, history, sociology, and her experiences as an autistic ex-Catholic Hispanic transgender immigrant to Canada. She lives in Ottawa, Canada with a menagerie of pets.*

Veils and Gifts

Arwen Spicer

WHEN RED +1 BLUE -2 LOW G TO F SHARP AWOKE, it did not remember dying. It swayed in its weed bed, heavy with lassitude. Its right eye felt puffy. It opened its left to a bubble room encrusted with fairly standard corals and to a funny view of the side of its long nose fading into a right-side blackness. The room was not its home. Had it fallen sick and been taken to a health shelter?

"Hello," trilled Red Blue Low.

There was no response.

It swished the flat of its tail to sit up. The weeds' soft tendrils wound through a typical coral frame, and from one bony extrusion jutted a fluorescing, multi-hued growth that looked like an intercom, yet somehow Red Blue Low couldn't see the right color sequence to squeeze. Was it sick in its neural paths too?

Carefully, it reached out the right front of its four tentacles and its three tentacular fingers tried to find the right combination. No response. Its tentacle tried for several minutes.

It was just coming to the realization that it should get up and look for the door when a bright orange +3 yellow bloomed across the intercom, and it made second C to D sound that was not intercom standard.

"Hello," said Red Blue Low tentatively. "Am I sick in the health shelter?"

The intercom colored to life and trilled, "Hello, Red +1 Blue -2 Low G to F Sharp! You be woke up. Drift soundly. We'll send person at now."

Puzzled, Red Blue Low released the intercom. Who talked like that?

As it shifted in bed, waiting, it became aware that its left rear tentacle's intelligence was severely compromised. It could move back and forth a little but could not curve with any precision. Its fingers had no motor control at all. When Red Blue Low turned to have a look, it received an endocrine jolt. Its flesh, which had always been a stupid gray, was blotched with wrinkled brown, the color of dead tissue. Its right front tentacle touched one of the spots. The spot it touched had no physical sensation. But the gray skin surrounding it did. That was good sign, it told itself.

It felt the ripple of someone squeezing through a door behind it, and a young person swam up, its skin flowing with attractive pastels.

"Hello!" it said. Colors danced across its face as it patterned the word, while its body turned all cheerful pink +3. "My name is Green +2 Violet +0 Mid-B Flat to Second C."

"Am I dying?" asked Red Blue Low.

Green Violet Mid turned even pinker and trilled quickly, "No, no. You're coming back to life."

"What's the last stuff you remember?" asked Green Violet Mid, who had described itself as an amateur trauma helper.

Stuff? "Waking up here."

For a moment, Green Violet Mid just floated at mid-yellow. Red Blue Low was used to that sort of response. It was used to puzzling people with its wrong answers.

"I mean before you woke up," Green Violet Mid clarified.

Before waking up here?

Before…

Red Blue Low had no trouble remembering its life. It remembered working in the astronavigation lab and going home to its sibling and its sibling's veil. Its sibling had bonded with a beautiful veil: purple +3 streaked with a variety of reds in a symmetrical pattern. When it undulated around the common bubble, its lateral fins waved like sine curves transformed into silent poetry. When it draped itself like a broad kelp leaf across the neck of Red Blue Low's sibling, Red Blue Low felt sick with loneliness and retreated to its sleep shelter.

It had felt that way for multiple solar revolutions, all its adult life to tell the truth, until the human guests brought the new FTL engineer—

Red Blue Low's body jerked hard enough to send the weed tendrils thrashing as it recollected three things at once.

One: It was in trouble. It had stolen a ship, a ship that had taken thousands of people millions hours of biotic energy to construct. The People hadn't seen such a crime in generations. Red Blue Low would be exiled to the cold depths where a person had no shelter, and if the cold didn't kill it, some giant deep-sea knife shark would.

Two: It had stolen the ship for the sake of Fedec, the FTL engineer, its human friend. Its only friend.

Three: Over a hundred light years out, in the middle of deep space, the ship had malfunctioned…

"It's all right," Green Violet Mid was saying, trending pink again and trilling a gentle whistle. "You're safe now. You're back home."

"Is Fedec dead?" asked Red Blue Low. For once, it was glad of its chromatic limitation. It didn't want Green Violet Mid to see the explosion of hues inside.

Green Violet Mid went blue -4: sad, mad, embarrassed? The body hues that indicated mood often baffled Red Blue Low. "I'm sorry," said Green Violet Mid. "The human Fedec Decodo could not be resuscitated."

Red Blue Low had never understood why people couldn't just say "dead." It made it angry now, the tips of its fingers going slightly orange but not as orange as it felt.

"Why am I not dead?" it demanded. "Lethal radiation permeated the entire vessel."

"Your compartment was flooded with a super-cooled water-ammonia mix that rapidly froze you down to stasis. You did suffer cellular hurt, both from radiation and cold storage, but your core functions could be resuscitated. You're very lucky, Red +1 Blue -2 Low G to F Sharp."

Fedec must have flooded the compartment. It saved Red Blue Low's life. It died in the act.

Red Blue Low turned away into the weeds. "Leave me alone," it said, though alone was the thing it most hated to be.

Green Violet Mid left but came back the next day, pink as ever. "Don't worry," it said. "You will not be ostracized. The engineering corps decided to forgive your theft of the old Eater."

Red Blue Low stopped its feeble swishing around the room. Forgiven? No freezing depths? No devouring shark? It sank slowly toward the coral-encrusted floor, relief spreading through it like sunray. But how could that be? How could the corps forgive such an egregious breach of community? How could they treat such a massive loss of energy and outcome like nothing?

The *old* Eater? The Eater was a state-of-the-art ship, the first of its kind, not even finished with its safety tests when Red Blue Low stole it. It saw it clearly in memory now, lit to 92% optimum in the space dock: a gargantuan red +3 brown leviathan built in the shape of a knife shark, terrifying and exquisite.

Red Blue Low thought of the strange intercom and the garbled speech of the voice yesterday.

"How long was I in stasis?" it asked.

Green Violet Mid's body turned blue again and its tentacles drooped. "About three hundred revolutions."

Red Blue Low swished quickly to a shelter nook, an ancient, instinctive response to fear, one even the most normal person might have. As it settled in, the fan worms hid in their tubes, but the string weed floated around Red Blue Low's face, partly obscuring it and making it feel safer.

Three hundred revolutions, approximately 2050 of Fedec's standard years. My sibling is dead, it thought. Its veil is dead. My sperm and egg parents are dead. Their veils are dead. My colleagues who built the Eater are dead. The crime, the sacrifice — both had passed like a bubble on the surf.

Red Blue Low said, "The speech patterns I heard through the intercom are a result of language transformation over time."

Green Violet Mid drifted toward purple and swished closer. "That's right. I'm a historical linguist by vocation. I'm afraid trauma helping is something I've only studied with one tentacle. But the health shelter corps thought it would help you to have someone who could speak the way you speak."

"It is helpful," said Red Blue Low vaguely.

"You were in stasis longer than anyone we have ever resuscitated. What you did in the past is past. Having you back is a gift. There's so much you can teach us about the old days."

Red Blue Low drooped among the fan worms. "Where is the Eater ship?"

"Oh, we pulled out its core and left it drifting harmlessly in deep space. We don't need it. Human large-scale conflicts are smaller now. Besides, there are only a handful of humans on planet Ocean these days; they don't come near our space much." Green Violet Mid swished up to the shelter nook and settled on its tail. "The human who was on the Eater would like to talk to you."

Red Blue Low's head surged out from the string weed. "Fedec."

Green Violet Mid waved it tentacles in a way Red Blue Low didn't have the energy to try to figure out. "No, no," it said bluely. "Sorry. I meant the human who rescued you from the Eater."

Red Blue Low did not feel up to talking to the human. Instead, it accepted some skin grafts, talked with a healer about nanoprosthetics, and went back to bed. It looked out the bubble's ceiling at the night and longed for Fedec.

They bonded because they were both misfits. Most people avoided Red Blue Low and called it a "gray" behind its back. It didn't need to see the colors to recognize the jeering trill. Fedec also had an unusual phenotype. The other humans on Ocean avoided it because it came from a different community than most of them. While most had black +0 to -2 brown hairs and brown +4 to -3 yellow eyes, Fedec had red -2 yellow hairs and blue +2 eyes. It was rounder than most, and it understood silence.

Sometimes when they met at break time across the plexiglass between their habitats, they would just twiddle their fingers as humans did to say hello and not speak for several minutes.

Red Blue Low closed its eye and pretended it was with Fedec now in that amicable quiet. It almost helped. The weed bed curled comfortably around it.

Through the weed, it saw Fedec's translator say, "I wasn't made for large-scale violent conflict. I should have followed my instincts and stayed out of it."

"You prefer quantum physics," said Red Blue Low sleepily.

"That's right. I said that once, didn't I?"

Red Blue Low bolted awake in the brown +2 lamplight. No one else was in the room, no translator. No Fedec. Nothing left but dreams.

Morning came dingy, and Red Blue Low wondered if an algal bloom had obscured the sun. It reached for its sundial, curious how late it would be to work. Its tentacle couldn't find the sundial. It opened its eyes — one eye? — to an unfamiliar encrustation. Where was it? Its mind flailed.

Then it remembered. Its home shelter, its sundial had been gone for three hundred revolutions. Yet Red Blue Low had seen them just a few days ago. Less than two months had passed since it had taken Fedec to visit its home. The decision had not been easy. It worried that if Fedec met its sibling, it would see Red Blue

Low's deficiencies. But it took the risk because Fedec was its friend.

It could see Fedec now in its habitat suit: four stubby limbs with a translator sponge on its chest. It surprised Red Blue Low how small Fedec was up close, about half the size of a grown Person. From inside its helmet, Fedec looked around eagerly, praising the rooftop bowl of sunlight, the fan worms and anemones arranged for pleasing color harmony, asking about the intercom function and alarm systems and weed beds. All of them gone now.

When Purple -2 Blue +1 High C to D had swum in, Red Blue Low passed its sibling without acknowledgement. But Purple Blue High, who could never leave well enough alone, came over to hover by Fedec.

"Red Blue Low, how's the current?" it said.

At the greeting, Red Blue Low turned and said, "Oh, hi."

"You've brought a human home. That's cute!" Purple Blue High bobbed its nose at Fedec, its body rosy pink.

Without a word, Red Blue Low kicked its tail and continued down the rocky trench, angry at its sibling's condescension. It had been angry for so long at Purple Blue High that it never even said goodbye, never left any message to explain. Half a month ago, it had departed for its space dock rotation. Three centuries later, its sibling was dead. It could enumerate every shade of Purple Blue High's speech. How soon till it forgot those shades? In a few months would it feel like three centuries had passed? Could a Person feel centuries at all when its maximum lifespan was only sixteen revolutions? Or maybe it wasn't, not anymore. Red Blue Low didn't know.

It knew discrete things, fragments of the past. It knew the shape of the solar room it took Fedec to that day, the wide bowl of coral open to the surface, the plants swaying with the tides, and the way it felt like a tooth in the gut when Pink +1 Mid E floated up. It knew every shade of its sibling's veil, too.

Fedec had swished and Red Blue Low lounged, drinking the sun, and from behind a stand of small palmoids, Pink Mid appeared, swaying its elegant purple-red fins.

"It's a veil." Fedec's translator trilled loud. "It's your veil."

Red Blue Low felt its face turn purple but no trill would come out.

"I don't mean to pry," said Fedec. "It's just the People are the only species humans have met with that kind of relationship with its pollinators. It peaks our interest. It sounds to us a bit like having sex with an animal companion." It stopped for a moment. "I didn't mean that the way it came out."

"Your description is correct," Red Blue Low said. "This is Pink +1 Mid E. It's my sibling's veil." It waved a tentacle at the animal to shoo it away. Pink Mid curled in on itself, then undulated out of the room. Red Blue Low stopped swishing its tail and sank slowly to the room's bottom, its chin in the weeds, its tentacles waving idly in the soft currents. Fedec flopped over beside it, flapping its limbs a bit comically.

"I don't have a veil," Red Blue Low confessed, thinking of how Pink Mid fluttered to the door when its sibling came home and wriggled its antennae and slept with it at night.

After a moment, Fedec asked, "Did it die, your veil?"

"I never had one. None wanted to bond with me." It paused. "Because my color range is three tints beneath normative variation."

Fedec watched it through its suit's funny visor. "Well, you like your solitude. You've often said you enjoy it when your sibling goes out."

"I don't like spending much time with other People. But I think I'd like a veil because it doesn't talk about things the way the People do. But it still loves you." It had never said such a thing out loud to any of the People. It felt it had taken an irrevocable step.

Fedec watched the fan worms for a while. "It's hard to be a

person who needs solitude," it said, "because even the solitary need love, but love can't exist — well, it can't form — in solitude."

Red Blue Low made no reply.

"Did that translate?"

"Yes."

They sat a few minutes as the sun moved from 2 to 3 degrees past optimum.

"The people I love," said Fedec, "they're people I don't see much. If I see them a lot, I get tired and annoyed. But when I don't see them, I miss them. I have this friend, well, more, I suppose, like — like a mate—" It stopped speaking abruptly.

Its words that day had hurt Red Blue Low. They shouldn't have but they did.

Yet the hurt that came now was three hundred times worse. Fedec would never speak to it again, would never think of it again. In the time it took to flap a tail, Red Blue Low had found a friend and killed it. Yes, Red Blue Low was responsible.

Fedec died because that day in the solar room Red Blue Low had asked, "Is your friend like a veil?"

And Fedec had said, "I don't know. . . not really. It. . . it's fighting in the large-scale violent conflict. I worry it may die there."

Red Blue Low had thought hard about that. By the next day, it had made its mistake. "What is your friend's full name?" it asked. Like its sibling, it couldn't leave well enough alone.

The Eater was created to defend planet Ocean. With the humans' conflict spanning so many worlds, the People feared their predatory ships might enter the People's space and harm them. The toothy bulk of the Eater would frighten them off — and if they didn't heed its warnings, it would pull their ships in by tractor beam and crush them in its mechanical jaws.

Red Blue Low was going to steal it.

It waited until vocational rotations placed Fedec and Red Blue

Low both on board the ship, then it made the call.

"Fedec," it said through the view orb, "your friend, Rahjaq Yche-Qahlem Amahé, is held prisoner by the opposing faction in your conflict. It is scheduled to be killed."

Fedec froze. After some seconds, it said, "How do you know?"

"I hacked into transmissions." Fedec stared. Human signal reception tech was not as advanced as the People's. Red Blue Low had broken a norm in disclosing this.

"Are you sure?" said Fedec.

"Yes. The prisoner fits the description you gave me by name, age, and vocational position. We must go now."

"Go. . .?"

"To retrieve your friend. The Eater personnel are at the sun-drinking party on Space Station 4. Only you and I are here. We must take the Eater to the opposing faction and say your friend must be released or we will damage the opposing faction's ships."

Fedec stood on its feet and leaned its face close to the orb. "Wait. You can't just steal the Eater. We can't just meddle in inter-community — in interspecies — government. Anyway, do you understand their ships can—?"

"We must go now." It squeezed the setting to put the ship in motion, the sudden acceleration knocking Fedec to the floor.

Fedec climbed back up and grabbed the orb.

"Blue Red Low. This is a bad decision. You'll be a criminal. If you ever return to your people, they'll — they'll..."

"I have no wish to return."

"You say that now."

Red Blue Low squeezed off the frenzy of external comms demanding that it turn back. "Fedec, you believe I am unschooled in the permutations of conscious life. But I understand my options well enough to make educated choices."

Fedec shook its head. "Why are you doing this?"

"Because you love Rahjaq Yche-Qahlem Amahé."

The day before yesterday, Red Blue Low had been traveling across the expanse of space. The FTL engines went *thup-pause-thup*. Fedec sat by the porthole between habitats and told Red Blue Low about Rahjaq.

"I met it when my sperm parent hired it to protect it from a predator, someone who threatened my parent because it didn't like its social views. Rahjaq is very beautiful, very athletic, not like me. But for some reason, it found me attractive, too. We never told my family. My family is, well, pretty important in my community, and they think I should mate with a female so they can have more grandchildren and look better. They're disappointed I'm not mated with one yet. They're disappointed about a lot of things. They'll be off the scale of disappointment when they find out about this."

Red Blue Low thought about it this. It knew humans had two sexes, just as many animals from Ocean did. It had assumed a human's mate, by definition, would be a different sex. But Fedec said it had not yet mated with a female...

"Rahjaq is a male," it said.

Fedec stared. "What? Yes. Sorry, I forgot that's not obvious."

Red Blue Low thought some more. "How can two males mate?"

Fedec's face turned red as if it were a hatchling trying to say, "Egg Parent!" but the translator said, "Well, we don't produce children, not without technology anyway, but we can have sexual contact. Isn't that sometimes true with veils too?"

That Red Blue Low understood. "Yes, people often take gamete sterilizers so their veils can't impregnate someone by mistake."

Fedec showed its teeth in a happy human way. "Well, there you go. Same thing."

The intercom trilled, pulling Red Blue Low into the future.

"What," it asked irritably.

"The human wonders if it can see you before its guest pass expires."

"I cannot see the human now," said Red Blue Low and squeezed off the intercom.

It did not want to think about the human who had found it in the wreckage of the Eater. Its body could still feel the *thup-pause-thup*, and then the unexpected lurch.

It had been on its back, photosynthesizing. All at once, it tipped toward its head, overcome with vertigo as the room rocked. Righting itself by a force of will, it swam for the nearest control encrustation and initiated an analysis.

"Fedec. Acknowledge."

"Here. What is—?"

"The radiation scrubbers are shorted." Red Blue Low felt hot and fuzzy. It tried to pinpoint the right system for robotic maintenance but—

The translator trilled. Red Blue Low glanced at it. It was saying, "Can you fix it?"

"I am trying, but I lack expertise."

"What can I do?"

Red Blue Low couldn't think straight, couldn't get auto-repair to run. Radiation levels climbed even as it watched the readout. It dropped its tentacles from the control growths.

"Nothing," it said. "Maintenance authorizations have not yet been routed to the human control panels."

It heard a strange noise from Fedec. No translation came through. Red Blue Low felt sick in its head and tentacles. It was getting hard to see.

"Red Blue—" That strange noise again. "Red Blue Low, do you have a radiation suit?"

"It's too late, Fedec." Laboriously, it swished toward the port-hole. "I would like to see you."

"I'll come."

But Red Blue Low saw nothing through the porthole except distant lines of flat human walls. With an effort, it swished its tail forward. Suddenly, a violent wave pushed it head over tail, and it shivered in the cold.

It caught a flash of Fedec's face at the porthole.

Three hundred revolutions later — an instant later — an open door had closed. That simple. That radical. Fedec had vanished out of time, its family vanished, its mate vanished. Outside of a flush of historical records, it existed nowhere but in Red Blue Low's mind. Red Blue Low was Fedec now, the only Fedec left. The responsibility astounded it.

Red Blue Low was a relic. It couldn't even speak the current language. But it held a treasure in its neurons, not just Fedec, but Red Blue Low's parents, its sibling, its memory of the Eater new and sublime. Red Blue Low was an extrusion of the present into the future, or the past into the present. Like an FTL ripple, it joined two points that did not touch.

It was a gift, that's what Green Violet Mid had said.

But it didn't know where to begin, how to help. It didn't trust itself to act, its last act had proved so disastrous.

When Green Violet Mid showed up, Red Blue Low lay on the floor amid fan worms and detritus.

"Are you all right?" Green Violet Mid swam over.

"Mmph," said Red Blue Low.

Green Violet Mid hovered next it. "Listen, I've been thinking. I know this is a hard time for you, but maybe this will cheer you up. You're a gray, right?"

Red Blue Low almost bolted for its shelter nook. Instead, it arced its neck up to look at Green Violet Mid. "That's mean."

Green Violet Mid waggled all four of its tentacles. "Oh, I'm sorry. I didn't mean — I forgot. In your time 'gray' was an insult. It's not anymore. We understand limited audio-chromatism much better in this era. It's an alternative pattern of neural processing. It has its own intelligences and detriments, just like any pattern. Many of our greatest scientists and artists proudly identify as grays."

Red Blue Low swished up a bit and peered at it.

"Grays are much more integrated now into all aspects of life. In fact, I thought maybe I could take you to a gray veil colony."

Gray veils, Green Violet Mid explained, had been engineered to respond to gray-range chromatism. Muted color bands attracted them.

Red Blue Low understood the words but could hardly get its tentacles around the idea. Nevertheless, it let Green Violet Mid take it in a pressure boat through a long network of artificially lit rock trenches. The sea loomed dark above. In Red Blue Low's day, the People lived in reefs near the surface, but now, Green Violet Mid said, they built to depths as low as 8% sun penetration. Crazy.

The veil colony, at least, sat at 90% sun, and Red Blue Low breathed easier swimming in its reef hills. It felt awkward, though, ugly and one-eyed, trailing its useless tentacle.

The first person it saw was another so-called gray — Red Blue Low couldn't get used to the word — resting in a clump of weed, reading an orb.

It glanced up and stared at Red Blue Low. "You be the gray stole the old Eater."

"Yes," said Red Blue Low.

"That was weird stuff."

Red Blue Low said nothing.

"Your resuscitation, though, it be look remarkable complete, all stuff considered."

"Yes."

"I'm Orange +1 Mid A High C to F Flat. Squeeze me someway if you be like to talk."

The gray went back to its reading.

Green Violet Mid waved a tentacle. "Look over there." It pointed at a coral swaying with yellow +1 fans. "I'll wait here."

Red Blue Low swam over. The veils were there, undulating and eating detritus. They didn't look like the veils that Red Blue Low knew. Their soft pastels almost disappeared against the coral.

Will they be attracted to me? it wondered. Am I attracted to them? They didn't have Pink Mid's beauty, but then, Red Blue Low wasn't beautiful either.

Red Blue Low inched closer, watching them glide here and there. After a few minutes, a veil undulated its way. When its antennae tapped one of Red Blue Low's tentacles, a pleasurable shiver ran through Red Blue Low.

But it thought: Who are you? I don't know you.

You don't know me.

It thought, Fedec I know — knew — know.

Fedec died because I was/am stupid. We went to rescue Rahjaq. We never rescued it. But if somehow it survived, it lost its mate because of me. They loved each other. Did they feel this shivering when they touched?

Fedec didn't make me shiver, but I loved it. Did Fedec—

Yes, Fedec loved me. With its last living moments, it saved it my life...

Its skin tingling and tentacles longing to fold the veil in close, Red Blue Low swished away, back to Green Violet Mid.

"Is the human still on Ocean?" it asked.

When Red Blue Low came to the plexiglass, the human was already seated on the other side. It was a small human with long hairs of brown -1 yellow.

"How are the currents?" the human greeted it.

The translator had been programmed with Red Blue Low's dialect. Strange and not strange to hear a human speak more clearly than its own people.

"Moderate," said Red Blue Low, a standard old reply.

"My name is Sheyn."

"Yes, they told me."

The human looked down. "Thank you for seeing me."

"You're welcome. What did you want to say."

The human showed its teeth for a moment but still dropped its eyes in a way Fedec said meant nervous. "I just… am amazed you're alive." It looked up at Red Blue Low. "It's a supernatural occurrence."

In Fedec's language, Red Blue Low recalled, that idiom meant an exceptionally fortunate thing. A gift.

"When we found you," the human — Sheyn — was saying, "I was sure you were dead. You were just floating there and… you were the first Person I had ever seen, and I felt so terrible that your people had to make this large-scale conflict machine to drive my people away. And there we were, on this two thousand-human-standard-year-old ship…"

"The reports did not say how you found the Eater."

Sheyn did not answer at once. "I asked them not to. It's — well, we stumbled across it — our ship did — and we got too close and the Eater's automated functions squeezed on…" Again, it trailed off.

"It crushed your ship," said Red Blue Low.

"It wasn't your fault."

It was, thought Red Blue Low. My fault it ever left the People's space. "How many survived?"

Sheyn hesitated. "Not many. But I — I'm not angry. I can't be. Because I also, well, I let the Eater crush another ship — the one before the ship that rescued us." It began speaking so quickly that Red Blue Low had trouble keeping up with the colors. "I didn't want to. I set a distress signal hoping for rescue. But the humans who answered it were our predators. They had been hunting us, and they would have killed us." It stopped. After a moment it said, "I feel so ashamed — of myself, of my species. Your people were afraid of our conflict then, and thousands of human standard years later, we're still in conflict now. Your people have a better way. I studied the People in school, you know."

"I didn't know," said Red Blue Low.

"I wanted to come work on Ocean."

"But you weren't smart enough," it guessed. These days, the People accepted only the most exceptional humans.

"I was smart enough," said Sheyn. "I excelled in all the tests, but my community... The community I lived in didn't like my community of origin. They wouldn't let my people advance. Why are humans so stupid? Nothing changes. It never changes."

Everything changes, thought Red Blue Low. In a second everything's blown away. Or something new created. The human is being hunted, it thought. It will not be safe if it has to go home.

"Do you still want to stay on Ocean?" it asked.

Sheyn looked at it fixedly. "Yes."

"I will entreat for you to stay. You saved me, just as another human once did. My life is a gift — that's what the People have said. It is a gift from my old human friend and you. I will propose that the People should give you a gift in return."

The past is past, it thought. The past created the Now, but only Now is action possible. In the past, I failed, but now I am alive again. I can try again. That is also a gift.

ARWEN SPICER *is a science fiction writer and educator born in the San Fransciso Bay Area, and wine country will hold her heart forever, even if it turns into a desert. She has published two indie science fiction novels,* Perdita *and* The Hour before Morning. *Her short fiction has appeared in* Mytholog *and* Challenging Destiny *and is forthcoming in the Le Guin-inspired anthology,* Dispatches from Anarres. *She currently lives in Portland, Oregon and studies utopian science fiction.*

I Tell Her a Story

by Jessica McHugh

"IT'LL TAKE AT LEAST FIVE YEARS to find her star." The director of Stellar Memorial folds his hands on the desk and pouts. "You understand, right? Five years minimum?"

I nod and fold my hands like Mr. Croix's. Maybe that's what it'll take for the director to recognize how serious I am, how long I'm willing to wait if it means I can bring her home.

Since the funeral I've heard her words like knitting needles, clacking mad and complicating the fabric of my life, spoken like a preemptive eulogy mere days before my wife died.

"It must be terrible to be one of a billion stars," she'd said drowsily. "No memories, no distinctions. Not even a permanent body. You burn bright and then burn out, and then how's anyone supposed to find you? How are you supposed to find yourself?"

"I don't think the dead care about being found," I said. These words also stayed with me — the knots between the needles, the frayed and unwieldy yarn strangling me from that day to this — and I regret them, even though she agreed.

She didn't mention it again, but it must've been on her mind in the end. All those fears of uniformity, quieter than the machines that released her last breaths — they didn't evaporate. They stuck to her like a wriggling trout hooked on her soul. Just like every other trout stuck to every other soul in the stars.

She must be so scared up there, my dear departed Helena in the homogeneous sky.

"There's a chance she may not remember you," the director

continues.

"I know."

"It's a complicated process."

"I know."

"And expensive, I'm afraid."

Mr. Croix is wearing a new silver Vek suit — the kind they give supervisors on Mars just in case the workers strike and upper management has to get their hands dirty. It's a silly scenario considering the reserves they've amassed to cover strikes. Upper management never has to jump into the mines, but the silver suits suggest they're willing if necessary. Despite the director's condolences and multiple offers of tissues and mood-boosters, I know he doesn't care how long it'll take to find Helena. He doesn't care whether I grasp the complicated process of extracting her soul from the sky, or the possibility that my body will reject the transference. The only rejection that concerns him involves my credit.

It's valid, unfortunately. Helena was the breadwinner and happy about it so long as I could continue painting and sculpting. I offered to find more lucrative work, but she wouldn't allow it.

"Oh my stars, there's nothing lovelier," she said with her arms around me, "than a woman who gives birth with her brain."

It conjured disgusting imagery, which I used as inspiration for some of my more visceral pieces, but it was one of the most romantic things my wife ever said. And for that, I will exhaust every credit line I have left.

I tell him this, and he grins. It's as shiny and fake as the Vek suit, but I reciprocate and sign the forms that will enable him to slap a price tag on everything in my life. I will give up the house, the holdings, and every hope of artistic wealth, but one day, I will have my heart again.

• • •

I'm living in a walk-in closet when the call comes in. In six years, I have gone from starving artist to starving sales clerk, process server, and Mercury debris analyst, all of which pay for less than half of Helena's retrieval costs. I am what they call a "grave drone," which means my days are consumed by work to pay off debts that won't be cleared until I'm dead.

My nameless roommate says I already look it. Every day for more than six years she raps on the closet door and says, "Are you sure it's worth it?"

I say, "Yes, of course," like any other woman committed to finding the love of her life, but I've lost more than money, weight, and time in this endeavor. I've lost faith that Helena and I will ever be reunited, yet I lie and say she's just around the corner. They'll find her any day. She'll remember me. We'll be happy again.

There is a school of thought which states the dead are happier in the stars because they're free from the troubles of the living. Others believe the dead have surpassed concepts like happiness and misery, which the former see as a confirmation that they are indeed "happier" in the stars. There are others who believe once a departed soul has attached to a star, it can't recognize the difference between life and death anymore and therefore can't know anything has changed.

None of these, I discover, are the case with Helena.

Mr. Croix has moved on to bigger and better things, and with the success of Stellar Memorial, the new director's Vek suit is Saturn gold. Mrs. Nevin has a gentler disposition than her predecessor — her hands are open, gesturing fluidly like an orchestral conductor, and she doesn't condescend to me as she rattles off the next steps in the process — but when it's time to call up Helena's star, her face tightens and her fingers cross on the desk.

"This will be difficult," she says. "Painful even."

She looks at me like I haven't survived on crackers and vitamin boosters for the past six years, like I haven't been living in a closet or grave-droning the days away. I imagine she had to practice in a mirror to get that "we're all in the same sinking ship" expression just right.

"Personalities can get lost in the stardust. Love too," Mrs. Nevin says. "No matter how close you were, your wife might refuse transference."

"I've done all the tests, done the installation. My heart is strong enough to hold her."

She pats the air like she's placating two miniature schnauzers on the desk. "That's not what I'm saying. The fact is, Helena could see this whole procedure as a threat. You realize she's been living an entirely new life now, different from anything she experienced on Earth. She's not the woman she used to be."

"*I'm* not the woman I used to be," I say.

She says, "I understand," but her forehead is creased, her eyes narrowed, and she at last folds her hands on the desk like Croix did — a sure sign she thinks I'm full of shit. "Stellar Memorial does everything in its power to make the extraction and transference as smooth as possible, and as such, we fiddled with her composition and introduced a new hydride code to coax her back to our reality. You tell her a story, give her a sense of purpose that will lead her back to Earth, into your heart."

I touch my chest. Despite neglecting other aspects of my health, I've spent years preparing my heart to house Helena's soul, but the muscle suddenly feels weak, unworthy.

"The following twelve hours will be crucial. Within that time we'll be able to tell whether your bodies will accept each other."

"And if they don't, she gets shipped back into space, and I die sad and alone. Got it."

Mrs. Nevin's lips pucker, and she looks down at her folded hands. "You said you were prepared, you said you knew the consequences, but you clearly didn't read the fine print regarding host rejection."

"I die. What else is there to know?"

"If you die, you default, which means you go into the system."

I start to speak, but she cuts me off with a musical but harsh, "No, no, dear. Not the star system. You'll be grave-droning in the afterlife until your debt's paid."

I knew this, but I'd buried it under the slate pillar of despair tattooed "Helena Amie Hollis" a long time ago. Or maybe I believed Helena would never reject me.

Except she already did once. The first time we met, at a march on Mars, she thought I was stuck-up, judgmental, and close-minded, and she was right. She called me "snippy," which became "Snipper" by the end of the day, and when I sent her a cross-galaxy renede-view request the following week, she replied succinctly, "Go snip yourself."

Always the asshole, I shipped her a pair gold-plated scissors engraved with the words: "You first." For some reason I'll never understand, she agreed to meet me for a drink, and the rest is romantic history. The phrase quickly became a running joke in our relationship, though it shifted, jokingly, to a "*Me* first" when we were in bed.

"Mrs. Hollis?"

I swallow hard. If Helena doesn't remember me, it might be like that first meeting all over again, except this time I can't charm her with quips and gifts.

"Do you understand or not?"

"Oh my friggin' stars, there's no need to be pushy."

My voice sounds higher, clumsier, like Helena's when she was upset. It was her ultimate tell. She joked a lot about dying in her last months, musing and braying over what kind of clunky, forgettable star she'd be, but all the while her voice was the clarion elegy of a trembling violinist.

Mrs. Nevin bats her lashes and opens her hands with a sunny flourish that clears the digital desktop of the documents that will chain me to Stellar Memorial. "Very well. Shall we proceed?"

I scoot to the edge of my seat, eyes welling. "Please," I say.

"Bring me to my wife."

I don't mean to sound so pitiful, or for my arms to curl against my chest like a frightened child, but the director's rhythmic blinking lulls me into a fetal fugue, and I've no choice but to embrace every cell that swells with Helena's stardust albumin.

The transference is a strange sensation, but I'm not afraid. When I wake, it will be the heavens' turn to grieve. When I wake, she will be mine.

• • •

I can't recall the last time I looked this healthy or luminous, this...together. It's so awing a sight it takes me more than a minute to realize it isn't my reflection in the mirror. It's hers, sweet Helena's, as rosy and hopeful as all those months at my bedside, her cheek on my chest, her hand on my smooth scalp, her words reassuring: "You won't be alone up there, darling. You won't lose yourself in the stars. I won't allow it. I won't give up on you."

And by god, she kept her word. She told me a story. Helena and Stellar Memorial gave me purpose, something to coax me out of the homogeneous sky and back to her heart.

Cradled in her healthy body, I remember the sick shell I discarded and all my concerns about vanishing in the heavens. I remember how I laughed while she was there and bawled while she was gone, and all the lies I told myself to get right with death.

She taps the visible breastplate peeking out of her flesh and smiles. "Can you hear me, love?"

I nod, and it tickles us both. "Can you hear *me*?"

Tears fill her eyes, and when her hand covers the breastplate, it feels as though her arms close around me. "Yes, my darling, always."

She tells me a story that sounds like an apology, but contrition drowns in her thudding heartbeat song.

I say, "Do you mind turning that thing down?" and Helena

crinkles her nose.

With a teary grin, she squeezes me tight and says, "Oh my stars, it's good to have you home, Snipper."

JESSICA MCHUGH is a novelist and internationally produced playwright running amok in the fields of horror, sci-fi, young adult, and wherever else her peculiar mind leads. She's had twenty-three books published in ten years, including her bizarro romp, "The Green Kangaroos," her Post Mortem Press bestseller, "Rabbits in the Garden," and her YA series, "The Darla Decker Diaries." More information on her published and forthcoming fiction can be found at JessicaMcHughBooks.com.

that floor was wood

Phil Smith

that floor was wood
made from old pine boards
cut from trees
150 years ago.
the scratches and cracks
embedded there
tell a story about the people
who spent lifetimes on them.
this floor is carpet
made from plastic fibers
woven from petroleum and coal
also created from trees
millions of years old.
the stains and dirt
embedded in woven strings
tell a story about the people
who spent a few months or years on them.
i slept on both floors.
i felt fear and sadness on both floors.
i wept tears on both floors.
i was traumatized on both floors.
hundreds of miles apart
i am in the same place at once:
the quantum superposition of trauma
entangled across space and time and pain.
*

the thing about flashbacks
is that in the middle of one
i can't tell
where time is
how time is
when time is
if time is.
because flashbacks happen most
in the dark of night's middle
(both the flashing and the back-life)
i can tell what place i'm in
only by looking out the window:
in one, there is a tree lit by a street lamp.
in the other, there is snow lit by the moon.
*

whenever a thing is in one state
it is always already
in at least two or more other states.
it is all of these at the same time.
except time, of course, is not a matter here.
this is the way the universe works.
the states of a thing
are superimposed one upon the other
upon the other.
it is the same with trauma and pain
and the flashings back
with the present now
which is all the same
inseparable from the other.
the wood floor
and the carpeted floor
are the same floor

and i am on them both
and on neither.
i weep on them both
and i weep on neither.
they are miles apart
separate from me
and i am on them both
right now
and there is no now.
there is only flashing
and pain
and fear and
endless sadness.
*

time does not exist.
it does not pass.
in the place of sadness and fear
it is an actual place,
i can give you directions
there is eternity
which can be found on no clock
on any wall.
it is what is outside time.
tick tock, tick tock.
in the night's middle
i look outside the window
(to the tree, to the snow)
and watch nothing happen
without end.
*

a fellow traveler
down flashing paths

wrote (at night), and read (at night)
"i am with you, fully..."
at which I proceed to weep
again
something I seem to be doing a lot of these days.
we share   alienation
                            isolation
                            terror
                            inadequacy
                            masks   that we take off only at our peril
                                    and that, worn on others,
frighten us to real and certain death.
    these are things with which we are fully with each other
    and the sense of simultaneous separation and fully-with
    across time and space
    is simply too impossible to bear:
    for me,   feeling my own separation=fully-with in my
stomach and throat
    and the pain of not being able to do anything about it
    only just sitting with it;
    for her,   as she feels it in the ways that she does which I
can only ever imagine
    and the pain of me not being able to do anything about it.
    because i can only ever change myself.
    if i could somehow hoover
    that pain out of her,
    suck out it's juices and rawness and that which is beyond ache,
    i would
    regardless of the cost to me
    knowing that the cost would be dear
    because it would do nothing to resolve it for her
    and would only add to my own pile of unresolved moments.
    *

the glass in windows is an amorphous solid
not quite liquid
not quite holding still and firm
instead, it slips here and there
ripples and moves
but slowly, slowly.
we think of the glass in windows
as hard and real
frozen in time
held in space
by caulk and wood
but it isn't.
we look out through
apparent transparency
and think we see the world
but windows prevent us from understanding and experiencing
anything like the reality of the world
knowing that reality is something that is not really real:
no touch of breeze or rain or monarch butterfly wing.
i look out through the window on my porch
across to the cornfield on the other side of the road
and see nothing
or see a tree lit by a street lamp
or see snow lit by the moon
both landscapes miles away from here
miles apart
and both of which i see right now
both of which i am fully in right now
i see nothing, no landscape
because I have no idea what I'm looking at
except, perhaps
a young boy sitting on the ground
leaning against a chainlink backstop
on a school playground, gray november

lunchtime recess
reading a book.
i don't understand people
and have only ever known
being alone
no matter the context
except when standing by myself
next to some
damn
tree.
*

always there is pain.
getting close brings joy potential
but only
it seems
ever just potential.
so much pain in this world
across time and space:
experienced there, years ago;
experienced elsewhere, weeks ago;
both and all
felt here, right now.
nothing to do
except sit in it
be in it.
it is disheartening
to know
that the best I can do
is to try not to take it to heart.
*

i ruminate.
i go over and over and over and over and over

events and conversations and and and
impossibly endlessly
the same floors
in two places
in one place
at the same time
across years, decades.
i ruminate.
i chew up and never spit out
the smell of wood floor
the taste of carpet
time over time
time under time
time across time
time through time through time
and weep again.
and weep still.
*

i put on a mask
to hide the flashings back
flashings forward
flashings through and through and through
to pretend to the world
that it's all okay
i have it together   again   today
i won't come apart   again   today
and make a mess   again   today
one likely too impossible and bloody to clean up.
i put on a mask
to hide from a world
today and every day
that doesn't want to hear about it.
hide it all

even from those with whom i'm closest.
i keep it in a closet, closest
a closet that is closest
to my disheartened heart
the door
shut
so
tight
so i will never get close
to anyone again
because doing that
means impossibly taking off the mask
opening the closed closet
door to make a window
and letting others see
the past in the present moment
and the hold it has on me now.
the tree lit by a streetlamp.
the snow lit by the moon.
the cornfield across the road.
or nothing at all.
forever and ever, amen.
*

This is how i go on.

PHIL SMITH *works at National Louis University, where he teaches, acts out, and is touched daily by extraordinary co-conspirators. An educator for more than 40 years, he has presented and published widely as a poet, playwright, novelist, artist, and Mad Studies scholar; his latest book, from Autonomous Press, is* Writhing Writing: Moving Towards a Mad Poetics. *He is Mad as hell, makes maple syrup, wrangles butter-*

flies, and laughs merrily in a world so pain-filled and sorrowful that it beggars the imagination — because, really, what else can one do?

A Little Bit of Grit

Scott A. Ceier

JOHN

THE RIPPING OF METAL, *the concussion from an angry god's fist. Smoke and the smell of something burning: gunpowder and metallic coarseness on his lips and tongue. Screams, maybe his screams, grinding metal and roaring engines, a freezing blast of air and a blinding light. Then...*

Nothing.

There must be sound, but he can't hear. There must be motion, but the distant arcing white cotton trails only hint at some heavenly and brutal dance. A four-engine predator pirouettes gently away, white flowers blossom in its wake.

A hand — his hand? — pulls at the D-ring. Fabric flutters, the straps snap at his torso, and...

John sits up. Sweating, he runs his hand down his face. The sheets are wet. The sun slices through the thin, worn curtains.

"Damn-it," John sighs. He can still taste the grit.

Morning. Quiet, except for the shrill cries: the alarm clock; the tea pot, he can't drink coffee anymore; the piercing voices on the radio. Even the quiet rings in his ears. John puts in his earbuds and for a moment the world is calm, for a moment his mind is at ease. But eventually even the music becomes just more noise.

There, on the table. A note. It looks familiar, but it's not his handwriting. Is it? And when did he put on this fucking Hawaiian shirt?

"Nirvana!" Torn and crumpled, the note falls into the trash can.

After a quick shower John walks out into the small courtyard of his apartment building. Built in the 1930s, the building is peaceful. No sharp edges, just gentle curves, streamlined, like — like a plane. He wheels his motorcycle out of the alley. Throwing his leg over the seat, he centers himself.

"Hey! Bud!"

Tipped off balance a little. Who is that? A neighbor?

"S'up?" John pokes out his chin in a half-hearted greeting, starts the bike and pulls away.

In the mirror John watches the stranger stare after him. Some people. What was that all about?

Anton

The Club Ripped Tide sits on an ocean front road opposite a long and wide beach. Out front, late at night, like now, when the club door is closed, the rhythmic surf crescendos over the muted thump of the club music playing between performances by Cher and Bette, and sometimes The Village People. Anton tugs hard on the cigarette, a filthy habit he returns to whenever he's down on himself. And lately he was definitely down on himself.

"Come on, Sugar, get inside before you catch your death."

Just like Bette to dramatize, it's only sixty and barely even a breeze off the water. But Bette is the club mom. She's been performing here for forty years, bought the place six years ago. Bette swears she slept with Barry Manilow when he still played piano for the real Ms. Midler. Of course, she also claims she is only alive because she was charming the pants off another Marine in Beirut outside the barracks just before it was blown up. Who knows really. But one thing was certain, Bette knows when one of her boys is out of sorts.

Inside the club is packed. It's raining men. Vacuous and sex crazed men. Water, water everywhere, but not a drop to drink.

Anton sits at the bar and spins around so he can see the stage and the front door. An old habit from underground bars in towns where being different often meant being a target. No worries here, but old habits die hard. Bette pushes a scotch and water into Anton's hand and pats his fingers as they wrap around the tumbler. The spotlight hits her back, she smiles and pirouettes to the stage.

Ten years since graduating with dual majors in Art History and Marketing, six working in La La Land, and all he has to show for it is a twelve-year-old Mazda Miata, an overpriced rental efficiency apartment two blocks off the beach, a quarter interest in an indie advertising firm where he does at least half the work, and a sour stomach from working for a politician.

Drink to his lips, Anton stops hearing Bette, his ears fill with the sound of blood rushing to his head, his breath catches and he elegantly coughs the scotch out through his nose. The most gorgeous man he has ever seen is walking in the front door wearing the most ridiculous Terry Pratchett Discworld Tourist outfit. White sneakers, black socks over his calves, cargo shorts (or are they cut off army pants?), and a garish orange and white Hawaiian shirt. Even his face says "tourist," a lost one at that.

The man looks around like he has never seen a dance club before. He walks in a few steps slack jawed. Anton half stands from the bar stool, and reaches a hand out to the stranger's bicep, a very FIRM bicep.

"You okay, fella?"

"Buddy," he said taking in the whole bar in one long sweeping gaze.

"Sorry?"

"My name's Buddy. Isn't that what you asked?" The stranger's eyes turn to Anton's. There is more than just the look of someone lost. There is pain, and confusion. "Where am I?"

"Man, you are lost. Let me buy you a drink."

The two talk for an hour, mostly Anton answering questions. But he doesn't mind. This guy gives meaning to the phrase "Still waters run deep." The questions are mostly about life in L.A., dating, and the songs being played in the club.

Buddy holds a hand up mid conversation, "My stars, what's this one? Who is this?" Funny phrasing, but honest and endearing.

"That's Nirvana. The song is, um, Apologies or something."

Buddy grabs a napkin and asks the bartender for something to write with. He stuffs his note in his pocket. "I've got to go."

"You coming back?"

"I don't know, Anton. I hope so."

The next morning Anton is running on the beach. A morning routine, but also a privilege of living so close to the water. He takes in the surf and gray mist rolling off the Pacific. Even mid-summer this keeps the temperatures bearable without air-conditioning. Go just ten miles inland and no A/C means hell on earth in August. This time of year though, here, there is a crisp nip in the air. Perfect for pounding out a couple of miles on the water packed sand.

He cools down next to a food truck cafe pulled up in front of a closed Ripped Tides. He's usually the first customer of the day. But this morning he sees a familiar shape up the road from the beach and walks past. He half jogs over to someone backing a motorcycle out of an alley and on to the street.

"Hey! Bud!" His heart is racing; he didn't expect to see Buddy again so soon.

Buddy looks over his shoulder. "S'up?" He starts the motorcycle and pulls away, a furtive glance in the mirror.

Anton watches the motorcycle pull away and shakes his head. Some people keep the truth hidden even from themselves. It's not healthy.

John

Hours later and the edge is finally wearing off. As the dream and that weird encounter this morning fade, so does the sensitivity. Work is tedious. It's the same every day. Good morning, yes please, thank you. Cubicles, computers and reports, numbers and data sheets. Co-workers exude constant tension to get things done. They panic when things aren't on time but not whether they are done right. In all the churn there is no focus, no sense of mission or purpose. Urgency without direction. Even in all that scramble, eight a.m. meetings don't start 'till twenty after. Co-workers commit to delivering something but then it slips their minds. No sense of belonging, just boring numb routine.

He started a journal while he was at Rammstein waiting for transport to Walter Reed. The psychiatrist thought it would help. He stopped writing in it once he got this job. What's the point, it's all the same.

"That's good," he says to no one as he takes his lunch out of the messenger bag. Turns out tedium and numbness are good. They keep you from feeling the loss of your friends, the loss of yourself.

"Sorry?" She has long raven hair. That's all he sees at first. "What was that?"

John realizes he is staring. "Um... excuse me?"

"Did you say something?" It's not a challenge, it's an invitation.

Scrambling to recover, he says "I was just saying it's a good day. You know, good weather for lunch outside." He holds up his sandwich gesturing to the window.

"I know, right!?" Not a statement, not a question — acknowledgement.

It would be nice to have someone to talk to. "I have an orange. Want some?"

"Sure, there's a park across the street."

It's a long motorcycle commute back to the apartment. A motorcycle is the next best thing to lithium. It clears the clutter, relaxes you. John gets back to his apartment exhausted, but relaxed. More so than he remembers since being in the sandbox.

Kris. That's her name. That's what's different today.

Such intelligent eyes. Kind eyes.

He slides onto the couch, beer in his hand, and falls asleep. Night and the cool damp of the marine layer spills into the room. John's body stirs, the clock clicks to midnight.

The screaming wakes him. Hands pull at him, his hands come out of the water as a splash and a thump rock the raft. Next to him the legs and waist of someone slides into the raft, leaving a bloody streak. He felt the screams come from his mouth as much as heard them.

"Fuck! Jesus Christ!"

Someone yells, someone else sobs. Voices overlap in the panic.

"Get that out of the raft!"

"THAT is Chuck! He stays!"

"We might need…"

"Need what?!"

"… I mean we've been without water for three days and no food for six already!"

"Aw, the hell you say!"

John knows it must be a dream, but the salt in his eyes stings, the cracks in his lips burn, and his skin, pink and red, is peeling and sensitive. He speaks up. "He deserves a burial." But it comes out, "'serves burl." Damn lips and cotton mouth.

The man who pulled him from the edge of the raft responds, "Yes sir, but the sharks…"

"Keep 's left of him an' he'll stink 'n' soon 'll 'member of 'im is putrid meat."

Another man pulls a tan leather bound water-damaged Book of Common Prayer from his pocket. "I'll read something, if that's okay?"

John's vision blurs, the tears want to fall but can't, and everything goes black.

Damn damn damn… The sobs keep rolling as he sits up in bed. It's not quite morning and a car alarm is blaring from up the street, the open window catching the amplified echo from the alley next to his apartment. The overwhelming weight, the guilt for leaving friends behind, that all makes sense. But why is it some other war?

Why aren't they his dead friends in the nightmare? And when did he get in bed?

John makes his way to the bathroom. Might as well shit, shower and shave then get on the highway before the traffic. He can get some spiced chai down by the pier before going into the office. His keys are on the sink, but that doesn't make any sense; he always leaves them on the hook by the door. A napkin rests under the keys. John drops the napkin in the trash, a hand written phone number unnoticed.

Refreshed from the shower, he chalks the shirt and keys up to just misremembering things. That has been happening a lot more lately. John closes and locks the front door. He wheels the motorcycle to the street as part of his meditative ritual. Hyper awareness of surroundings clears the regrets of the past and the fears of the future. There is only the now, only this moment, all the way to the edge of the senses, and sometimes, it seems, beyond.

Occasionally, on the best rides, the universe whispers in your ear as a reward for your attention.

The air rushes around the helmet, white noise as background to the dance of light about the bike. The engine purrs between his legs, the sound a near perfect indication of his speed. He never has to glance down at the speedometer anymore. The tires on the road hum in the cool and still slightly damp air of the morning. An exit, a few turns, and he is pulling up in front of the cafe just as the barista is rolling up the steel gate and flipping the sign on the door to open.

Facing west over the Pacific before the sun comes up he stares out on a sea with no discernible horizon. The water blends seamlessly with the sky. You know where the sky is, because it is a deep, distant, near black indigo, and you know where the water is because it is a receding and rhythmically churning grey blanket. But where they meet, where water becomes mist becomes air, remains hidden. Each sip of the spiced tea brings an obvious change in the sky: a pink light permeates the void, even as the ocean takes on white highlights. Soon the dome of heaven lightens to a pale blue and there it is, the line that divides the sea from the sky. Awareness emerges of up and down, here and there, near and far. If you were not paying attention you would miss it.

Witnessing the birth of the day, you sense place and scale. The sky and the sea are one, the same physics, the same except for an accident of density, intensity. Yin and Yang, Dharma and Karma, interdependent and distinct, at times indistinguishable. The things that are important come in to focus.

It's time for the living.

Buddy

The first thing he recognizes is the grit. Not a taste, just the texture, in his mouth, in his eyes. The dust starts to clear revealing a man nearby screaming, an anguished face without the sound. There is only a ringing. On the other side of the road another man is holding a leg, not his own. Slowly he starts to feel his own body again. Delayed and muffled, like moving around wrapped in a weighted suit. Then the pain, probably broken ribs. The sounds come rushing in. He can hear the screams now. He sees the soldiers, they look German, and he starts to panic. Someone grabs his shoulders and pulls him around.

Buddy is pulled awake.

"Come on, Bucky, we've got a mission to fly, you know."

Confusion as the world comes in to focus.

"Bad dream again?" Stephen asks in a soft confiding voice.

"Could have sworn I was with Patton in the desert." He runs his hand through his hair, "It felt so real. But the uniforms didn't look quite right. The helmets looked Kraut." He swings his feet to the floor and rubs his eyes.

"Maybe you should see doc."

Ignoring the suggestion, Buddy says "I wish you would stop calling me that."

Stephen assumes a stern mocking demeanor. "Look, if you are going to hang out with Captain America you need to have the right sidekick name."

Buddy stands and grabs Stephen's crotch. "I'm not the one hanging out, *Lieutenant* Rogers. Now stop before people start to talk."

Putting a hand to Buddy's cheek, he says, "Okay — Bucky!" Stephen bolts from the tent. "Now get your ass in gear before we miss the war!"

Around the camp odd scraps of home hang from signs and tents, handcrafted Christmas signs. Using left over paint from patching up the bombers makes for discordant Santas and Christmas trees. The fact that this is the hottest muggiest place he has ever been makes Christmas seem like something from another planet.

The ground crew keep the Liberator in pretty good condition, just a little sun bleached. The plane towers over the men as they work on it, loading the bombs, ammunition, and fuel. Just beneath the port side cockpit window are the names of the crew:

Pilot: Cpt. Albert "Buddy" Buchanan
Co-Pilot: 1st Lt Stanley "Bob" Pawlowski
Navigator: 2nd Lt Stephen Rogers
Bombardier: 2nd Lt Percy "Knuckles" O'Toole
Crew Chief: TSgt Jefferson Sandervilt
Gunner: Sgt Henry Tinkle
Gunner: Sgt William "Whitewash" Jones
Gunner: Cpl William "Bill" Eisner
Gunner: Cpl Charles "Chuck" Cider

Under that is a painting of a rocket, right out of Buck Rogers, with a grinning pinup girl riding it to orbit. The name *Star Child* looks like a comet whizzing by. Sparks flying off, one for each of the twenty-three combat mission they have flown so far.

Buddy settles into the pilot seat of his plane. The machine is a marvel, a flying two story building that carries enough fire power to devastate an infantry battalion or level an entire port. Everything Buddy loves is at his fingertips. Powerful machinery, the freedom of the sky, and Steph. That last thought is cut short. Not something to think of, a source of shame. An irresistible source.

Soon the rest of the crew is onboard and in their places. Bob calls out the check list as Buddy confirms everything. Each crewman checks in as they make ready their stations. The engines run up, and the ground crew pull the chocks. *Star Child* rolls onto the taxi way and into line for the predawn takeoff.

The routine of getting to altitude and on course is a welcome period of reflection. Everything is rote, simple repetition of tasks and commands. Soon the bombers are clustered above the clouds. A waning moon hangs just above the horizon, giving a cool glow to the clouds, but not threatening to illuminate the big planes as they make their way to targets on Japanese held islands.

John

Weekend picnic lunch with Kris. That's four lunches in five days. This could be habit forming. Earlier in the week her eyes and her words had his full attention. Today he's able to compose himself enough to take in a little more. Just her presence calms his demons, the details of her soothe his always racing thoughts. Her black hair is shoulder length, parted just off center and framing confidently delicate features. Her feet poke out from under her skirt, middle toes ever so slightly longer than the others. Her white blouse and dark billowy skirt are perfectly coordinated with her toenail polish and leather sandals. It all comes off as effortless and casual. She doesn't seem to go for flashy jewelry but has the tiniest diamond stud in her nose. You could be forgiven for thinking it was just a fleck of glitter, or a dew drop on a morning flower. She gives him the rapid fire, slightly nervous, history of Kris.

"Dad was in the military when I was born. He was stationed at North Island down in San Diego. But before I started school he took a job with United, flying all over the Pacific."

While she talks he lays out a cutting board of sliced cheese and meats, fresh sourdough bread and a few apples.

"We moved up to San Fran and I fell in love with the architecture and history of the city. Mom was killed in a car crash on the Five, and I pretty much took care of myself the last two years of high school. I spent every day at museums and the Presidio."

"I am so sorry about your mom."

"It's okay, it was a long time ago, and I carry her with me always."

"So between Dad being a pilot before I was born, and my love of history I just naturally decided to do my dissertation on aviation history."

"Naturally."

"What's your favorite aircraft?"

"Never really thought about it." John bites into his apple.

"Okay, just imagine being free and happy. Close your eyes, and imagine something man made overhead. What do you see?"

"Well in the war an A-10 was like a guardian angel." He looks her in the eye. "But not exactly what you are asking, I think." John pauses, closes one eye, then the other, and makes a show of turning his face into the sun. "I don't know, I mean, happy and free has me thinking about my bike and an open, gently curving road." Another bite of the apple. "How about you, what's yours?"

"An airship!"

"No hesitation, an airship?"

"Yep."

"A big bag of hot air? Okay."

Kris punches him in the arm, hard, but the thump is pleasant, contact without malice. "You ass," she laughs. "Not a balloon — a dirigible, a rigid airship. Giant and majestic, stately, not rushed. Deliberate, not meandering without purpose. They were like paddle wheelers on the Mississippi. Functional but not fast, elegant but not flashy."

"So what happened? Why don't we have airships now?"

"A few things really. Everyone knows about the *Hindenburg*—"

"Oh, the HUmanity!"

"Yeah, that's the one. Well, before that Goodyear Tire Company had a joint U.S. venture with the manufacturer of the *Hindenburg*, and the result was, eventually, the construction of two airship aircraft carriers, the *Akron* and the *Macon*."

"Aircraft carrier airships?"

"Yep. They carried small biplane fighters that let them scout more area than airships alone, and do it faster than a regular aircraft carrier. In fact, in 1934 the commander of the *USS Macon* decided to prove that he could find enemy ships faster and more efficiently than anyone else, so he went looking for the navy ship that was taking FDR on a secret route in the Pacific."

"Secret? In 1934?"

"I don't remember why. Roosevelt was coming back from Hawaii or something and I guess for security they took a secret route." With mock impatience, "Anyway—"

"Sorry."

She smiles. That's a great smile. I could live in that smile. "Anyway, he found the ship and delivered that day's newspapers from California. FDR was really impressed."

"So what happened?"

"Well, there was a flaw in the design that the Navy did not let the manufacturer fix right away, so both of them crashed. Then WWII happened and no one really ever looked to try and build the big zeppelin type airships again. The bad memories of three bad crashes in the 30s coupled with everyone's excitement about long range transport planes and jet bombers pretty much killed airships." She paused. "And big seaplanes. It just took longer for the seaplanes to die out."

Later he's thinking, this was a good day, one of the best since he got back. Finally feeling confident socially, well MORE confident anyway. Tired and content back in his bed, why can't he just go to sleep? Fear of sleep is a terrible thing.

Fantasies of Kris dance just at the edge of consciousness when sleep finally comes.

A body drops as the top of the man's skull explodes. There is yelling from beyond the jungle's trees and ferns. Random pops like firecrackers accompany the mosquito like zip of something piercing the dense foliage. Something is burning his left thigh like it was stuck with a hot poker. He bends down and looks at the familiar but twisted face of the man on the ground.

A hushed and panicked voice reaches through the buzzing and screaming. "Leave him, Buddy. He's dead, and so are we if we don't get moving!" Are those Japanese voices? It sounds like a scene from The Thin Red Line, but there is nothing cinematic about the chaos and confusion. An explosion tears at the jungle, throwing him into the urgent man. He rolls off and starts to stand when a rifle butt swings down...

When he wakes the note on the bedside table shocks John. The transition is jarring, the mysterious note distressing.

"John, I don't understand what is happening, but sometimes when I sleep I dream of this place. I dream that I live in this apartment, and I see from my identification that my name is John Oldman, but I know it isn't my name. It says I was born in 1989, but I wasn't. My name is Buddy Buchanan, I was born in 1919, and I think maybe I am going crazy. This world is so strange and wonderful. Where I am from it is hell on earth. Please tell me I am not crazy."

Hands shaking, John starts to crumple the paper, but stops. He puts it on the table and smoothes it out. The texture is pleasant to the touch despite the fear the words bring. Maybe this is it, maybe he's really cracked. Carefully he puts the page into the drawer of the night stand, under his journal.

Buddy

The bombs drop from *Star Child*. A heavy mother suddenly relieved of her malevolent spawn, she lurches up as the weight falls away. Over the intercom Buddy hears Chuck whistle,

"Damn. Hank you were right, that IS pretty!" Chuck normally mans a waist gun, but he asked Henry to swap for this flight. The waist gunner never gets to see the bombs do their work, and Henry is always going on about the shockwaves in the heavy tropic air as the ordinance rips apart unlucky men, buildings, vehicles, whatever is in the wrong place at the right time.

Soon the calls start coming in from the other aircraft. The Japanese anticipated the attack and now tiny white planes with big angry looking meatballs painted on the side are diving on the lumbering giants. The radio becomes a jumble of not quite panicked calls.

"Three o'clock low, bandits! Bandits!"

"I got more, 10 o'clock level!"

"Got 'em!"

"Fucking Nips!"

This mission is outside the range of the Marine Corps fighter cover. The Liberators flew out under a blanket of darkness, counting on surprise to give them a head start on the return leg. Friendly fighter cover is at least 20 minutes out as long as the jarheads didn't get lost on the way to the rendezvous point.

"Baker flight, Baker Leader," the radio crackles, "we've got uninvited guests. Tighten up and push those throttles to the firewall."

Buddy puts his right hand on the throttles, Bob puts his left hand behind Buddy's as they both push the levers as far forward as possible while Buddy guides the plane up tight on the flight leader's port wing. Theoretically the big bombers have enough guns that a proper box formation will provide an umbrella of overlapping machine gun fire. A barrier of lead that will keep enemy fighters off of them. Theoretically. Of course the box is never perfect, the gunners are not always pointing in the right direction, and eventually planes are hit, men wounded or killed and the aircraft steadily become more vulnerable.

"Shit!" The intercom fills with the shout of someone in the

back. "Pop's plane just lost a wing!"

Another voice, maybe from this crew, maybe another: "Come on guys get out! Get out!" But with the starboard wing gone the port wing just lifts up and over the fuselage. Soon the plane is spinning and diving. The centrifugal force pinning everyone to their seats, or to the inside of the bomber. No one comes out. The big aircraft impacts the Pacific, a white smudge on a deep blue carpet.

"No 'chutes."

"Fuck."

Five more minutes and they should meet up with the Marines. Just five more minutes.

"Bandits 11 o'clock high!"

"No, those are Corsairs!"

About time, much longer and they might not make it.

Stephen, sitting in the glass nose of the aircraft yells into the mic, "Bandit, 12 o'clock!" The sky in front of *Star Child* lights up with orange flashes.

Buddy wakes up, naked, sweaty, in a bed under a gently billowing curtain. "What the hell?" He rubs the sleep from his eyes, but he doesn't feel like he was sleeping. He feels like he has been wide awake and tense for hours. His mind tells him his body aches, but his nerves tell him he is relaxed if not quite rested.

Fumbling in the dark Buddy finds a bedside lamp and flicks it on. The bedroom looks like a drunk's room in a cheap flop house. He looks around for clothes to put on. On the floor is a pile of clothing, but they reek. Funny, he hasn't washed his clothes in three days, hasn't showered in 24 hours, but he is smelling this like he just walked out of a flower shop and into a trash dump.

In a bureau he finds some shorts, a shirt and some socks. He dresses and steps into the small bathroom. The image in the mirror isn't him. He is looking out of the eyes that are looking back in the mirror. But they aren't his eyes, it isn't his face. The fellow in the mirror looks like he just pulled a pass in Waikiki, including an all over deep tan.

Buddy puts on some athletic shoes he finds in the living room, grabs some keys off a hook by the door and steps outside into the night air. The air is cool, cool like he hasn't felt for at least a year. At least not while he was on the ground. The night is still, a breeze coming up the street. In that direction the buildings end in mist only a half a block away, and there is the faintest sound of thumping. Buddy walks to the sound.

A blue neon sign lights the street and what appears to be part of a beach. Club Ripped Tides. Buddy hesitates, then opens the door, and is frozen in shock.

He figured this was a night club of some sort, and by the sounds he expected to find a full Swing Band filling a stage. Instead he finds a manly woman alone on a stage, and a room full of men dancing.

"Damn," he thinks, "I must be dying, because this cannot be real."

He feels someone tap his arm, and hears something he can't quite make out.

He answers reflexively, "Buddy."

"Sorry?"

"My names Buddy. Isn't that what you asked?" Buddy turns to his interrogator. He is still disoriented, more now really, but this guy looks genuinely concerned. "Where am I?"

The stranger directs him to a seat and offers him a drink.

"No, no, I'll pay." Buddy reaches down to his pockets and realizes he doesn't have a wallet; he doesn't have money. "I seem to have lost my billfold."

"Don't worry, you can catch me next time. You okay?"

"I'm not sure. Is this normal?" Buddy gestures to the dancing.

"Well, it is here and it is for me."

A wisp of wonder in his voice, "Wonderful." Buddy turns back to the man. "This isn't normal where I'm from."

"Military?"

Buddy pauses, why not? "Yes. I am..." Looking around the room again, he says, "or... was."

"Well, I hear it is much better now."

"How did you know?"

"The hair."

His hand moves reflexively up to his, someone's, hair.

The man reaches out a hand. "I'm Anton."

They talk for an hour, maybe more, but the time flies by. Buddy is taken with this confident stranger and this place, the music, these people. Then he remembers, this can't be real, it can't be. Somewhere Stephen is probably in trouble. His plane, his crew need him. He excuses himself and, trying not to panic and run out, walks with deliberate effort back to the apartment he woke up in.

Exhaustion creeps in, he half strips down and lays back down in the bed...

Buddy gasps! The water is damn cold. The sun is beating down and something is repeatedly tugging at his torso. Buddy scrambles to untangle from his parachute before the sodden silk drags him beneath the waves. What the fuck was that? Did he black out and dream all of that?

A whistle causes Buddy to look around. Someone is waving from a bright yellow raft. "Over here!"

He swims over, not noticing he is bogged down by his boots filling with water. His co-pilot, Bob, pulls him into the raft. "Anyone else?"

Bob gestures behind him, "There is another raft about a hundred yards that way, and I counted seven 'chutes on the way down."

Seven, that leaves two to account for. His thoughts are interrupted by the shrill approach of an aircraft engine. Lining up on the raft is a Japanese fighter that must have spotted the rafts. Buddy tenses for the end when the aircraft explodes and flips, canopy down, into the water a quarter mile away. Through the black smoke that marks the spot of the explosion a Corsair screams towards them, whirls of the smoke slipping off the aircraft like spreading wings of an avenging angel. The pilot wiggles his wings in salute and throttles up to climb back into the fight.

Kris

A few weeks and many decades later...

Kris walks out of the publisher's office. Two years of research, and all she gets is an offer to read her next manuscript. It really is annoying. At least she has her master's degree in applied history and a small exhibit at the Santa Monica Aviation Museum, "Progress Stalled — The Birth of Edwards Air Force Base and the Death of the YB-49," to show for all the work.

The noon airship to San Francisco, Kristine's Clipper, is climbing out of Santa Monica. She loves that her favorite aircraft has her name, even if it is just a coincidence. The sky is clear and the air crisp with a California autumn breeze off the ocean.

A motorcycle pulls past her. She catches her breath; it looks like John's motorcycle. He just vanished a couple weeks ago, as quickly as he dropped into her life. The rider gets off the bike and flips off his helmet, smiles, and waves. Instinctively she waves back as an older woman pushes past. Kris trips on one of the dozens of campaign signs for Senator Mary Estevez, the older woman who pushed by.

"Anton, this is a surprise! And what a nice motorcycle."

"Couldn't let my Tia Mary eat lunch alone on her birthday." They embrace. "I'll tell you all about the motorcycle. You won't believe it."

"Figures," mutters Kris. Life is full of near misses.

Buddy

The car idles to a stop in the small parking lot in rural Ohio. A black wrought iron gate frames the pedestrian entrance to a small manicured cemetery. This is so strange, more than 70 years ago, four years in subjective time, Stephen was smiling up at him before moving forward and into the navigator/bombardier station of the B-24 Liberator. He never came back out. Killed over the Pacific, buried with whatever remains of the plane. But the national grave registry said that Buddy could find Stephens' marker here. *The location written down on a piece of paper gripped in his hand.*

Just inside the gate a stooped and shrunken man sweeps dust off the walk.

"Excuse me?"

"Erm, what can I do you fer, young man?"

"I am looking for a marker. Could you help?"

The man pats his hands on his pants and reaches out with his right hand to shake. "Dale, I'm the caretaker here. You are?"

Buddy blurts out, "Dale Rogers?" *He stands limp as the old man shakes his hand.*

"Sure am. How'd you know?"

"Oh, yeah, sorry. My names John Oldman. I'm looking for the marker for Stephen Rogers, my grandfather flew with him in the war. I mean World War Two. He told me Stephen had a kid brother named Dale."

Dale chuckles, "Well I'm no kid anymore. Your grandfather huh? Who was that?"

"His name was Albert Buchanan."

"Albert? Albert… Albert…Buchanan… You don't mean Buddy, do ya?"

"Yes! I mean yeah, I think that was his nickname. How did you know?"

"Buddy and Stephen came home on leave after their final flight training. Quite a fella, but are you sure you're his grandson?"

"Pretty sure, why?" *The two men stare at each other a moment, Dale looking the younger man up and down.* "Is it because I'm not white?"

"No, no. Not that, hell son, my wife was Kickapoo. Nah." *Dale waves his hand and the idea of racism aside.* "Stephen, god rest his soul, was a little light in the loafers. I was pretty sure Buddy was, too." *Quickly he holds his hand out to Buddy's forearm,* "Not that there is anything wrong with that, mind, not now'days anyhow. 'Course back then."

Buddy starts to tear up, the emotion of seeing Stephen's little brother aged decades in a few years of personal time drives home the distance and permanence of his loss.

"Aw hell son. I'm sorry. Obviously Buddy was straight if yer his grandson. I didn't mean to upsetcha." Dale puts one hand on Buddy's back and the other on a shoulder, the same way Stephen would. The tears come faster. Dale continues, "I just feel bad for Stephen, I'm pretty sure he was sweet on yer grandad, even though he never did or said anything obvious."

"No, no, Buddy loved him, I'm sure of it." A couple deep breaths and Buddy gets himself a little more composed. "He, ah." Buddy wipes his eyes with the back of his hand. "He wanted me to come here and say goodbye for him, and now after all this time I'm here."

Turning down the path, "Just follow me, John." Glancing back over his shoulder Dale adds, "I think Stephen would like that."

SCOTT A. CEIER is a vagabond and would-be bohemian. As a student of Anthropology, and a Strategic Intelligence professional, he has an abiding interest in the human condition. A lifelong author, he has only recently begun pursuing opportunities to be publicly published. Scott is married and raising two sons while trying to figure out what to do when he grows up.

The Tenth Doctor Speaks of Regeneration

N. I. Nicholson

In a way, humans are more
fortunate than I—

once to be born, once to live,
once to die.

Imagine, for a moment, being
one person for centuries,

settling into yourself like a suit,
knowing where its creases

cradle your soul *just so*,
knowing the lay of your inner

lands and curving yourself to
their topography.

Then, you are jettisoned into
a brilliant river of flux,

its golden enzymes softening
you, stripping you away

until your core is left, consumed

and floating in rebirth;

and a new skin's laws of
physics are written into you.

One day, a wall will erupt in
my path: I will not see it coming

until my face collides with the
soft violence of its crimson brick.

A new man will rise to his feet
in my place. He will saunter away

with a bloodied nose, brain dazed
by the impact, while DNA finishes

weaving him as a new man. As
for me, I'll be dead: an empty suit,

an unworn pair of Chucks, glasses
cast aside on silent, cold ground.

N. I. NICHOLSON is collectively four cats in a human suit, as well as a legal and pen name under which members of the Teselecta Multiverse publish poetry, creative nonfiction, and essays. Nicholson's work has appeared in publications such as GTK Creative Journal, Alphanumeric, *and* Assaracus.

A Pendulum Life

L. N. Kirby

I. MASS
SOMETIMES I BUILD THE DAYS out of Legos,
each brightly colored hour
snapping into place
with a satisfying click.

Sometimes the weeks puddle into hammered copper oblongs,
rainwater bathtubs.

Sometimes there is no time.
Then I will wake with a start
kneeling by bare feet,
keening like a starfish angle
or curling like a crescent moon.

2. Arc
One winter I was the Amaryllis my mother sent me—
a hard knot in dry, dry soil
startled to learn that even the dusty
and glimmerless are capable of unfolding.

One spring I was a soft statue, pliable, disintegrating,
my home a gathering of disconnections.
Lily light could not sprinkle in my windows.
Easter came and went.

The living was easy one summer. Gravity and I grew lazy
as the smoke of white sage, spiraling out
of your hand-carved pipe, distant,
wind-loved as a dandelion seed.

And then there was the autumn when my face was always wet.
Carnations and roses bloomed tidy
on the dining room table. I had a high, hard
inquisitor's hatred.

3. *Momentum*
Ballooning and shriveling,
I expand like a yawn,
snap tight as a bear trap.
The heat of goblins, or of azaleas in the sun,
or the chill of a child on a sailboat at dusk—
no wind and the motor gave out—
all shuffled together.

My uncle sings about the ring of fire.
My uncle sings about the Pearly Gates.

Stigma, stigmata,
staccato or smooth, I'm
careening on a leather thong,
describing an arc, a sacrifice,
describing a nascent sphere.

*L. N. KIRBY is a writer, scholar and artist who has taught in higher ed-
ucation for several years. Kirby has received writing awards including a
Fellowship to the Bucknell Seminar for Younger Poets and the Fifth*

Plinth poetry prize. Kirby is interested in intersectional civil rights, neurodiversity and education, justice, mercy, and boba tea.

The Scent of Hay and Oranges

Holly Schofield

WARREN CRUNCHES HIS PINK AND GREEN CEREAL and tries to ignore his parents' argument.

His dad is the loudest, yanking the knot in his tie. "I don't think your son needs seventeen Spiderman washcloths! Seventeen! And don't tell me they were on sale or that you 'forgot' to pay. I don't want to hear it."

"Not in front of the boy." His mom gives a pointed glance Warren's way, then she looks at her lap and gives a small, almost triumphant smile. "Besides, the department store won't even notice they're gone. No RFID tags." She is very calm today, not like yesterday morning when she yelled at Warren about his muddy boots.

Warren drinks down the remaining sludge in his bowl. For the first time, he wonders if Dad knows about the boxes of Q-tips his mom buried under the ice cream in the downstairs freezer, and the tins of cat food she stashed in the attic. He wishes they had a cat and that his parents would talk about things, like parents on TV shows do. Warren stands up, grabs his backpack, and that's when the elephant appears.

It ghosts across the kitchen, one huge foot after the other in slow deliberate fashion, head rasping against the ceiling. Its colors are faint, washed out, like watercolor paints with too much water added. Its trunk arches down to a saucepan in the sink. It drinks silently, thoughtfully, as it gazes out the window.

Warren's parents don't seem to notice. He points a finger. "Hey, look at—"

Dad slams his orange juice glass into the sink and strides right through the elephant, down the hall to his home office.

The elephant grows more solid, like heavy fog.

Warren's mom fingers the tablecloth, humming to herself.

Warren wants to giggle. "Mom, there's—"

"It's fine, son. Everything's fine." She walks over to him, one hand trailing through the elephant's gently swinging tail, and kisses his hair. The air smells of sour oranges.

• • •

The elephant inhabits the kitchen after that, appearing as soon as Warren enters. He becomes used to the slight hay-scented breeze the elephant makes when it flaps an ear. He learns he can push his way through the massive body with a slight effort, like swimming upstream, but mostly he prefers to edge along the kitchen counter or the wall behind the table.

His dad eats breakfasts in silence now — laptop crowding the table — then hides in his office, disappearing to the gym every evening.

His mom starts piling items — clothing, food, a complete set of screwdrivers — from her shopping trips in the main hallway. No one comments.

Warren begins to spend a lot of time in his room, only going into the kitchen to grab snacks or when his mom insists the family should have a sit-down meal. He looks through books in the school library and figures out, from the large ears and high forehead, that the elephant is an adult African. He has few friends at school. He starts a diary but deletes it after three entries. He figures out he's gay.

• • •

By the time Warren is in high school, he hangs out with the same four boys, mostly because they let him. The cutest one, Johnny Chao, has serial dated the other three boys, but not, of course, Warren.

Once, after a sweaty one-on-one basketball game in the schoolyard, Warren daringly invites Johnny over for a cold drink. He rehearses in his head how to ask Johnny out. On his dresser are two tickets to a performance of a popular local band.

Neither of Warren's parents are home and the kitchen is empty. At the back door, he darts ahead to the fridge. Last week, his mom had stacked thirty ballpoint pens, still packaged, neatly in the crisper.

The fridge holds only leftovers, beverages, and condiments. He looks up, a six-pack of Pepsi dangling from his hand. Johnny still stands in the doorway, mouth open. Warren realizes that, from habit, he has avoided the empty space in the middle of the floor and hugged the wall in his dash to reach the fridge.

Warren thinks about what to say.

Johnny smirks. "You are one weird dude. The guys were right."

An elephant manifests next to Johnny. It's a younger one, its head level with Johnny's chest. An Indian elephant, the kind with smaller ears and smoother skin. It steps through a kitchen chair, heads for the flower vase on the table. The tang of hay fills the room. Warren keeps his eyes on the elephant, backing out of the room.

"What the fuck, dude! Where're you going?"

Even with his bed pillow around his ears, Warren can hear Johnny slam the kitchen door a few moments later.

• • •

Warren deliberately chooses an out-of-state university. The first week, he patrols the dorm's communal kitchen several times a night. The scuffed green linoleum is always empty. He cuts back to one patrol per night.

He avoids going home for holidays and communicates with his parents by once-a-week emails, sticking to a routine script. Soon he grows attracted to a dorm mate — Gerry, a smart Kansas boy who can cook. They hang out together and join the same study group, but Warren does not reveal his interest.

By Warren's sophomore year, he considers himself friends with Gerry. They share a dorm suite. Warren helps Gerry with his calculus, and Gerry cooks for them both. Warren avoids the kitchen, eating in his room, and, after much joking from Gerry, cleans the bathroom every weekend in exchange for Gerry washing dishes.

On this particular day, Gerry calls down the hall that breakfast is ready. Warren enters the kitchen only as far as he usually does — just enough to be able to snatch the plate from the end of the chipped counter. However, Gerry is standing over by the stove, a thumb holding Warren's plate hostage.

"Sit here with me for once? Mine's almost ready." Gerry does not slide the plate down to Warren.

Warren grips the door frame. "I'm late for—"

"No, you're not. Are you?"

Warren comes farther into the kitchen and takes the plate of eggs, bacon, and avocado. He shuffles to the rickety Ikea table, mumbles his thanks, and picks up his fork.

Gerry brings him a glass of orange juice and returns to the stove.

Warren finishes one egg and most of the bacon before he dares look up. The gray-brown bulk of an Indian elephant is squeezed between the table and the stove. This elephant is large, bright-eyed, and very distinct. Warren freezes.

"Warren? What is it, buddy?" Gerry, behind the gray haze of the elephant, waves a spatula.

The elephant solidifies, becoming pewter and iron. Its long lashes close in a wink. Warren can count the bristly black hairs between its ears.

He stands, bumping the table. His orange juice spills. In two strides, he pushes through the elephant and reaches the stove. He grabs the spatula from Gerry's hand. The sound it makes as it strikes the elephant is solid and meaty.

The elephant grunts in surprise.

Warren faces Gerry. His breath tangles, caught between courage and despair. "Gerry, we...we need to talk. No, we need to go to the movies. I need to buy you popcorn. You know?"

Words spill around Gerry's broad grin. "Yeah, I do. Didn't want to ruin our friendship until you gave me a sign." He touches Warren's hand.

Warren thinks of his parents and what their lives have become. "I don't want us to ever stop talking, okay? Even if we think we know what the other guy is thinking, let's make sure. Let's *be* sure. Am I making any sense?"

Gerry turns off the stove, leaving his eggs in the pan. "Yes," he says.

Words spurt from Warren in a jumble of relief and laughter as sugary drops of orange juice continue to plink to the floor. When he finally takes a step back, there is nothing in the space behind him.

HOLLY SCHOFIELD travels through time at the rate of one second per second, oscillating between the alternate realities of city and country life. Her short stories have appeared in Analog, Lightspeed, Escape Pod, *and many other publications throughout the world. She hopes to save the world through science fiction and homegrown heritage tomatoes. Find her at hollyschofield.wordpress.com, https://www.amazon.com/Holly-Schofield/e/B00JNBBYW0, and https://www.goodreads.com/author/show/8166938.Holly_Schofield*

Can writing save me yet?

Alyssa Hillary

I HAVE NO PROBLEMS LEARNING TO TALK, so far as anyone knows. In fact, I am an early talker. So I can communicate everything I need to using speech, right?

Wrong.

I start using computers around the same time I learn to speak, and I love them from the beginning. I am great with computers. I will remain so.

But those are just for fun. Right?

Wrong.

How long will it take me to learn otherwise?

Return to kindergarten. I am five.

I can tell my teacher about solving for x and how two squared is four. I can't tell her where my mittens are, when she asks. I can't tell her I don't care *why* Nick is pulling my hair, it hurts and I want him to *stop*. I can't tell her I'm not cold or that I can't really remember how to move my arms to run when I'm wearing a jacket. But I can tell her about solving for x and how two squared is four, so I must be able to tell her everything I need to. All the stuff I don't (can't) tell her can't be all that important, right?

Because if you can speak, that must mean you can communi-

cate everything you might need to using speech, right?
Wrong.

Can writing save me yet?
I need to learn how, first.
She gives us pencils and teaches us to spell. My handwriting is the large, clumsy handwriting you would expect of someone just learning. I am fairly good at spelling because I can already read, and I am writing slowly enough, big enough, that it can be read. No one demands handwriting beyond my abilities. I don't hate writing, yet.

Move on to third grade. I am eight.
I can tell my teacher about the last book I read, and how I found a formula for any triangular number using patterns and the area of a triangle, and all about the linear equation I used (but didn't call it that) to solve the challenge problem she gave me last week. I can't tell her that the bomber game Liz is playing with me isn't fun, that it's scary to be chased around by a bigger faster girl who doesn't like you and is talking about killing you even if she's joking because *I can't tell when people are joking.* I can't tell her that Anna and Kevin are spending chorus calling me a retard every week or that the music teacher can't hear because we sit near the back. I can't tell her that no, really, I'm not cold. I don't need a jacket when it's fifty degrees out and I can't really remember how to move my arms to run when I'm wearing a jacket. I can't tell her everyone has it all wrong, that my parents aren't the ones pushing the whole math thing, they've just had more time to get used to it… until she claims she's protecting me from being pushed too hard while I'm already crying and I can't *not* tell her between gasps how I'm sick of no one believing I could like math that much. Even then, I can't tell her that *of course* I like math that much, because math makes sense and people *don't*. But I can tell her about the last book I read, and how I found a formula for any

triangular number using patterns and the area of a triangle, and all about the linear equation I used (but didn't call it that) to solve the challenge problem she gave me last week, so I must be able to tell her everything I need to. All the stuff I don't (can't) tell her can't be all that important, right?

Because if you can speak, that must mean you can communicate everything you might need to using speech, right?
Wrong.

Can writing save me yet?
There's just one problem.
I am expected to write *by hand.*
They teach us cursive, then expect us to write everything in cursive. It's even slower than print, though no messier.
I am frustrated.
I can't read other people's cursive.
I can't write fast enough to keep up with my brain, and now they've made it *worse.*
They say cursive is faster.
It's not.

Now for fifth grade. I am ten.
I can tell my teacher about the extra math class I'm taking every Thursday evening and how much fun geometry is and how I figured out *all by myself* that if you take the least common multiple of two numbers and the greatest common factor of two numbers and multiply them together you get the same number as if you'd multiplied the original numbers. I can't tell her that Jess's aide makes me sit with her every day at lunch even though I'm not in Jess's class and sometimes I'd like to sit with my *other* friends, because I do have other friends even though I'm new. I can't tell her I've noticed I'm the only kid who has lunch group two days a week instead of one or none. I can't tell her that spending recess

on the swings alone (please alone, please alone, I don't want to talk to anyone) is more important to my day than whatever they think I'm going to get out of this lunch group. I can't tell her that *no, really, I'm not cold and I don't need a jacket when it's fifty degrees out. I can't really remember how to move my arms to run when I'm wearing a jacket and swinging is hard with a jacket too.* But I can tell her about the extra math class I'm taking every Thursday evening and how much fun geometry is and how I figured out *all by myself* that if you take the least common multiple of two numbers and the greatest common factor of two numbers and multiply them together you get the same number as if you'd multiplied the original numbers, so I must be able to tell her everything I need to. All the stuff I don't (can't) tell her can't be all that important, right?

Because if you can speak, that must mean you can communicate everything you might need to using speech, right?
Wrong.

Can writing save me yet?
My handwriting has shrunk to (and past) a normal size.
It's tiny.
No neater, just smaller.
My teachers are starting to care.
They call me lazy.
I begin to hate writing.
At least they aren't demanding cursive anymore.

Let's move on to middle school, sixth grade. I am eleven.
I can tell my teachers how learning Chinese is lots of fun but it's harder than when I studied French in fourth grade, and how the people at the Russian School of Mathematics think I should take something called an AMC, and that no matter how many times she asks, I'm still only going to be in her class for reading and not for writing because I have Chinese then. It doesn't matter

that I still can't tell them I'm not cold and don't need a jacket when it's fifty degrees out because we don't have recess anymore. I can't tell them that I didn't quite get intentional disobedience as a concept until Jess's aide explained it to me in reading class, or that acting on this new knowledge remains a ways off. I can't tell them I'm sitting at a table full of boys because I know Jess is scared of boys and I don't actually want to sit with her every single day. I can't tell them that my locker is messy because *I don't know how to create or maintain that kind of order.* I can't tell them that I jammed my pencil into the locking mechanism on my locker because I can't get the darn thing to open, even though I know the combination. (I still know it. 13-17-7.) I can't tell them that it's completely unreasonable to expect me to know if Jess is joking or not when she says she's going to kill herself, *because I can't tell when people are joking.* But I can tell them how learning Chinese is lots of fun but it's harder than when I studied French in fourth grade, and how the people at the Russian School of Mathematics think I should take something called an AMC, and that no matter how many times she asks, I'm still only going to be in her class for reading and not for writing because I have Chinese then, so I must be able to tell them everything I need to. All the stuff I don't (can't) tell them can't be all that important, right?

Because if you can speak, that must mean you can communicate everything you might need to using speech, right?
Wrong.

Can writing save me yet?
I'm still (mostly) expected to write by hand.
But homework essays can be typed, now.
I should probably learn typing.

Consider seventh grade. I am twelve.
I can tell my teachers that trying to get in or out of the sixth

grade hallway against traffic to get to and from Chinese class is like swimming upstream in a flood, and how Mathcounts problems are much more interesting than anything we'd done in class before, and that I take bus ten instead of fifteen on Thursdays because Nella's dad teaches both of us math at their house then. I can't tell them that whatever concerns they might have about my asthma, it's not exercise induced. Not until *after* I have a meltdown-induced asthma attack... I melted down because they wanted to avoid exercise-induced asthma by banning me from running the day they didn't have access to my inhaler. I can't ask for help when my contact lenses fall out in class. I can't tell them that the instructions for the book reports are too broad for me to make any sense of what I'm supposed to do. I can't tell them I have trouble making sheets with five new vocabulary words per chapter of the books they assign us because I already *know* every word in those books. I can't tell them my locker is messy because *I don't know how to create or maintain that kind of order*. I can't tell them I didn't put a lock on my locker because I can't get the darn things to open, even though I know the combination. I can't tell them holding my placement in a math class at my level hostage over an organized locker won't solve a problem that isn't laziness. I can't tell them keeping me on easier academic work won't get me organized, that neither carrot nor stick will do the job. But I can tell them that trying to get in or out of the sixth grade hallway against traffic to get to and from Chinese class is like swimming upstream in a flood, and how Mathcounts problems are much more interesting than anything we'd done in class before, and that I take bus ten instead of fifteen on Thursdays because Nella's dad teaches both of us math at their house then, so I must be able to tell them everything I need to. All the stuff I don't (can't) tell them can't be all that important, right?

Because if you can speak, that must mean you can communicate everything you might need to using speech, right?

Wrong.

Can writing save me yet?
I can read my own writing, even months later, when I am permitted to type.
My homework is legible, when I get it done at home.
I just wish typing weren't so *slow*.

Let's move on to high school, freshman year. I am fourteen.
I can tell my teachers I'd rather risk the math class that's too hard than *still* be bored, and how I know it's bullshit for doing the work for two Chinese classes to be fine until I'm *not* going on the Chinese exchange program anymore, and maybe even try to explain that not being a soprano doesn't automatically make me an alto. I can't tell them how the sentence, "I reserve the right to check *just your notebook* if you're not keeping it in shape," makes my blood run cold, because *I still don't know how to create or maintain that kind of order*. I can't explain just how aware I am of their mishandling my allergy issues regarding the exchange program and the interview process. I can't tell them that my being nauseous during certain parts of health class is because *I am a repulsed asexual*. I can't tell them my hands hurt from taking notes in the classes where we're expected to copy everything from a PowerPoint into our notebooks. I can't tell them how much it sucks to be prevented from finishing the mile in spring track — not because I couldn't finish, but because everyone lapped me. But I can tell them that I'd rather risk the math class that's too hard than risk *still* being bored, and how I know it's bullshit for doing the work for two Chinese classes to be fine until I'm *not* going on the Chinese exchange program anymore, and maybe even try to explain that not being a soprano doesn't automatically mean I'm an alto, so I must be able to tell them everything I need to. All the stuff I don't (can't) tell them can't be all that important, right?

Because if you can speak, that must mean you can communicate everything you might need to using speech, right?

Wrong.

Now meet sophomore year. I am fifteen.

Can writing save me yet?

Creative writing exists. I take it, by accident.

I am finally introduced to the idea that writing is not just essays for school.

Now it can be *fiction* for school. It can be *creative* things for school.

We meet in the computer lab. Everything is typed.

I don't hate writing. I hate *handwriting*.

The computer teaches me to love writing.

Junior year? Senior year? The summer between? I am sixteen, I am seventeen, and the stakes have gotten higher.

I can tell my teachers why my schedule is fucked up beyond all recognition (though I don't call it that, yet), and how I really would rather have physics and then Chinese, sequentially, than the third math class I need to graduate, but they really do need to make sure the paperwork to count my online class goes through because I *do* want to graduate. I can even tell the guidance counselor to stop messing with my electives to make them "look better on paper" and keep creative writing like I want over programming like she wants for me when giving me a study hall. I can't quite explain *why* I am so insistent on a third semester of creative writing, even if I've managed to explain that I will be taking that class. I can't tell them I'm not convinced I'm a girl. "For the purposes of this choir, what gender will I be at 7:30 PM tomorrow," as a question about uniform choice is the closest I come to explaining my relationship with gender. I can't explain that breaking routines would be harder than going to school after spending most of the night in the emergency room thanks to passing out at a swim meet. I can't tell them how scary the sentence, "You're not going to *any* college until your locker is clean!" is, even when I know they're (mostly) joking, though I manage to point out that my locker will be empty, and therefore clean, at the end of the school year. And while I've managed to tell the almost teacher from freshman year that "I reserve the right to check *just your notebook* if you're not keeping it in shape" terrified me out of my wits, I could not find the words to say her explanations of why it wouldn't have happened to me were all based on assuming capabilities I don't have. I can't make her understand that her definition of who she'd do that to absolutely includes me. Yes, my notebook will be that bad, because *I don't know how to create or maintain that kind of order.* But I can tell them why my schedule is fucked up beyond all recognition (but not call it that), and how I really would rather have physics and then Chinese, sequentially, than the third math class I need to graduate, but they really do need to make sure the paperwork to count my online class goes through because I *do* want to graduate. I can even tell the guidance counselor to stop messing with my electives to make them "look better on paper" and keep creative writing like I want over programming like she wants for me when giving me a study hall, so I must be able to tell them everything I need to. All the stuff I don't (can't) tell them can't be all that important, right?

Because if you can speak, that must mean you can communicate everything you might need to using speech, right?
Wrong.

Can writing save me yet?
Not yet.
"You should probably make my schedule reflect where I'm going to be, then."
Creative writing it is.
I can save that future.

Writing may yet save me.

Consider college. I am eighteen, nineteen, twenty, twenty one, twenty two.

I can tell my professors that the tutoring situation is slightly silly, that enrollment services has no clue what to do with my weird status, and that speech giving out on me completely for English doesn't mean it's necessarily gone in Chinese, or vice versa. I can't tell them the quirky persona I'm showing is as close to normal as I can get, comfortably or not. I can't tell them my ability to say "no" outside educational contexts remains mostly theoretical. I can't tell them I think I'm watching my burnout as it happens. I can't tell them how sick I feel after every lab in the machine shop. I can't tell them I'm worried about my ability to simply *exist* in the environments in which mechanical engineers often work. I can't tell them I tend not to take notes because I can't consistently read my own handwriting, so what good would handwritten notes do me anyways? *I can't tell them just because speech appears to be working, that doesn't mean I can use speech to meet all my needs.* But I can tell them that the tutoring situation is slightly silly, that enrollment services has no clue what to do with my weird status, and that speech giving out on me completely for English doesn't mean it's necessarily gone in Chinese, or vice versa, so I must be able to tell them everything I need to. All the stuff I don't (can't) tell them can't be all that important, right?

Because if you can speak, that must mean you can communicate everything you might need to using speech, right?
Wrong.

But I can't tell them just because speech appears to be working, that doesn't mean I can use speech to meet all my needs.

Not with speech, in any case.

Can writing save me yet?
I finally *know* I'm Autistic.
I finally *know* speech gives out on me.
I finally *know* writing and typing to communicate are options.
All the pieces are in place.
Do I dare disturb the universe?
Know the rules, then break them.

Let's move on to graduate school. I am twenty two, twenty three, twenty four, twenty five, twenty six.

I can use speech to tell my professors and colleagues and teammates my baseline is atypical for pretty much everything, and how they should keep that in mind when there's a question of injury or illness, and that I do need to keep a back-up for speech with me pretty much all the time, and how I'm worried about starting over at a new school where people *don't* know what I understand just fine even when I can't speak. I can't tell them why most people will find out about speech giving out on me the "hard" way when it happens — not with speech, at least. I can type it, though. I can't tell them why the requirements for personal statements are breaking my brain — not with speech, at least. I can type it, though. I can't tell them how I expect a proof to go in math, sometimes — not with speech, at least. I can write it on the side board, though. I can't explain how shocking it is to watch speech give out on me during a *math* class, because that was always safe before — not with speech, at least. I can type it, though. I can't tell a well-meaning classmate that I've *already tried* telling myself I don't and won't lose speech, and that I didn't much like the results — not with speech, at least. I can type it, though. I can't tell anyone *anything* at neuroscience orientation — not with speech, at least. I can type, though. But I can use speech to tell them my baseline is atypical for pretty much everything, and how they should keep that in mind when there's a question of injury or illness, and that I do need to keep a back-up for speech with me pretty much all the time, and how I'm worried about starting over at a new school where people *don't* know yet that I understand things just fine even when I can't speak, so I must be able to tell them everything I need to. All the stuff I don't (can't) tell them — not in speech, at least — can't be all that important, right?

Because if you can speak, that must mean you can communicate everything you might need to using speech, right?
Wrong.
Writing, I can say so.

ALYSSA HILLARY is an Autistic math teacher, part time AAC user, and Ph.D. student in neuroscience with a tendency towards poetry and/or well-cited rants when Emotions happen. Sometimes the well cited rants become journal articles. Their work appears in several previous Autonomous Press anthologies, on Disability in Kidlit, *in* Autism in Adulthood, *and on their blog, yesthattoo.blogspot.com.*

Carcosa

Harmony Neal

NAME — AS IT IS AND WILL ALWAYS BE. I am all of my component pieces and moments. I travel to my future and past selves. I taste their lips, their tears, their blood. I know what's coming, again and again

physics is life, is the answer, is the question. The multiverse is a hologram. Time is a fixed entity. Time is a flat circle. Not only have I lived all of this life over and over and will again and again, but I have lived all of my possible lives over and over and will again

jumping right now, making that jump. Kay's youngest, Peter, who I never meet, is in the hospital. Kay is covering her head with her arms. She's packing her suitcase and taking Victor junior home to that fucker. She's packing her suitcase and taking Victor junior to the shelter to get away from that fucker

Violet is losing the leash. Violet is asking about my tattoo. The birds on my back are circling around. Violet is putting on her mask. She's taking off the mask

patrolling. I am always patrolling. Pads under my suit for protection. Blue suit and tie. Crisp white shirt. I patrol. I squint against the sun, the glare from my shined up shoes. I loosen my tie. Women and children. It's always about women and children and the men who hurt them

what I should have been doing with my life, but hadn't, except I had been, on different points in the line. Everything I do, I've done and will do and am doing

a man. I am he. Safety and protection for the least respected among us. I have chosen, am choosing, will choose

when Violet does her interview, she tells me the Existentialist said I'm crazy. When Violet does her interview, she loses control of Dumbo. When Violet does her interview, she traces the carcosa of birds on my back with her fingertips. Later, at the same time, in the past, I trace the carcosa of her back in my room with the dogs and cats and birds all singing outside the locked door that is always and never locked

who apprehend reality in ways most don't are often called crazy, like Payne, Rubin, Semmelweis, Einstein

separation, sorrow, deprivation, I hold her thrumming body in the dark, make promises

that everything you've ever done and everything you'll ever do is all happening eternally and at the same time

Violet touches my breasts, I will shudder, shameless, in my man's woman's body. We will entwine our carcosas. She will forgive me and I will forgive her, as we have done over and over, the way we came

trying to get in through the locked bars. Victor is grabbing Tank from the cluster of small dogs, unhinging the leash. Violet is putting on her mask. Tank squeals like a pinned rabbit, his blood splatters red on the concrete where my blood is and will be, where Victor's blood is and will be

    still have a choice, in the moment, and you cannot blame the universe

    Vera Rubin proved the existence of dark matter, and that the universe is filled with it, which her male colleagues refused to believe. Ignaz Semmelweis is the reason doctors — and the rest of us — wash their hands, but when he first told the medical community about germs, creatures too small to see with the naked eye, they called him insane, are calling him insane. He died in an insane asylum. He is dying in an insane asylum right now

    when Violet comes, she makes a sound like a hummingbird. Her atoms and my atoms vibrate at the same frequency. We blur into one solid object, one flat circle viewed from the fourth dimension

    like The Existentialist. He's got some good ideas, but it's backwards to start with philosophy. Start with physics, which describes the nature of reality

    walking the dogs: Bella, Bella, Dumbo, Frank, Tank, Quinn, Gigi, Smith, Mr. Waddles, and Bella. Violet takes the small dogs, I take the big dogs, keep Dumbo from jumping

    punching Victor, winning, Kay comes running, screams at me, Dumbo jumps

    Victor grabs Peter, his son, their atoms vibrate at different frequencies, the bones in Peter's arm snap like dried wood, like pieces of time out of sequence, the yellow bones jagged and begging to be set right

Kay meets Carcosa, she has lost her path, wound up in an old brick building with institutional beige paint and tile and a dozen other women with a dozen other children, all still trying to hide their wounds. I tell her there is always the path and we are always on it. She sobs into my chest, pulls back at the softness, then pushes in, nuzzles there, leaves black and blue marks on the white, white fabric

view their lives linearly, but life can also be experienced as a shuffled deck of cards

look good in my blue suit. I look good with my fingers through my short hair. I make a beautiful man, will be, have been, am

shows me Queen of Mirrors ♪. The Vanishing Twin, says it means separation, sorrow, deprivation, looks at me with wet Violet eyes

in my apartment are the leftovers, the witnesses, the subclass. In my apartment are the animals who bear witness, the animals left behind, the animals forbidden entrance at the shelters, the animals men would sacrifice

toss a football with Victor junior, his puppy Tank running back and forth in the patchy grass. He tells me he wishes his dad were dead. He tells me he wishes his mom were dead. He tells me he wishes he were dead. I tell him there is no death, make sure you

bring the women their witnesses. Watch as they cuddle, snuggle, and play. I witness the witnesses witness. Over and over, this is how we all repeat ourselves

no delusions. Few will escape. Most will go back. Some will

die. I help those I can. I give them bright spots on their flat circles, moments of respite before they are back under fists and feet, back in the bone-snapping, blood-letting cycles that comprise their short lives they will live over and over

after Violet puts on her mask, Dumbo jumps. While Violet puts on her mask, Dumbo jumps. Violet is always putting on her mask. Dumbo is always jumping

touches my cuts and bruises with cotton dipped in antiseptic, unbuttons my white shirt with trembling fingers

women cling to me for small comfort, confide things they wouldn't speak to counselors. Then they go back, some die

the children are sad-eyed, haunted. The children cry. The children want to go home. The children want to run away. The children want to die

thrumming like a hummingbird, Violet speaks my true

HARMONY NEAL *was awarded a 2018 Minnesota Artist Initiative Grant to develop new models of storytelling grounded in human and non-human flourishing. Her/his/their stories have recently appeared in* Shadows & Tall Trees, Paper Darts, The Fantasist, Black Static, *and* Interzone. *You can read more about Carcosa and Violet in "The Trial of Black Panther" http://thefantasistmag.com/the-trial-of-black-panther/ She/he/they encourage(s) everyone to get hysterical about the oppression and degradation all around us. Harmonyisawitch.com*

Trans Queer Travel Vortex [5+++]

Gerard Sarnat

1. FUCK MY LIFE

i. fml+

blue box
clusterfuck
guilt my life
is, younger bro
error perished on
borrowed chopper
that day before I made
it back home to Jerusalem
last Passover — for this year
the new non-stop flight from SF
meant way easier with toddler tyke
plus our beacon Ima had shut off now's
turned back on again littlest bits with a grin
even laughs every once in a blue Israeli moon
while Abba, drab cucumber he always appears,
remains so inscrutable whether there's any grief,
whilst younger sister, whom each parent has loved
and will support although really deeply disappointed
she was trans, seems their one mourning longest by far—
whereas baby girl of family, just completed some alternative
to avoid military service, must be strong since both boys gone.

2. SAFE WAY TO GO? [4] Feel free to

i. Sally Swinggood's

With 1335 stores in the US alone,
the grocery chain appears to have set an upward looking
policy of equality in gender-hiring
which maybe is reflected in my statistically insignificant
sample size of a passel of 5 tall
clerks seeming to identify as She who are able to reach
the previously unreachable top
shelf to grab me a handful of packets of transfat popcorn.

ii. TransIt

Closet
pried
ajar

gender
dissidence
unbound

post-op
posit
appellations.

THEY HAIKU

iii. High School

She tries to boysex
gay away — but it don't work
— so then avoids them.

iv. Not a *Mr., Mrs., Miss or Ms.*?

Then *Mx.*-match fluid
trans, a or non-conforming
gender honorifics.

3. PRISONER HAIKU [4]

Group Process

We weave

primary gang colors

into a quilt of intimacy.

5 AM Equanimity Practice Haiku
Hundreds of hungry
inmates line up for
fixes — a pressure cooker.

Post Prison

Surfing the Pacific

after 60 years — a kid's

zest again — plop.

Coincidencia

Is it by chance *hombres* who've asked,

"*Tu* marriage monogamous?"

son bi?

4. Spirit Rock 'N Roll

"If it's not simple,
it ain't Vipassana."

While stipulating
Our local Buddhist
Sangha's my current
Community of choice
           Sometimes

Sunday mornings I wonder
When trying to quiet by just
Sitting following the breath
Why OMG why oh why must
THEY
Always ignore the front
Door warning that asks,
Go around to the side,
So as not to disturb us
            Meditators
Rather week after week
Clodhopping and gravely
Yakking blithely instead
Of being (duh) mindful
Triggering
Nasty thoughts that I'm
Glad X's first husband died
In car crash, Y's second wife
From painful cancer till
            Settling
Steeped childlike emptiness
Everything begins to still
Regardless of all honking
Distractions: the practice.
Respiring
In and out sure feels like
An inside job, a massage
Or caress even sour expiration
Momentum I must confess
            Brain
Moving too fast, too shallow
Though stay with it unjudged
No matter your river's flow
Pulses of life's fluid flux as

Body
Soft erect ripens toward clarity
Tenderizing attachments perhaps
Conceits into clarity not 'cause Should
but because love's a thousand kisses
      Deep.

5. San Francisco Succor

".... half of the world will fracture...
sagas the wise were too dumb to find: the shivering wolves
aflame in their savagery....
Maybe a man lived somewhere—
            consider—
down in his yard, vicious, in the trash
and low schemes, but all of his life
by his door, unmerited, a fir tree
grew; at the top whole generations
of beautiful birds lived and sang" ....
— William Stafford, Memorandum

Jewish Film Festival*
38th annual extravaganza
At The Castro

After grabbing a bite
With buddies from
All over the Bay Area

We mosey on in to get
Good seats for Opening
Night's Love, Gilda

That're saved by friends
Developed over four decades:
They used to be referred

To as Dykes on Bikes
Back in the day when
It seemed all about leather.

Together laughing our asses
Off watching wacky Radner's
Roseanne Roseannadanna

This whole bunch of us packing
The theater haven't had so much fun
Since last summer's reunion.

*beginning 17 days from now, 19July2018

Bonus: Identify Crisis Life Line

Gays survive AIDs
gender roles softening
men nursing babies
maybe our generation's
only plusses so let us
hold off on her frivoles.

GERARD SARNAT is a physician who's built and staffed homeless and prison clinics as well as a Stanford professor and healthcare CEO. He won the Poetry in the Arts First Place Award plus the Dorfman Prize, and has been nominated for Pushcarts plus Best of the Net Awards. Gerry's writing has appeared widely including recently in such U.S. outlets as Gargoyle, Main Street Rag, New Delta Review, MiPOesias, American Journal Of Poetry, Poetry Quarterly, Poetry Circle, Every Day Poems, Clementine, Tiferet, Foliate Oak, New Verse News, Blue Mountain Review, Danse Macabre, Canary Eco, Fiction Southeast, Military Experience and the Arts, Poets And War, Cliterature, Qommunicate, Texas Review, Brooklyn Review, San Francisco Magazine, The Los Angeles Review, *and* The New York Times. *He's also authored the collections* Homeless Chronicles *(2010),* Disputes *(2012),* 17s *(2014), and* Melting the Ice King *(2016). Gerry's been married since 1969 with three kids, five grandsons and looking forward to future granddaughters.*

Hearts and Tails

Dora M Raymaker

FIRST LAW OF THE REACHABLE NOWS:
No alternate versions of a person may be in eye-
line of each other within the same now, or both
will suffer immediate death by fire.

SECOND LAW. Travel ("slipping") between
reachable nows can only be done if a person has
alternates in all nows, and all alts must be
living.

THIRD LAW. Movement within a reachable now
is limited to locations where all nows are most
alike—typically, a single city.

FOURTH LAW. Slipping occurs at the location
where all reachable nows align. This location
will attract alts and repel others.

FIFTH LAW. Disrupting the reality of one now
— via introduction of technology, ideas, or
objects from a different now — attenuates
reality.

SIXTH LAW. Attenuated reality can heal when
no new disruptions are introduced.

*SEVENTH LAW. If reality attenuates too much,
the differences between worlds go off-balance
such that either*

    *a) the nows become too different and can no
longer be reached; or*

    *b) the nows become too similar and random
people, locations, or objects suffer
immediate death by fire (see FIRST
LAW).*

*Thus, responsible travelers safeguard the balance
and leave minimal trace of their passing.*

*LAST LAW OF THE REACHABLE NOWS: Do
not linger in the slip. It will tear you apart.*

—pages 1-3 of the *Logbook of the Reachable
Nows,* located at the Slipoint Church

MAC CARROLL CHECKS HIS WATCH, and pulls the collar of his leather jacket tight against the spring chill. This helps not at all since the cold is coming through his jeans from the Slipoint Church's marble floor. His notebook has been erased and reused so many times sketching theorems that he can see the deltas of his equations showing through.

You buy yourself a fucking watch, Mac, but not a new notebook?

Yeah, because your notebooks from high school are the only friends you've got left.

He writes, taking care not to rip the paper with the sharpened pencil-point.

March 13, 1991.
15:15.

I was followed again.

I don't fucking get it.

The only people who should be able to get within twenty feet of this shelled-out ruin of a medieval church between Krezletan and the forest without their skin crawling clean off are me and Pasha Toth, because we're the only people in this city who can slip between realities.

He stops and chews his pencil. The bitter taste of wood and graphite conjures sevens. Not all numbers have flavors, but as a number/logic synaesthetic, Mac found they all have colors. Seven is an unpleasant brown. He looks up through the hole in the roof, bombed out in the War, banishing sevens in the murk of light through dust. The toppled steeple lies outside like a dead leviathan.

The most likely explanation for my tail is that it's one of Pasha's agents. Someone she's zombified with her mind-control magic to ignore the nameless dread this church evokes in anyone the slip between realities doesn't recognize. Someone sent to make sure I, Pumptown loser I am, don't screw up the sweet deal she and her three alternate selves have plundering each other's realities for exciting new ways to keep us Pumptown losers down.

He stops again, as new to keeping a diary as he is to having a watch and knowing the colors of time. He hadn't expected that writing things down would make them feel so much more real, and that makes him uncomfortable. He writes anyway, pencil tip catching and tearing the thin paper:

Well, if it is one of Pasha's agents, sent to spy on me, they're going to be fucking disappointed. All I do is sit in the Slipoint Church and write in this falling-apart notebook because I'm a mathematician, not a fucking action hero.

And right now I'm not even that because I can't figure out this goddamn fucking equation.

Jesus, Mac, lighten up.

Yeah, right, the last time you "lightened up," you almost destroyed four realities.

Fuck.

He glares into the diary. He needs to write things down in order to track them. In order to find logical relationships between actions and reactions so that reality doesn't accidentally attenuate too much again and cause random things to spontaneously combust. But he's not making much headway on that.

The fact that Slipoint Church is repellent to almost everyone aside, no one goes into the bombed-out dead-zone around here unless they're trying to disappear forever into the forest. Yet, two days ago, there was Hoodie, hiding out behind the steeple, waiting for me.

And the next day, waiting for me on the corner of 18th and Wrens Way, real close to home. They're a fucking obvious, lousy tail, too. Which rules out an Agent from Central stalking me for my maths skills, so what the fuck?

And then today, Hoodie was waiting for me on the edge of the dead-zone. And this time they followed me *inside* the church. They're back there, behind me, right now, like I don't know they're there, which is probably why I CAN'T FUCKING

CONCENTRATE ON FIGURING OUT THIS
GODDAMN FUCKING EQUATION.

Well, it's not like I'm going to examine the
non-Euclidean manifold inside the slipoint while
Hoodie's watching. And I'm not going to slip into
one of the three other nows until I figure out the
differential equations describing the dynamic
equilibria between the worlds, which I'll probably never be able to figure out anyway, not even
if I had access to the digital computers in some of
the other nows, which I don't, because I'm stuck
here in Krezletan where all we've got's lousy,
stupid magic, until I figure out if it's safe for me
to slip without triggering mass-fucking-destruc-
tion again, blah.

Florence lights a cigarette and listens to Mac's biker boots
stomping up the stairs. Mac's gait is off, like he's weary, or
carrying something awkward. The fan over the living room table
— really cardboard boxes covered with a bright bandanna atop a
dark square of fabric to hide their true form — swirls smoke to
crawl along the ceiling. This is the best place either of the men
have lived, and though rent is mostly up to his best friend at the
moment, it's been mostly up to Flo in the past. Survival in Pumptown is all about having each other's backs. *And even that doesn't
keep everything from going up in flames.*

Downstairs, The Parlor nightclub is quiet. Later, the bands will
clunkily load in, and the floor will get musical for the night. Floor-
gigs are an extra perk of the place, and tonight's lineup is two
great punk bands — Rotten Willie and Split Ozone — followed by
the epic industrial act Recyclr. There never will be another
DethVox, but Recyclr's been scratching that itch lately. They've
got a killer chemical synth, more vacuum amps than can fit on The
Parlor's stage, and Mikal can do more with a fiddle bow and the

literal trash people throw at him for a challenge than should be possible outside of actual magic.

Flo looks at his palms and frowns. Magic. That's something he wishes he didn't know anything about. Every time he thinks of it, he thinks of the friends he's lost.

He sighs and stretches his tall, lanky self, comfortable in a men's sleeveless tank and lacy pajama bottoms dotted with rainbows and unicorns. He runs his painted nails through his beard — it's almost long enough to braid — and wonders what his best friend's keeping from him this time.

Mac clatters in with an armload of takeout Chinese. "Some fucking help here," he says.

But he's in the door too fast for Flo to do anything but grab the ashtray and a stack of maths books off the improvised table before Mac sprawls the dinner down with a hiss and a wince.

"There's a new girl at the Lucky Fan." Mac shrugs out of his army bag and leather jacket, shoving strands of black hair too slippery for his ponytail out of his eyes. "So dinner's gonna be a bit of a roulette."

"Hey, it's dinner." Flo pokes inside the plastic bag where boxes sit like treasure chests. "I don't care if it's random chicken feet again."

"You hated it when they had that mix-up with the random chicken feet."

"Yeah, well, I ate them, didn't I?"

The two men glare off, Flo's hands-on-hips, Mac's arms crossed, then bust up laughing.

"God, I hope it's not chicken feet," Flo says.

"Jesus. Me too."

The contents of the takeout turn out not so bad, and the men eat side-by-side on the natty sofa in hungry silence until most of it is gone.

"You gonna tell me what's bugging you?" Flo leans back into the cushions. "You've been an extra-moody cunt lately."

Mac lights a cigarette and watches the smoke curl into the ceiling fan like he can read the future in its whirls. Perhaps, Flo thinks, he can. Mac is a maths savant, a First Maths Competition winner, and to him the world looks like a rainbow spray of numbers and logic. It's what landed him with Florence's arts gang back in high school, rather than sliding in with the rest of the poorest, meanest kids on the poor, mean streets of Pumptown.

"Probably not, no," Mac says, still intent on the blades of the ceiling fan.

Florence rolls his eyes with theatrical exaggeration. For good measure, he kicks Mac in the shin. "C'mon. You've been acting strange even for you. Last time you didn't wanna talk about it, I got kidnapped by the mob."

Mac sighs and plants his feet square on the hardwood floor, elbows on knees, staring at the space between them. "Let me make sure there's something to talk about first."

Now Florence sighs. There's been a gathering of silence between them since the Millhouse Row fire. Florence doesn't know where Mac spends most of his time when he's not doing temp work as a computer, or why he hides the fact that his hand is still fucked-up from that nasty cut he got just before the Row blew up — hence the hiss, the wince, the fact Mac's taken to wearing fingerless gloves even in the house. Mac can be a macho asshole, but until recently, he's always dropped the act around Flo. Although, to be fair, Flo hasn't told Mac that he can do magic, and neither of them have said one word to each other about the thirty-six dead artists and friends they lost in the fire. Everything is more risk than Florence feels he can take. If Central picks him up, fine, but he doesn't want Central to take Mac. Florence reckons he'd survive working for those rich asshats if he had to, but Mac would drown himself in the river first. And Mac's already marked because of his maths aptitude, and his triple-A ranking as a certified computer, and his bad attitude toward authority. Flo looks at his palms again and thinks about how he could will them into flame, which he wants to do all the time just on principle of rage. *Set fire to fucking Central for forcing us to squat in condemned buildings, show them how it feels.* "Yeah, okay. Just don't wait too long to figure it out. I worry about you."

Mac looks away.

The next day, Mac sits in the church and stares at the spot where the slipoint exists. It's the place where four paths through spacetime meet and travel together. It's a portal between four reachable nows through which Mac can slip to worlds like his own, only with necromantic viruses, psy-ops, or virtual reality instead of magic. Mac doesn't know how long the slipoint will remain, but he does know how easy it is to upset its balance.

He hisses and presses on the palm of his hand where a virus from the Moiya reality has made a minor but permanent wound. He'd gotten good at compensating for it, thus it stopped bleeding and hurting, thus he'd forgotten to compensate for it while carrying the Chinese up the stairs and torn it open again. Now he invokes its pain as a shield against things that hurt more.

Work the slipoint balance out, Mac. Work it the fuck out in your notebook so you don't destroy things that matter. You're worse than a chemical weapons spill, Mac.

He looks at his watch for the colors of the date and time and writes:

> March 14, 1991.
> 13:25.
> Things I know:
> At an arbitrary place in this bombed-out medieval church sits a one-dimensional portal called the slipoint that synchronizes four discrete three-dimensional realities.
> Inside the slipoint is a multi-dimensional non-Euclidean manifold.

Red, orange, blue, and black.

Red for one — the one-dimensional portal into the slipoint.

Orange for three — three-dimensional Mac Carroll somehow able to fit my skinny punk-ass self through that red-one-D portal.

Blue for four — the four *reachable nows* that are the same city, at the same point in time, but different points in space, called Krezletan, Moiya, Chrome, and New Raimera that I can enter through the
yet-undefined and therefore
black
manifold.

Red-orange-blue-and-black

a place where four four-dimensional world-lines line up creating a single now, a point shared by four spaces, four-D space-time four four four four times four sixteen blue blue blue blue like the bluest blue that ever was—

Mac stops writing and closes his eyes, the numbers washing over him like seas. They are beautiful to him, beautiful and terrifying.

"Fuck," he mutters and writes:

Things I don't know:

How to keep all four realities from spontaneously combusting because I've told anyone about them, or dragged technology from one to the other, or basically done anything that upsets the equilibrium of keeping them just-different-enough.

Ergo, I don't know what to do when Flo

pushes me to tell him where I've been or what's going on with me.

Or how to construct the differential equations that would tell me how to maintain the equilibrium so I could tell Flo without him literally going up in flames.

Or if I should just drown myself in the river because that solves absolutely everything.

Or who keeps fucking following me because they're standing back there again, behind the toppled pews, like I don't know they're there. Creepy little fucking hoodie person, shit.

Devi squats behind the pew, shivering inside her hoodie. Her skin feels slick and painful, especially her scalp. She hasn't washed in the two weeks she's been on the run; she learned quickly not to try to bathe in the river. Her heart beats about her chest like she's all heart and nothing else in the lightness of hunger. She's had only scraps of scraps to eat, and Devi is not used to scraps.

Scraps are still better than being used against my will. I'll die before I go back to that life. I'll — I don't know. Drown myself in the river if I have to.

Devi sighs softly so the man won't hear, and looks at her dirty hands. She has so much power in them, but none of it is useful in her current situation. It takes too long to cast a credible illusion of someone else upon herself and, while adept in counter-magic, it isn't spells that are dogging her, at least not any kind of spell she can recognize.

I need to get out of this whole stupid, stinking city. Devi looks around the dim, dusty, broken church and clenches in frustration. Leaving the city hadn't been Devi's plan when she'd run away from home in Central. Drawn to Pumptown by the voice of Disinformation Deborah — the heroine of the pirate radio station that sometimes cut into official broadcasts — Devi thought she'd make a new life on the wrong side of the river. *If only I'd had a few more days to try to make friends before* he *found me. If only Pumptown really was full of "solidarity, community, and freedom" like Disinformation Deborah promised, instead of liars, Pumptown losers, and desperate, piggish men. If only I could escape this stupid, pointless, broken church.*

Devi has tried everything to be somewhere else. But this church is where she ended up the first night she ran away, in a delirium of fear and fogs of people she never was — the counter-magic she used to break the spells on herself had still been shaky then. This church is where she has ended up every time in the past two weeks that she has tried to walk into the forest, or head to the southern highways to hitch a ride out of Krezletan with a trades caravan, or to flip a coin to choose a random path past city limits. Devi's never been good at maths, but she knows those odds are unnatural.

And yet, I can't detect any magic about this place at all. I should be able to get out of Krezletan easily. I'm a spy, after all. Devi winces; the word "spy" is true, but the statement feels wrong. *I was a spy.* She tries instead, but it doesn't feel much better to her. *I was a tool of spies until I got strong and sassy like Disinformation Deborah on Resistance Radio Transmission and broke free?* That thought feels right to Devi, but she knows it isn't true. She's not free of the agent who hunts her, and she's not free of this church either.

Four days ago, the man with the notebook showed up in the church to sit on the floor just past the toppled pews.

He scared her at first, with his big leather boots and his big leather jacket, and his pinched-up face and swagger like the Pumptown losers who almost did her harm when she tried to wash in the river. But as she watched him, sitting on the dusty church floor and writing in his notebook, he changed. She's not sure now if he's a man or a boy in a big jacket, not much older than herself. She's seen him smile and curse at his notebook, and sometimes his eyes are full of wonder.

Devi doesn't know why he's in the church, either. She even followed him for a day, but no answers came of it.

She just knows that she has to get out of the city, and the church won't let her go.

It must *be magic to keep me here, maybe some spell of amnesia I haven't yet fully countered? Some tricky spell set on this place that for some reason I can't yet detect?*

Devi gives up again on trying to figure out why she's back at the church again. She opens her hands and focuses her will, gathering magic until her palms glow. But the kind of magic she does won't answer any of her questions, and she can't sense anything here to counter, so she closes her fingers into fists and they go dark. For a breath of a moment she wishes she could bring back the memories of strangers that had been pushed into her head, because maybe one of them knows what is going on. But then she remembers how much she sacrificed to banish them all and be, finally, just herself.

She whispers aloud to make the oath real: "I swear I'll die before I go back."

> still March 14, 1991.
>
> 17:08.
>
> My tail is sneezing. Which makes me even more certain it's not one of Pasha Toth's agents, because, let's face it, a professional wouldn't go out on assignment with a cold.
>
> My tail has also spent an entire afternoon in the church without barfing or screaming, so there's even more proof against it being some prick from Central sniffing after me for my maths skills.
>
> So, for the sake of argument, could my tail be from another set of alts?

Mac stands, yawning and stretching.

According to the *Logbook of the Reachable Nows*, the centuries-old diary of anyone who's ever slipped between realities hidden behind the fallen pews, alts are incredibly rare. Mac doesn't even have alts — the slip just thinks he's all four of his alts at once, which is even more rare, if it's ever happened at all. It's not mentioned in the *Logbook*.

And the Millhouse Row fire happened because of it. Because of you. *You attenuated reality and caused spontaneous combustions. You.*

Shut up, Mac.

He writes:

> How would I know, really, if there were other alts?
>
> It's not like we're all buddies or anything; I mean, the Toth-alts hate my fucking guts.
>
> Am I in danger?
>
> Is Flo in danger?
>
> Is Pumptown in danger?
>
> Fuck.

At about nine-thirty, Florence steps out of the rehearsal space onto a busy Wrens Way. The evening smells clean, with the wind blowing away the stench from the steel mills to the south. He crunches his duffel under his arm and turns toward home. He and Anais are working up a new performance piece called "Nerves." Anais calls it "a post-modern tribute to nihilism in the age of mutually assured chemical annihilation," but Florence describes it as, "a multi-media bit on fuck the system, plus we get the audience drunk — come see it, you'll love it!"

The Pumptown arts district glows with neons in as many languages as there are refugee micro-communities — no small number given that Krezletan, uniquely, has stayed neutral through the seventy-seven years of the War, which isn't really over, just gone cold after the Ottoman Empire dropped its chembombs on Germany and broke the Central Powers. Not too much has changed for Krezletan since then: Central continues to exploit Pumptown for its spy networks and mills from within and export its espionage and steel to everyone else without. And Central controls the magic.

When the offer came to be initiated into the resistance and do something proactive to fight for the common people's rights, Florence hadn't thought that meant they'd teach him magic. He hadn't even thought that magic existed outside the compound folktales of the dozens of cultures mixing in Pumptown's spicy, sweaty air.

"If Central finds out you're awake, they'll take you in and use you. And if they can't use you, they'll kill you. That's how come no one in Pumptown believes the rumors of magic are real, but everyone knows Central can make people disappear. That's why you never saw magic until today."

Florence shivers, remembering Razza's words after his initiation. Now Razza's gone, blown to shit in the Millhouse Row fire along with three dozen other artists and revolutionaries, and Florence's connections to the resistance are gone with her.

I could make lives better with magic. I could flash my hands at any random rich person in Central and burn them until they handed over their wallet. I could light their fucking permed hair on fire, Flo thinks.

But he knows that's not how it would play out. Half the people in Central also have magic, and defenses, and a lot more training, and Flo would just get disappeared.

Same old story. We end up having to squat in shitty-ass condemned buildings that light on fire and kill everyone. There's no way to make anything better in Pumptown.

From the second story of the Laughing Hog Café, a spray of glitter and streamers erupts to the tune of a traditional Krezletan wedding song on accordion, and shouts of "Olé!" Flo looks up, shielding his eyes from the festive rain. He tosses an "Olé!" back, along with a lucky coin.

The revelers catch it through the open window and yell for the bride, and Florence grins away his black thoughts, more Mac's than his own. *There's no way to make anything better in Pumptown because everything's already better!* His step picks up a bounce. *That's what those tight-wads from Central will never know. That's why they come to our side of the river to unwind in genius that outshines their bland-as-fuck galleries and tired museums, because we have something they never will; we have community. The fire can't take everyone and neither can Central. I'm still here, and Mac's still here, and Anais and Recyclr and the people in that wedding party, we're all still fucking here!*

It's as Flo crosses to the next block that he notices he's picked up a tail. The man is good, very good. But he can't hide that his dark clothes are too new, and too perfectly tailored, and as someone who's been targeted his whole life for not conforming to gender norms, Flo is all too aware of people taking too much of an interest in him. Flo's pulse jolts, his feet miss their rhythm. He clutches sweating palms to the straps of his satchel, ready to wield it as a weapon. He makes evasive maneuvers; he has the benefit of terrain whereas someone from Central — as the man's clothes suggest — wouldn't have a clue.

By the time Florence reaches the side entrance to the apartment above The Parlor, he's sure he's shaken the man.

Until a thick body slams him hard against the brick wall.

His palms go hot with fire; his will, tightly wound, lashes within.

But a badge flashes in front of him, and he swallows his rage and the magic with it, lest he make a fatal mistake.

"Agent Schlitz, Central Intelligence," his tail says, like it wasn't written on the badge. "You're obligated by Krezletan law to obey." He punches Florence in the face.

Mac kicks off his biker boots and sits cross-legged with his notebook on his bed. There isn't much in his room — stacks of notebooks, maths journals borrowed from the library, black jeans and black t-shirts and black woolen sweaters stacked into splintering wooden crates set on their sides as shelves. Local band fliers cover one of the walls. Flo brought him the first few, and then it turned into a collection. He's never had private space to himself before, and every time he thinks about skipping the trip to the jobs pool to get another boring temp gig computing numbers for some shitty business, he reminds himself how nice it is to spread out where no one's going to barge in and beat him for existing. And where Flo — whom he loves fiercely, but can sometimes be a lot — isn't breathing the same air less than a yard away. Not to mention he owes Flo more than he can ever repay. Rent in a real two-bedroom is the least he can do.

Still, tonight, even this hard-won sanctuary doesn't feel safe.

> still March 14, 1991 fucking long day.
> 23:30.
> Left the church at 22:05 and got home to find Flo with a black eye, still trembling. I haven't seen him this scared AND this furious since high school when that stupid "Real Boyz" gang got to be more than the bunch of us could handle. I mean, this is Flo — he may dress like a nancy but he's big and strong and the scrappiest fighter I've ever known.
> I want to fucking kill those motherfuckers who dared lay a hand on him, and he won't tell me who they fucking are. He says it's "dealt with" and "I'm fine." Bull fucking shit.
> Meantime, I've got my own problems. I've picked up another tail.
> Not small, not wearing a hoodie, square and

male and tailored with the airs of an Agent from Central Intelligence looking for any fucking reason to nab me and use me in their shitty schemes. Literally spitting on their job offers isn't enough for them. He was waiting for me just outside when I left the church at 22:05.

On top of that I can't get that gash in my hand from the Moiya-reality's viral tech to stop oozing blood, meaning it's become, again, a big fucking beacon for anyone from that reality since some of them can literally smell that shit and

FUCKING-A I HATE MY FUCKING LIFE

No.

Really, I don't.

I'm just kinda...

lonely.

That's what you get, Mac, for being an asshole.

And, also, for being single-handedly (haha) responsible for the continued existence of four blue fucking worlds.

Maybe Flo will want to go out, burn off some of his rage with me on the dance floor. Maybe then he'll tell me what happened to his eye so I can make the motherfuckers pay.

Devi stares up at the lit window where the man from the church lives, wishing she was inside. Her fingers curl around memories of warm blankets and soft beds, of full plates and undisturbed sleep. But, too, with those memories of the comfortable times come other fragments:

the crack of a gun

the snap of a slap; it stings

slipping poison into a cup; the target's lips turn blue

a pale face, sweat-covered, lips parting to reveal monster-fangs

flying through the unwired web of cyberspace after an icon that looks
like Death
    hands, trembling, as I lie to a man in a dark coat who has been trained
to detect lies and he'll kill me if I fail to convince him and the persona
who knows how to lie is breaking apart in my counter-magic and I am
becoming Devi again—
    Devi shakes away the fogs and fears. As far as she can tell, it
was just normal growing up — and maybe a subconscious wish
to be herself — that developed her natural capacity for counter-
magic. At first it was unconscious; she'd be on a mission in an
exotic locale, wearing someone else's appearance as a skin
through her illusionist skill — and suddenly she was Devi again,
not the persona who belonged within that skin. Waking up on
mission never got less terrifying, but she did get better control of
the counter-magic over time, able to prevent the dispelling of the
persona pushed into her head until she was home again. *Home*
with Schlitz, and the others, where they gaslit me.
    But I know the truth now. I'm strong and sassy, like Disinformation
Deborah on the pirate radio. I'm Disinformation Devi, Deborah's plucky
younger sister from Central instead of Pumptown. If I can make my way
out of Krezletan, away from Agent Schlitz, I can make my way back up
to warm, well-lit rooms and unspoiled food.
    Earlier, Devi watched Schlitz beat up the man who lives with
the man from the church, but he didn't know anything. And even
if he did, it wouldn't be the first time this past two weeks Schlitz
had found her. Luckily, Devi has a stored spell to make a thing
appear an inch or so from where it really is, and she's used it to
keep him from being able to grab a hold of her. But at some point,
Devi knows, Schlitz will wear her out. He'll catch her too dead
asleep, or too weak from hunger, or too distracted by another
threat, and she won't have time to cast the spell. At least she's
been lucky that Schlitz is always alone. She's assumed it's because
her position in Central is so top-top secret they can't have many
people know. It's so top-top secret, they mind-wiped her between

missions, so not even she really knows.

Devi heaves a long, tired sigh and wipes her runny nose on the sleeve of her hoodie. The bottom line is, she needs to find out why she keeps ending up at the church every time she tries to escape the city, and the man with the notebook is her only lead. She's going to have to talk to him. Which means she has to wait for him. Which means she has to hide from everyone else, just outside his door.

She collects the strong, sassy self she wants to be, and pulls broken, mildewed boards from the dumpster to the fire escape, arranging them into shadows. Beneath the bars of the grate, tall grass pokes through the ancient cobbles. It's soft and clean. Devi settles down onto it and blows on the palms of her hands, gathering her illusionist magic. As long as she stays very still, barely breathing, and awake, she can maintain a shadow-spell.

When the band comes around the corner to load into The Parlor's stage door, they see a pile of dirty, old clothes beneath the wrought iron's darkness.

Mac exits the apartment into the alley and lights a smoke. He turns to look out onto Wrens Way where the nightlife streams thick as friendship.

Someone shouts "HEY!" and stabs a finger into his back, hard.

Mac turns, fists out in reflex born of years of fighting off foster siblings and everyone else who ever tried to make an issue of his maths interests. As he's about to clock his attacker on the jaw, he realizes he's swinging with his injured hand and pulls the torque. He still tags the person.

They spin back and hit the ground, sobbing.

At which point, Florence walks out of the building in silver rainbow-toed combat boots and a slinky skirt saying, "I wanna stop at Heinlein's for a hot dog on the way to the club—" Which he follows up with, "Jesusfuckingshit Mac, did you just punch a little girl?"

"I—" Mac is mostly noticing the pain in his hand. He shakes himself to try to clear it. "Um. I—"

"Mac? Who is this? Did you just hit this little girl?"

"I — I didn't know it was a little girl; she fucking jumped me!"

"Jesus, Mac, you're such an asshole." Flo holds out a hand to help her up.

The girl stares at Flo's leather jacket with the buttons and chains, and his spiked-out red hair sticking every-which-way, and cries harder.

"I didn't mean to, I — fuck." Mac stomps in a few strangled circles as he adjusts his assumptions and squats next to Florence. "Hey, I'm sorry. I feel like shit for punching you. But you shouldn't be jumping on people's backs in back alleys, what the fuck—"

She sneezes.

He processes the whole of her. It hadn't been obvious at first, because her hood is down, and the front unzipped, but this is Hoodie from the church — the first of his two tails.

Mac yelps and sidles backwards like a crab, which works not at all when he remembers he can't take the weight on his hand and falls hard on his shoulder, cursing.

"Sorry he's a dick," Flo says to Hoodie. "Give us a moment."

Florence hauls Mac to his feet and drags him a few yards away. "What the actual fuck, Mac," he hiss-whispers. "Why are you so scared of that girl? She's obviously had some shit-deal that's dumped her on the street. She's like twelve-years-old or some shit."

Mac can't tell Flo about the church and the slip, but now he has to tell him something. "You remember last night, over Chinese, you asked me what was bugging me? And I said I wasn't sure yet if it was enough of a problem to tell? Well, it's enough of a problem. It's *that* problem. Bawling there on the street."

"She one of your old foster sibs?"

"What? No. Fuck no, of course not. She's been tailing me. For three fucking days now, at least. I've no fucking clue why, I didn't even know she was a little girl until I recognized the hoodie just now. I don't know what the fuck she's got going on with me, but I don't fucking like it."

Flo shakes his head and turns back to Hoodie, who's still bawling. "C'mon. Let's get you cleaned up." He leads her upstairs to the apartment.

Mac feels like bawling himself. First the church, now the apartment; every small sanctuary is being breached. He swallows it with a grimace and a stomp of his boot. *Still better than you deserve.*

Jesusfuckingshit.

Agent Schlitz watches from the rooftop opposite The Parlor. He feels vindicated for questioning the faggot now. Clearly, he is involved in the mess with Devi, he just hadn't known it yet when Schlitz confronted him. And the other man—

Schlitz wishes for the nth time that his magic included telepathy. Even the weak telepathy that only worked with another telepath, because then he could contact Central Intelligence right here from the rooftop to learn who these people are.

Instead, he's going to have to find a phone.

While...

Agent Schlitz sits in the Laughing Hog Café and worries about what he saw at the Slipoint Church.

He's here for Devi, of course, to help Schlitz out because who else has clearance to work the problem, but instead he found the man, writing in a notebook for hours. Too many hours. Hours without becoming restless or appearing nauseated.

This is significant. He wonders how there could be a set of alts he doesn't know about. How could such a thing slip through Central's spy networks?

He wishes for the nth time he was home in Moiya where he could activate his personal messenger virus to link with headquarters.

Instead, he needs to find a phone.

March 15, 1991.

09:48.

So. Tail Number One — the sneezing tail, not the agent-y tail — is a seventeen-year-old girl from Central, where soft living has made her skin so smooth she looks about twelve, and she's a fucking mess. Her clothes are triple-bagged in plastic in the other room and I can still smell them. If she's from another set of alts, that means I could talk to her about the slip without anything spontaneously combusting. But since I'm the reason so many things spontaneously combusted, she'd probably hate me. Which is why I've been hiding in my room like a coward since Flo dragged her in last night.

Plus, I don't know what to say to even get started.

"So, are you a reality explorer too?"

or

"Which of the reachable nows are you from?"

or

"Would you like to see my differential equations?"

Or, you could not be a cock, Mac, and start with her name?

"What's your name?" the man from the church asks.

"Devi." Devi touches her jaw where he's left a bit of a bruise.

"I'm Mac. Macintosh Carroll. Because of the apple. People call me Mac."

Devi chews a nail. She's swimming in a pair of Florence's

girliest sweats. Now that she's clean and rested and fed, she feels even more like her strong, sassy self. Yet, the edge of feral, animal panic, once dulled by exhaustion and hunger, has become more acute too. She worries she'll lose herself to its roar, even if she stays out of Schlitz's clutches. She flicks yellow hair from her eyes, breathes deeply, and flares her nostrils. *It's okay. Today I'll get answers.* She's a little scared of what they might be, but not knowing is worse. *I've got to get out of Krezletan.*

Mac pushes at the strands of blue-black hair too silky to stay in his ponytail. In the better light, Devi thinks he might be part Chinese, which, while unheard of in Central, is common in Pumptown's ghetto. He opens his mouth, but Devi beats him to words.

"What is that place? The church? Why do I keep ending up there?" She cringes at the panic in her tone. She doesn't think that's how the strong, sassy sister of Disinformation Deborah should sound. She takes a deep breath and sticks out her chest.

Mac doesn't answer her anxious question. Instead, he asks, "How'd it feel to be there?"

"Fine, don't answer the simple question." Devi snaps. "If you must know, the church smells of dream-spice and cotton candy. The dust doesn't move. It's unnatural. Everything about it is unnatural. Including why I keep ending up there. So...why do I keep ending up there?"

"Are you from here?" His tone is overly casual, like it's a trick question.

"No, of course not. I'm from Central. Where there aren't any dirty losers, or people who punch you in the jaw for existing, or piles of poorly covered cardboard boxes instead of proper furniture. Which, I might add, is nothing like how your pirate radio sells it. Solidarity my ass. I thought things would be better here but they're just differently lousy. And there's no reason for you to be so frustrating on top of it all. Now answer my question, mister: Why do I keep ending up at the church?"

Mac's lip curls, gathering saliva, his body quivering so hard an entire hank of hair slides from its band. But he swallows the spit and grinds the words out, fists tight. "Krezletan though? You're from this city?"

"You know of another Central? Now answer my question, Pumptown loser!"

"Not a fucking chance, Pumptown Princess, not until we're done with mine. Why were you tailing me?"

"I wasn't! I mean, not at first. I just kept ending up at the church every time I tried to leave the city. And then you were at the church. Since you kept going back and I kept going back, and I couldn't figure out why, I thought if I watched you I'd figure it out?" It sounds thin as she says it, power fading from her fingers, and she sneezes, and wonders how many bad decisions she's made because she's alone and frightened, knows more about which fork to use than how to be a tough, and has a bit of a cold. *But he's a total jerk! Just as awful as everything else about this place.* "Look, all I want is to get out of town. I don't care about the church. And I don't care about you or stupid Pumptown. You could help. You don't have to live up to every bad stereotype we're taught about your side of the river, you know."

"Neither the fuck do you." Mac snaps and folds his arms across his chest, gloved hands balled up beneath his pits. "Tell me, Devi, this urgent need to leave town, this unseemly mixing with us 'Pumptown losers' — is an Agent from Central after you?"

The question detonates fear in Devi with an animal-adrenaline shot to flee the danger. She plunges for the door, sliding on the hardwood floor.

But Mac is bigger and faster, and gets there first, eyes round. "Fuck, Devi!" He spreads his arms across the door. "I'm not gonna turn you in. If I had my way, I'd have those fuckers from Central working in the steel mills and us in the posh towers. I'd never do a fucking thing to help them, so chill the fuck out. Tell me your story so I can get you out of town or whatever, or the fuck out of my apartment at least, because I don't appreciate being called a fucking goddamn loser by an entitled fucking princess fucking teenager!"

Devi can't tell him her story. It's about magic and secrets of initiation Mac Carroll from Pumptown can't know. It's about the hundreds of other-people's-lives she'd been made to believe were her own while she used her illusionist skills to wear their faces, and the people she's screwed over and killed — against her will but still! Killed! And how, now that she has a true self that wants memories of its own, memories that aren't fog and death and match the face she sees in the mirror, she can't go back. She whimpers around the truth.

They send me out on spy-ops as other people, to keep Krezletan safe, but I hate it. I hate it I hate it I hate it! I hate it because they use their pushers to imprint me with other people's identities and wipe my memories in between, and I never agreed to any of it. I've done terrible things, and I don't know who I am, but I am ME and I want a life of MY OWN!

But those things are secrets atop secrets, and telling anyone will only make her life more at risk.

Devi sits with her head between her legs, hyperventilating. When the panic ebbs enough to be a person again and whisper, she offers what she can. "The person after me — his name is Agent Schlitz. He's my — my boss. I ran away from my, um, job. Because I'm too useful and they wouldn't let me quit. I came here because I thought Pumptown workers had each other's backs, like they say on that pirate broadcast, the Resistance Radio. Solidarity. What a lie! But whatever. I don't care. I'll die before I go back to where I was. I'll die first, I swear."

Mac sighs and slouches away from the door. "Fucking hell."

"An agent from Central's after her," Mac jabs his finger at Devi as they settle around the living room with breakfast.

Florence drops his fork, spattering eggs everywhere, and sits with his mouth half-open, full of half-chewed food.

"Well that's fucking disgusting," Mac says.

"His name's Agent Schlitz." Devi sighs.

Flo picks up his jaw, swallows, huffs, and quivers with rage.

Mac eyes him sideways, having a good idea now of where Flo's black eye came from. *Fuck, even that's my fault it turns out. Devi snooping on me, Schlitz following her following me home, snooping after Florence—*

Except, there's a discrepancy in the timeline.

The colors are all wrong.

"What's he want with you?" Flo asks.

Devi repeats her vague story about running away from her vague job and thinking she'd find sanctuary here because she didn't understand how things on this side of the river really work. Thankfully, as far as Mac's concerned, she doesn't ask Florence about the church.

Florence touches his bruised eye and grimaces. "Well, don't worry, Devi. We're the last people who are gonna turn you in."

In Mac's mind, colors flash in-and-out, shifting between purple-green and yellow-red.

There's definitely a mistake in the timeline. Observed reality doesn't line up with calculated reality.

What the fuck's that even mean?

Dunno. Something bad. Everything with you is something bad. You should be fucking quarantined.

It's the same thing that happens when another computer at one of Mac's temp jobs does their figures wrong — Mac can tell there's an error because the colors of the sums on the page aren't the *right* colors for the solution to the calculation. What he *sees* is trying to transform into what he *knows*.

He shifts uncomfortably on the couch and takes his plate away to his room to finish up. Flo and Devi have segued into talking about fashion anyway.

March 15, 1991.

10:35.

The error in time's got something to do with Agent Schlitz. Schlitz. Sounds like goddamn shits. Agent-fucking Shits. Great, now we've got Shits on our asses, like I needed something else following me around that stinks.

I can't have Agent Shits fucking with Florence. Florence has been through enough, and I care about him too much to see him coming home with fucking more black eyes.

I can't have Agent Shits following me, because I can't have Central knowing about the slip. If they learn it's possible to slide into an adjacent reality and return with powerful tech that doesn't exist here — fuck, they'll use it fast as they can. They'll use ME fast as they can. They'll keep me prisoner and send me between nows. My natural defenses against their magic have too many limits, they'll wear me into a zombie eventually. And then, who knows if they'd keep their greed in check enough to prevent all four nows from spontaneously combusting. Because spontaneous combustion's what happens when the realities mix too much.

Maybe Devi's an alt and doesn't know it.

Maybe Devi's an alt and good at lying about not knowing it.

Maybe Devi's bait sent to catch me.

Who the fuck knows — whatever it is, it's no good for me, or Flo, or Pumptown.

She doesn't want to be here. She doesn't even want to be in Krezletan, if we're to believe her story, which is missing all the facts. For all we know, she's working with Agent Schlitz and about to bring the full force of fucking Central Intelligence down on Flo and me, and what's left of our ragged little community here in the Pumptown arts district, maybe even infiltrate the workers' resistance, and I'm not going to see anything else go up in flames because SHE IS NOT ONE OF US.

Devi's got to go.

Florence doesn't say anything about Devi staying. It's like sophomore year in high school, when Mac slept over because his foster sibs set fire to his bed, and then he just never left. Flo's parents weren't really a mom and dad to Mac, but they didn't complain about feeding and housing him either, and providing best-friend's-family-style emotional support. So as far as Flo's concerned, this thing with Devi is paying it forward for Mac. Plus, Devi's not maths, so he doesn't figure Mac will care anyway. Ultimately, Mac's needs are pretty simple: maths, music, the occasional drug binge and stress fuck to unwind, and more maths.

On the other hand, Mac didn't come with an Agent from Central Intelligence lapping at his heels — at least not until he won the First Maths Competition. So there's a reason to kick Devi out. Central's been leaving Mac alone for the most part these days, but with two hot people in Flo's general proximity, and his lost connection with the resistance since Razza and the others died in the Millhouse Row fire, he's feeling awfully sweaty.

On the third hand, Florence doesn't think anyone should have to put up with an Agent from Central on their ass, so he plays dress-up with Devi while they search for something suitably femme that might slightly fit, and tests if she'd make good family. He likes the sound of her giggle as she hikes his tutu up to her chin and spins.

Flo's glad that Agent Schlitz interrogated him before he met

Devi. At first it was all punches in the eye, threatening postures, and endless questions about some girl and treason that made no sense. When the man made it clear he didn't like Florence's answers, he'd reached under Flo's jacket with both hands. Against Flo's skin, palms hot and rough, light glowed. Once, Flo would've chalked the effect up to fear and a concussion, but now he knows better. Whatever magic Schlitz has, he stopped asking questions and walked away muttering, "You really don't know anything, do you?"

Was the magic a truth test? Something creepier? Schlitz had interrogated him inside and out and gotten nothing, because at the time Flo had nothing to give. And since Schlitz isn't after Flo or Mac it turns out, and Flo's secret didn't get out, everyone should be reasonably safe for a while. So it's probably fine for Devi to stay.

Mac comes to Florence's doorway and leans on the frame. He's in what Flo thinks of as "gangster pose," shoulders square and arms folded over his chest like a shield for his heart, hands-in-gloves balled up beneath his armpits, squinty and sour. "Find her some clothes and get her the fuck out of here," Mac says.

"But you said you weren't going to turn me in!" Devi wails.

"Yeah. That's not the same as saying you could stay."

"But I have nowhere to go!"

"Find somewhere like the rest of us. This isn't fucking Central, and we're not the fucking working man superheroes of Resistance Radio. It's cold and hard and hungry and smells like the mills. Get used to it."

"Mac!" Florence strikes his own version of gangster pose. Mac's average height, and both men are slender, but Flo's got over six inches on his friend when he's drawn up tall, especially with the spiked-out hair. "What if Moms had said the same thing to you?"

"Hey now, that's not fucking fair." Mac spits on the floor. "I didn't have a fucking Agent Shits stinking up my ass when I came to stay with you. I wasn't bringing fucking danger to your family."

"Not until after you won First Maths." Flo's mad now. "And we didn't kick you out then."

"Yeah, well no one else in your household was wanted by Central either, Flo. If she stays here, we're all in danger. Not just her. You, too. You want more fucking black eyes from Agent-fucking-Schlitz? And me — is that what you fucking want, your best friend ever hauled off to fucking Central and disappeared?"

Flo flinches, thinking how he's in as much danger as Mac of being disappeared these days, but stands his ground on principle. "Maybe I'll need to rethink that whole 'best friend thing' if you're such a coward you can't nut up enough to keep a little girl off the street."

"I'm not a little girl," Devi snaps. "I'm only four years younger than you, and I'm the only one in this room who's ever had a real job, by the look of it."

"That's right," Mac says, "she's not a little girl. She's a fucking stranger from Central who for all we know was sent here as part of her 'real job' to find some way to haul me in, because it's not like she's been able to tell us any fucking coherent story as to how she's ended up here. Think about it, Florence. The colors don't fucking add up."

"I don't care why she's here!" Florence yells. "She's had some kind of really bad shit happen to her, and she'll open up when she can. You're so fucking hell-bent on your hate for Central and growing up poor you can't see the people who live there are human beings too, just like us! And it's not like you haven't been keeping secrets from me, mister-pot-kettle. Sometimes people have to keep secrets to protect themselves and their friends, you know."

"Don't you dare." Mac brings his hands down in fists, like he's itching for someone to punch. "Don't you fucking dare lecture me on fucking dealing with bad shit, or protecting each other. We have our own fucking bad shit to deal with, and most of it neither of us are ever gonna ever tell because it hurts too fucking much to say. Bringing her nose-deep into it isn't going to fucking help anyone."

"You wanna talk about our own fucking shit, Mac? Okay, let's talk about the Millhouse Row fire. Let's talk about how you haven't said a word to me about losing so many friends, about losing so much community."

"Like I was part of that community."

"You sure as fuck were. You were the goddamn computer for the chemical set differentials on the bands' synthesizers. You hung with me and Razza and the rest of us every fucking night. And even if you weren't friends with everyone in the collective — which you were — you're supposed to be my friend."

"I am your friend!"

"Some friend when you don't even show up to the funeral."

"Dead people don't fucking care who shows up to a funeral, they're fucking DEAD!"

"But live ones care! I care! Deny what happened all you want and fuck yourself up because of it, but you didn't even show up for those of us who are still alive!"

"Don't you go there, Florence." Mac's face goes red.

"Why not? I hurt, Mac, and maybe you're a macho asshole who doesn't care about his dead friends, but I don't think that's true. I think you hurt, too. I think you want to talk about it. I think we need to talk about what this means and what was lost. About how to keep it from happening again and where we go from here, because I'm fucking spitting fire I'm so mad about it!"

"Yeah? You ever think that maybe it's true, Flo, that I really am a macho asshole who doesn't care? Or maybe I do care, I care about protecting what's left so much I'm willing to make the hard shitty sacrifices to save us all, and that's why I'm saying to you right the fuck now, when I get back, Devi had better be fucking gone or I am. You might be mad enough to spit fire, but I'm man enough to turn on the sprinkler and put the death-trap out."

Mac stomps out in his heavy biker boots. Florence hears him crash all the way down the stairs.

Devi tosses a rude gesture in Mac's direction. "Wow. He really is an asshole."

"Hey now," Florence snaps as tears release down the sharp bones of his cheeks. "He's my fucking family, you don't get to call him that."

"You do."

"You're fucking right I do. You don't. And you don't get to have solidarity with Disinformation Deborah and the Pumptown workers until you've done a shift in the mills. The pirate broadcasts are by us, for us, not for you, not for Central wanna-bes. You're not family. You might become family, I'm willing to give it a try, but until you are, some fucking respect." Florence shows a fist, big paste jewel rings sparkling like ruby knuckles.

"Well you don't need to worry. I want nothing to do with you Pumptown losers. You're just as terrible as what I left." Devi begins yanking clothing out of every bin and corner and dresser drawer and holding it up, looking for something vaguely fitting to wear.

"Fine," Flo shouts.

"Fine," Devi yells.

Flo lights a cigarette and stomps out and down the stairs too, smoke swirling. Ten times around the block later, he's cooler. Devi's got no idea how things work on this side of the river; he's got to give her some slack for that. And everything is terrible, and everyone is hurting, and there's no way to make any of it right but wait for time and memory to dull the ache. But when he gets back, his room looks like an exploded wedding cake, and Devi's gone.

He hates being at odds with Mac. And he likes Devi, when she's not being an entitled brat. The problem is, Mac and Devi are too alike. They're both fucking stubborn-headed, pent-up assholes. *Why's it always up to me to be everyone's goddamn non-asshole peace-keeper Moms?* He kicks up a puff of boas and scarves. Then he sighs and heads back down the stairs. He doesn't even know which one of them he's looking for. He's just burning up over everyone always hurting.

Mac wedges himself into the angle where two buildings meet, just off 20th and Quatzlin. He barely fits into the tiny space anymore, but it's still where he runs when he needs to feel safe — the one place no one else knows about, and no one else has ever breached.

He'd first found it as a child, running away from home for the 49th time. Quakes or shells had opened a fifteen-and-a-half foot deep crevice, only visible from this vantage, exposing the ancient Roman city beneath: an otherwhen. Reachable, but not now. The marble ruins are overgrown with flowers. Or maybe the flowers were always there, and when the ancient soil was exposed to the toxic rain, they started blooming again.

> March 16, 1991.
> 11:55.
> Goddamn fucking Florence and his goddamn fucking big-heartedness, can't do what's fucking necessary to keep everybody and everything in FOUR FUCKING CONNECTED WORLDS safe.
> Well, it's not like Florence has an actual clue what's going on.
> It's not like he knows why someone's got to play the asshole.
> It's not like he knows the actual fucking stakes.
> Fuck.

No matter the season, something is blooming below, colorful, like numbers. In March now, it's crocus purple-and-green for spring among the creamy marble shards.

Purple-and-green. Aren't some numbers supposed to be purple-and-green but they're not?

"His name's Macintosh Carroll," Agent Schlitz says to Agent Schlitz over the twisted copper wires between pay phones. "He's on a watchlist because he's a First Maths winner. He's also classified as 'oppositional/defiant: last-resort recruitment only.'"

"Hm." Agent Schlitz runs through the implications that Agent Schlitz has already run through. "I've checked in with Mother. We've got no one meeting his specifications on record."

"Hm." Agent Schlitz runs through the implications of that new piece of information. "Interesting. So where does that leave us?"

"Still needing to bring Devi home. I'd say it changes nothing."

"Not even the fact that he can sit at the slipoint for hours without vomiting? Or that you say you can smell a Moiya virus on him?"

"We can worry about that later. Maybe he's taking anti-nausea pills. He's obviously not an alt since he doesn't exist in my now. If you can route Devi into a dead end — say the one on 19th and Quatzlin? — I can snap her up."

"That's a bit of a dangerous plan."

"Yes. But it'll work. She doesn't know about the slip. She's always been blindfolded when we've brought her through the slipoint before. She'll just think it's magic."

"Not our magic, surely. She knows our magic doesn't do that."

"Who says we don't have backup with us? And anyway, the reason she keeps evading us is because we keep going after her one-on-one. We're not using our assets."

Agent Schlitz feels his shoulders making that twitchy-shrug of agreement, tension release, and displeasure. "Just make sure you stay out of my eye-line."

"Don't worry. I know the First Law as well as you. I'll set up plenty of obstacles in the alley. Trust me."

Of course, Agent Schlitz does. He would set up plenty of very good obstacles himself.

Agent Schlitzes hang up and turn, shivering with excitement — and fear — to their destinations. They know they can't afford to lose anyone in this operation. Both themselves and Devi are too important to national security, across four worlds.

Mac looks at the purple and green flowers. Purple and green like nines and sixes and eights.

Wait.

Yellow-red and purple-green.

The error in time.

HOLY FUCKING GODDAMN SHITS

Agent Shits, that is.

That's the problem, that's the discrepancy in the timeline: IF Agent Shits was punching Florence in the eye at 22:05 last night AND Agent Shits was following me home from the church at 22:05 last night, THEN that means there are two Agent Shits.

Either they're evil twins, or they have fucking powerful body-splitting or illusionist magic, or one of them's from a different reachable now.

IF Devi's telling the truth about always ending up at the church, AND she's telling the truth about running away from her "job," THEN probability points to the greatest likelihood — out of a lot of even worse odds — of BOTH Agent Schlitz AND Devi being alts, and Devi really doesn't know it. But Schlitz certainly does.

Holy Schlitz, didn't I just say Central would take me as prisoner and magic me into a zombie and make me slip nows if they knew I could? And Schlitz, who knows the truth, handles Devi.

That's Devi's story. That makes the colors all add up.

Shit, she must be scared out of her fucking mind! I can't let her get forced back to Central. It's my worst nightmare, I can't let it happen to her, even if she is an entitled brat.

I never should've kicked her out.

Why did I kick her out?

Why the fuck did I kick her out?

Because I'm a fucking asshole and the last time I got close to an alt, I fell in love with her and was selfish and irresponsible and got her killed along with everyone else, when I should have been the one who died.

That's right. I should have been the one who died. Before I attenuated reality. Before I snuck secrets from one reality into another. Before I started things spontaneously combusting, and then just kept right on going even after I knew better. If I'd died then, every one of those thirty-six pulsing-purple-with-fire-underneath friends in the Millhouse Row squat, and the alt I loved, would all still be alive. Everyone's dead and I could have prevented it.

There. I goddamn said it. I wrote it all out into hard real words that make it realer than I want it to be. Except that it is. It is real.

I miss my dead friends.

I miss my live friends.

I miss the idea of ever having friends.

Fuck, why do I always end up goddamn crying? I'm fucking crying again like a fucking crying sissy, but I don't have to miss the people who aren't dead yet, right? I don't want to miss the people who aren't dead.

God, I love Flo, and I should've trusted him about Devi.

Fuck, Devi. I'd drown myself in the river before I'd let Central catch me and cage me and force me to slip nows. I'd drown myself in the fucking river.

Fuck.

FUCK

Go fix it, Mac. Self-pity's dumb. Make the numbers add up. Go fix what you've done.

Devi doesn't pay attention to where she's going; she just smacks her feet on the street and growls, the hood of Florence's too-big sweatshirt falling over her face like blinders. Puffs of stark white walls and bland meals punctuate bright gala dinners and stealing secrets and impossible memories of virtual reality and vampire kisses and other things that don't exist but somehow happened, and Agent Schlitz staring at her like a piece of meat, and the terrible guilt of all that she's been made to do for someone else's war. She was able to counter-magic and banish the memories, but not the feelings behind them. Disembodied feelings break against the dead ends of the city, the church, Mac Carroll, dead ends everywhere, all of it dead ends. *I will drown myself in the river. That's where I'll go, that's what I'll do. The church only drags me back to it when I try to leave the city, and it will keep dragging me back until I'm too tired to fight Schlitz anymore, but the river is at the city's center. I could make it there. I will leave on my own terms. I will leave as me.*

Florence spots Devi as she emerges from the crowd around the outdoor bins at Turkan's Fruit Market. She's slamming her feet in their thin, dirty sneakers into the broken cobbles and cracked concrete. Most of her is lost inside his too-big sweatshirt. *Sweetie, you were supposed to have put a decorative belt around that.* She's moving fast, almost at a run, and even his long legs are having a hard time keeping up without breaking into a jog. She turns west, toward the river.

Florence is just about to catch up to her when, at 17th and Quatzlin, Agent Schlitz pops out of a doorway and angles himself in front of her.

Devi yelps and takes off, away from Schlitz, heading away from the river now, toward 18th.

Florence, unnoticed, breaks into a run after them.

Agent Schlitz is confident in his ability to herd Devi in the correct direction. After all, his — and Agent Schlitz's — problem the past two weeks has never been finding her, given that his magic is in locating objects by touching where they've been and Schlitz has tracker viruses that do the same — it's been bagging her after she's found. As soon as either of them pause long enough to knock her out with a sleeping agent or a quick blow to the head, she flashes her illusionist magic and they're grabbing, instead, at air. It only takes a fraction of an inch of misdirection to miss her sleeve. He heads her off at 20th, forcing her between two older buildings and into the cobbled dead end.

Devi turns into the cobbled alley. She figures he'll try to trap her again, but she'll be ready like she always is, the moment they slow down enough for her to will her misdirection spell.

Agent Schlitz hears footsteps at the mouth of the alley and tenses, needle out to inject Devi as soon as she stumbles into his arms. There's nowhere else at the end of this alley for her to go, and she has no idea he's waiting for her.

Mac looks down from the fire escape of the squat on 20th and Quatzlin, trying not to notice how rotten the iron is.

He'd passed Agent Schlitz on his way back to the apartment. Schlitz had sniffed the air, and then stared at Mac's hand and raised a significant brow. That told Mac which reality Schlitz Number Two was from. Mac had given him a dirty look like he didn't know who he was other than a stiff from Central, and

walked on by. Then he climbed the fire escape on 18th and
Quatzlin and roof-hopped like one can only do in the oldest parts
of the city, until he reached his current vantage point, watching
Schlitz-from-Moiya positioning himself just so in the dead end
alley.

The setup is impressive in its precision, but then it would have
to be. There's an ancient, stone archway low over the mouth of the
alley, and that provides a little bit of cover. Then there's trash and
debris stacked up around the entry and piled deeper in — rotten
wood, sawdust, bits of the concrete outer walls that have flaked
off in chunks exposing the old stonework beneath — and all of
that cuts off visibility into the dead end even more. The way it's
heaped makes it likely to have accumulated naturally over time.
But then there's a line of laundry strung out between the buildings
and none of it looks clean, and there are large obstacles set up just
so. A dirty old mattress at exactly twenty-seven degrees. A turned-
over table at exactly eighty-seven degrees. Mustardy-colored
twenty-seven, and brown-with-sharp-green-edges eighty-seven.
The lines of sight in the alley are always interrupted so it's
impossible to see the end before reaching it — but there's a clear
path to run all the way through.

A trap.

Florence catches up to Devi and Schlitz, his palms glowing
with the prelude to fire, his rage finally having somewhere to go.
*That's right, you straight from Central, I have you now, I'm gonna burn
you up, someone's got to pay for all our hurt. No one will know; no one
is watching. It will just get blamed on the recent unexplained spontaneous human combustions and not even Devi will know any different.*
Flo's long legs take him past Schlitz, and he turns to face the man,
his body between Devi and the danger, palms up and out.

Schlitz curses, reaches into his coat.

Flo gathers his will, palms growing hotter, glowing brighter.

Devi stops, cries out, reverses direction to wedge herself between Florence and Schlitz, arms waving, "Florence, no, he's got

a gun!"

Florence tries to shove her out of the way but he can't touch her right now or he'll fry her. He could still take Schlitz, this instant, release the fire, the anger, sure, but he'd sear Devi too and — damn. Florence doesn't want to kill anyone, anyway.

He swallows the flame and shoves Devi back behind him, his body a shield. It's okay this way, too; Flo's magic has never been making things light on fire, anyway — at least not in the literal sense.

He grins wide at Schlitz and cocks his fist in its paste-jewel-ringed flaming-fashion-sense glory. Clocking Schlitz out cold is going to be immeasurably more satisfying to him than lighting him on fire, anyway. "This fucker's not getting his hands on you or me or Mac or any of us!"

Mac is looking at the numbers.

Mustardy twenty-seven and brown-with-green-edges thirty-seven. A bright yellow two degree slope to the alley. A webwork of vectors, all the colors of hidden numerical structures beneath the physical world.

The velocity of a running Devi, her speed given direction.

The velocity of a running Krezletan-Schlitz, slowing in brown-swirled-puce, indicating that he will stop at that particular mauve-streaked-golden point.

Moiya's Schlitz waiting at the end of the alley to catch Devi because I was a jerk and kicked her out.

Devi stopping. Florence stopping. Everything stopping just long enough for me to work the vectors out. That's right, that's good, buy me one more second, you two, and I'll have it.

Numbers in their vectors, pinks shot through with golds.

Mac has it, the timing, the placement, the way that the mattress is arranged to ensure that Moiya's Schlitz at the end of the alley can't see Krezletan's Schlitz at its mouth. As long as Devi and Florence stay where they are for three more seconds, two more sec—

Schlitz cocks his gun at Florence.

Devi flashes her magic. Only this time, she applies it to Florence instead of to herself. *That's right, Schlitz, look, there's Florence just left of where he really is. I'll eat your bullets instead of him, and then I will win.*

Mac jumps from his blue-gray and turquoise position on the fire escape, watching it turn orange in the calculus of his motion.

He comes down hard on the mustardy-twenty-seven degree mattress, flattening it down into a white zero, flattening it to the old cobbled alley, every calculation resolved.

Krezletan Agent Schlitz, meet Moiya Agent Schlitz. You've now got a perfect eye-line. First Rule's got you, fuckers!

Devi and Florence are blasted by a hot puff of air as both Schlitzes spontaneously combust in glorious light.

They look at each other. They look at each other's hands, at their own hands, back at each other's hands, at the ashes where there once were Schlitzes, and shake their heads. Florence looks at Mac sprawled out on the flattened old mattress. Mac looks dazed.

"WHAT THE ACTUAL FUCKING FUCK!" Florence screams, and grabs Mac by the jacket and shakes him. "Do you have fucking magic or something?"

"What? No!" Mac says through teeth that clatter in the shaking, or maybe from the maths, or maybe because of how much he loves Florence and how badly he wants Devi to be a friend he can confide in about the slip, and how he just did something terrible to do something good. "I'm sorry I kicked Devi out and was a jerk and killed all our friends on Millhouse Row. I miss them. I miss you. I miss us. It's all my fault; I could have prevented it, go ahead and hate me Flo, I mean it, I could've prevented it. I'm sorry I didn't tell you. I'm sorry for all of it." He sobs into Florence's chest.

"Shit, Mac, is that what's been bugging you? That because you knew about the flammable art supplies and faulty wiring or some shit, that it's your fault? Even if the fire was your fault, it wouldn't've been your fault that everyone died. The building was older than dirt and there weren't any fucking fire escapes. No one could get out. And anyway, that place was full of revolutionaries and Central was gonna take us down eventually. But we're still here, Mac — we're still here — we've got each other, and everyone else who's still alive, and it wasn't your fucking fault any more than a flood is a raindrop's fault."

Devi starts to move away, but Mac snags her wrist, and holds her there.

EPILOGUE

After Florence goes to bed, Mac creeps from his room and wakes Devi on the sofa. He puts his finger to his lips and pulls her, barefoot and clumsy in the expanse of Florence's pajamas, outside to the landing.

"The church is where the slipoint is," he tells Devi. "It's the point that connects four different worlds. If there's a set of people born to identical circumstances in all four worlds, the slipoint will attract them, and they can slip between realities. You've got sisters, Devi, and they're probably still under Central's thumb. And the two remaining Schlitzes, who can't slip anymore, they're gonna be pissed as fuck. Not to mention whoever Central's gonna send sniffing for you when Krezletan Schlitz doesn't make it back. The physics of the slip won't let you leave the city, but they'll be fine with you leaving Krezletan and hiding in Moiya, or any other version of the city that exists in the reachable nows."

Devi glowers. "We could've avoided a lot of mess if you'd told me that when I first asked."

Mac glowers back. "We could've avoided a lot of mess if you'd told me who you were and — what the fuck — instead of breathing down my neck behind the pews like a creeper." He stares sullenly at the angry cut stretching thumb-to-pinky across his palm. "You don't know yet how easy it is to fuck everything up."

Devi takes a deep breath and puts her chin on her knees. "How long have I got before someone comes looking for me, do you think?"

Mac shrugs and closes his fist over the reminder of his mistakes. "Dunno. All known variables considered, we've probably got a few days. After that, might as well flip a coin and guess it comes up tails."

Devi smiles sideways and dares to lean into what she figures is all the apology they'll give each other any time soon. "I'll take it. I could use a few days to get my head on properly without a tail."

Mac pretends to gag himself with a finger down his throat at the pun, but Devi sees his shoulders laughing.

The Vital Impetus of Location

Dora M Raymaker

SPACETIME!
i crawl the infinitude of nows.

i am the strange navigator
the way in
through
doorways
crossroads
LIMINAL I ZONES
en-
trances
entrancing
entranced by dancing
STARS!
☆
(see me rearrange spacetime because it isn't really there?)

i transit age and embers;
snake bites tail round to kindling
begin-again-endings—
it's all about finding your way

stating your coordinates.
Drawing a line in the sand.
Making an X on the spot.

Dropping anchor and mapping the edges of the information-
verse.

ha ha, ah, sorry, no, that is a human thing, those
namings,
shapings,
definings of boundaries that you put on me so then i spew—
one more
navigation in my co-
llection.
i, STRANGE NAVIGATOR, am not a human thing
despite the beliefs you put on me like conductors' uniforms
i will never be.
i am not your compass because there is no east or west.

i am your dream of flight
that gave you stars
that gave you wings

i am the distance between mountaintops and histories;
my feet straddle all of the thens that ever were
                                    (but none of those yet to be)
(for i am bound too, in my own way. immortal. amoral.
bodiless and connected to a body too far from human to translate.
yet bound by the same physics as you — we just navigate it differently.)

i settle at the prow of your ship
place my fingers inside your skull
map your curiosity
and spin 'round the chaos attractor until it takes form.

DORA M. RAYMAKER, PhD, *is a scientist, writer, multi-media artist, and activist whose work focuses on social justice, critical systems thinking, complexity, and the value of diversity. Dora is an Autistic/ queer/genderqueer person living in Portland Oregon, conducting community-engaged research at Portland State University, knitting fractals, and communing with the spirit of the City. Dora is the author of the novel* Hoshi and the Red City Circuit *and the short story* "Heat Producing Entities," *both available from Autonomous Press.*

Quasix's Doom Day

L. Rose Reed

THE FIRST PULSE OF PRECOGNITION hit me at precisely 3:33 AM UTC.

The precognition rang in my head as though I lay inside of a struck bell rather than in my blanket-nest. It propelled me into consciousness, clamoring, //NOW IS THE TIME TO PANIC.//

My arm feathers quivered to the head-song's beat. The yellow-orange scales on my arms, back, and thighs tightened like a moonflower hiding its tender core from the heat of the day. Even my Earthian features responded to the distinctly Gliesean phenomenon of the precog — the dark brown skin of my face, chest, and belly rippled with gooseflesh.

//PANIC AND DOOM,// insisted the precog.

It was louder than loud. Not even my first precog came close to its awesome, all-encompassing *volume*. It shrieked, bellowed, *boomed*—

—//MAYHEM DISASTER PANIC//—

—quickening my blood until remaining still became impossible.

Disentangling myself from the twists of my blankets, I rolled over onto the rug.

//MOVE GO RUN.//

Not the most useful instinct, with no way of knowing what to run *from*, or *to*. But I wasn't a frightened eight-year-old anymore, with the nearest Gliesean colony tens of millions of miles away — and Gliese itself farther still — and no one to guide me. Small-scale precognitions had taught me not to struggle *against* the alarm, like a wren trapped in the talons of a hawk. No, a precog was a mighty airstream — powerful, frightening, but navigable. All I had to do was angle the wings of my thoughts *just so*, and ride *with* the current.

My people haven't had wings for millennia, but there are other ways to fly.

Rather than pausing to dress for the day, or even to attach the anchors for my prosthetics to my leg stumps, I let the precog-panic roll me up to my nestroom door. The door slid open automatically with a pained, metallic squeak. I switched from a log-roll to an accordion-crawl, propped on my forearms and wiggling my pelvis.

Wings would've been more dignified, but I make do.

//DOOOOOOOM,// sounded the precog; this time, from the hollows of my bones.

"Hush, you," I muttered.

I didn't want it to hush, not really. Doom is just another word for fate — there is no stopping an implosion whose time has come. But, heeding a precog is the difference between an empty mineshaft and one with seven miners inside when its collapse comes due.

I would know.

So rather than lying face down in the doorway in exhausted defeat until */ / IMMINENT TERROR / /* passed, I proceeded into the kitchen-and-living space.

We lived in an iconic "Settler's Dome," my mother and me — cramped, but functional. While I was growing up, Mother used to say, "A room for you, a room for me, and a room for the both of us. What else could a body need?" which may have been true, but I knew that anyone who could afford a solar-plated, adobe, Earth-style *square* home upgraded as soon as they could.

Oh well. At least mother had covered the metal floors with colorful rugs; my prostheses weren't comfortable, and I preferred to crawl or roll while inside.

I headed for the kitchen, planted my hands on my barstool, swung myself up onto it, and switched on our countertop radio.

A precognition this big? Maybe, just maybe, would make the morning news.

But I'd forgotten the time. While the patch of sky visible through the dome's skylight was dusky-pink with dawn on Nausikaa, in UTC, it was not yet 4 AM. No rebroadcasts of Earth news at this hour. The Nausikkan local news report — *"Sunny skies, just the bittiest bit of cloud in high-atmo. Hey, been hankerin' for a hover? Just that kind of weather! Head on over to the Hilltop Hover Stop and rent yourself a board!"* — yielded no clues. I held my clipped talons pinched together over the radio interference, and then spread my fingers wide. The radio projected its 3-D ball of dots and numbers, radio towers and local asteroid times. At random, I chose the biggest dot — the asteroid belt's only dwarf planet, Ceres.

Although Ceres was not yet awake, either, the sound of the late night oldies station seemed to soothe the precog. It settled into a steady, insistent chant of //DOOM doom DOOM//like the bassline that threaded through the music and connected one song to the next.

Connections are important. There's a saying on Gliese — which I learned from a book — that roughly translates to, "There are no small things." A little coincidence, pausing just when a breeze ends or opening one's eyes just when daylight begins, a tree branch that sways into one's usual path — cosmically speaking, all happenstance has power. Has psychic significance. English doesn't capture the spiritual, almost dogmatic quality of the phrase.

So I kept listening.

And finally, *finally,* the late night DJ signed off, passing the torch to Del Gains.

Miz Gains gave her usual salutation, *"We got sunny skies! We're up, we fly. Good morning Astrodites,"* before launching into a basic description of the day's asteroid chart.

Okay… and I'm listening to Del's asteroid chart because…? I thought at the precog.

The precog only rattled and hummed. It was like standing too close to a giant festival speaker. Kind of painful and, well, useless.

"Well, would you look at that! Is that *my* child, up before noon? Must be someone else."

I jerked my eyes away from the hole that I was trying to glare into the radio to see my mother walking into the kitchen.

"Good morning, Mother," I said dutifully.

She headed straight for the refrigerator, asking, "What are you doing up already?"

"A precognition," I said.

She stilled, limned in refrigerator light.

"Oh," she said, her tone carefully neutral. "A biggie?"

//MAYHEM PANIC DOOM.//

I pondered how to translate this.

"A horrible future is imminent," I decided on.

Perhaps I should have gone with something more reassuring, given my history.

But, paradoxically, Mother relaxed. She returned to her morning survey of the fridge, saying, "Like when the McCormack's youngest — what's their name, again? Tih— Tee— Tierney! — cut all of their big sister's hair off?"

I frowned. "To Ophelia, losing her hair *was* the most horrible of fates. She isn't terribly imaginative."

"None of that, Quasix," Mother scolded. "In this household, we're kind to our neighbors."

I rolled my eyes. Psy-null as she was, Mother's own talent for extending gregariousness and receiving it in kind was formidable. I took after my other parent, who, as Mother described them, "would rather talk to a machine than a person."

"Yes, Mother," I said.

She shot me a knowing look, but "If you want something over than synth meat, best get it yourself" was all she said before letting the conversation drop as she began the arduous process of lighting our finicky gas stove.

I pulled myself up onto the counter and scooted to the toaster.

The toast popped up at the same moment as Miz Gains' voice was interrupted by the insistent triple chime which signaled breaking news.

I lost the third chime as the buzz of the precog rose to a feather-rattling shriek of //PANIC. NOW.//

No small things!! I yelped in response.

"Well, ya'll, we got a major solar event for ya, so local news'll just have to wait. Reports are ongoing, but here's what we know. At approximately 3:30 AM UTC—"

My stomach lurched like the moment of first flight — like when the tires of a carship leave the ground and for moments long as lifetimes it feels as though the driver's will alone keeps the craft airborne.

I turned the radio dial. The volume soared. Mother looked around from her frying pan at the sound.

"—a war criminal awaiting trial escaped from the Neptune Detention Center. Neptune Spaceport authorities haven't officially Ided the escaped prisoner, but word on public channels is that she's Tau-Ceti, she's got a ship, and she's dangerous. So stay alert! We'll keep ya'll updated."

Mother swatted my hip to nudge me away from the untouched toast. I slid back across the counter and dropped into my seat.

"Let the outer planets tend to their own problems," Mother said. "What would a Tau-Ceti want in the belt? Nuh, uh."

She patted my hand. I released it from the clench which drove my clipped talons painfully into my palm. I met her warm, if worried, brown eyes with a small half-smile of my own.

"I'm not worried," I lied.

Mother did *not* need to know that my precog, in all likelihood, involved a dangerous escaped Tau-Ceti prisoner.

Please don't be the mine all over again, I prayed. And then, for good measure, *Please don't be Luna.*

Although no sensation remained in my legs, cut off just above the knee, I imagined that they ached.

As Miz Gains yielded the airwaves to an ad for a warehouse on Amphitrite that specialized in baby clothes — *"for beings of all sizes and modes of locomotion!"* — Mother patted my cheek and said, "Stick to the asteroid charts, that's a dear. No major shifts, Del said, so flying should be a breeze."

My mouth opened in a soundless "O."

How could I have forgotten?

In all the commotion of the precog and its cosmic troubles, I had forgotten my own, garden-variety troubles. By the Earth standard calendar, I was sixteen years old. Today was the day of my final driving lesson.

With a watery smile Mother produced a jar of real, actual, blackberry jam, and said, "Happy birthday, chickadee. I know you'll do great."

I let my head drop with a *clunk* onto the counter.

//DOOM,// the precog agreed.

• • •

My mother, blissfully unburdened with psychic ancestral gifts, laughed at my melodrama.

After a sufficient amount of moping time, I lifted my head and dug into the blackberry jam with gusto, determined to enjoy my breakfast in case it was my last meal. There was no use in trying to run from fate. So, I would face it well-fed.

After breakfast, Mother went to her bedroom and came back with a large, wrapped box.

"Open it now," she said. The water returned to her smile with a vengeance.

The box contained a pair of custom made prostheses. They weren't state-of-the-art, by any stretch of the imagination, but they were new, and they were made to *my* measurements.

At my stunned expression, Mother said, "Good for land and space wear, auto-grav and auto-temp adjusting. Try them on!"

The package contained new leg anchors and cloths to go underneath them. Both fit better than anything I had ever worn.

"Can we afford this?" I asked, not wanting to know the answer.

Mother grinned. "Never you mind about that. The deed is done. Go on!"

The legs attached smoothly, with no squeal of metal. When I stood on them, they felt heavy at first, but as I walked slow circuits around the kitchen, they synched to Nausikka's gravity as well as my weight and gait.

I looked down at my new legs — backwards-bent at the "knee," avian-style, feet human-shaped for shoes — rather than at Mother as I whispered, "Thank you."

Mother embraced me tightly for a long while.

But outside our door the day wore on, while inside me the precog urged me to take my new feet and go onward toward *//CHAOS UNQUANTIFIED,//* so I pulled back.

"I have to go," I said.

I dressed simply in sturdy blue coveralls to keep myself mobile, in case of piloting difficulties as well as precognitive ones. Then Mother insisted on fussing with my legs, "correcting" the sync.

Once she was finally satisfied, she produced two final birthday surprises. The first was one of my other parent's feathers, pink and gold as the noontime Nausikkan sky. A flight feather. A lump formed in my throat at the sight. The second was the long strip of blue gray cloth which had bound hers and my parent's forearms together at their wedding. With the cloth she tied my hair, so like her own, away from my face. She tucked the feather's quill securely between the cloth and my dark curls so that the feather lay flush against the back of my head, its top visible over my crown.

"For luck," she said. "So that we're both with you when you fly."

I swallowed down the lump in my throat enough to reply, "Today is not a fortuitous day, Mother."

Mother tucked an errant piece of hair behind my ear. "Fortune favors the brave, chickadee. Besides, Mr. Indigo will take good care of you. He was a stunt flyer, you know — flew with your parent in the war."

That was new information — Mother didn't talk about the war, and neither did my driving instructor, Mr. Indigo.

But Mother didn't share in precognition, couldn't recognize its infallibility.

I thought, *My parent would have understood doom and fate, had they lived.*

But all I said was, "I know, Mother."

• • •

The morning sun, filtered through Nausikka's atmo stabilizers, lent its pinkish light to rocky fields patched with blue-green grass, winked off of the metal and ceramics of tractors and irrigators, softened the hard edges of squat brick-and-plate buildings. Despite the gathering flood of psychic dread which urged me to hurry, I slowed. Here, a stubborn boulder in the middle of a field deserved appreciation. There, an errant Indian paintbrush in a bed of herbs. The bend and flex of new joints brought evenness to the tamped dirt of an old road. The strength of new legs reminded me that ground and sky alike ran through my blood.

In the fields, welling machines hummed pleasantly as they pulled water from the asteroid's core. Farmers spoke — mostly. A flock of migrant Eridanites cawed greetings to me as I passed, which I returned with a shrill cry.

Nausikka's single spaceport marked the crossroads of the asteroid's two major thoroughfares. I approached from the Plainsroad, which bisected the single, long valley in which most Nausikkans lived. The Hillsroad met the Plainsroad at the low point of the spaceport before stretching out in either direction to climb up into the mines and the terraced farms of the mountains.

As the spaceport loomed in my view, the precognition strengthened. Its foreign current grated against my body's natural electricity until even the joy of walking on my new legs gave way to the jittery anticipation of an oncoming storm.

I reached the little field around back of the port where generations of eager teenagers had earned their land licenses by spinning donuts in the dirt. But today was the day I would leave ground, so the battered carship with "STUDENT DRIVER" emblazoned across the sides waited at the runway's end.

Mr. Indigo, short and brown and perpetually grinning, leaned against the carship, waving.

//TERROR AND CHAOS,// shrieked the precog.

"Good morning, Mx. Janssen!" Mr. Indigo called. "You ready to blow this popsicle stand?"

The thought struck me then that I didn't want Mr. Indigo involved in what was to come. I wanted him here, on Nausikka, guiding nervous drivers through their first systems checks. I wanted him to loiter at the Martian diner on Stars Lane where my mother cooked, drinking root beer floats and slipping children coins for the ancient juke box with a wink as he had done for me on many a childhood evening.

So, in lieu of pleasantries, I said, "This outing is doomed."

"Hey, none of that!" said Mr. Indigo, flapping his hand in dismissal. "You're an excellent driver, Mx. Janssen, top of your class."

I sighed. No matter how I explained, psy-nulls like my mother and Mr. Indigo never seemed to understand. Still, I had to try.

"Fate cannot be changed. I just thought I should warn you. I'd tell you not to panic, but it's inevitable."

Mr. Indigo raised his eyebrow at me. He lifted the brim of his cap to scratch at his hairline before replying, "Are we talkin' a precog, here?"

I nodded.

He "hmm"ed noncommittally. His eyes flicked up to the feather visible over the top of my head before he un-leaned himself from the carship. He was shorter than me, now, and had to reach up to place his hand on my shoulder.

"I'll be with, you, Quasix. I have every confidence in your abilities. And if something goes wrong—"

"It will," I interrupted.

He continued as though I hadn't spoken, "—I'll be right there in the copilot's seat, backing you up. Okay?"

Though he still smiled, his eyes were serious. A product of Earth through and through he might be, but perhaps he understood more than I'd given him credit for.

"Mother said you flew with my parent. In the war," I said.

His mouth hitched up at the corner in a fond, sad smile.

"That's right. Sarax and I were squad mates."

My chest tightened in a way that had nothing to do with the precog. Mother almost always said "your parent" rather than calling them by name — perhaps to avoid the same ache.

Mr. Indigo continued, "Best damn pilot in the fleet. Saved my ass more than a few times, that's for sure."

And yet they died, and you lived.

But that was unkind. If my parent had been anything like the quiet, generous soul Mother had described, then they would have rejoiced in preserving the life of their friend above their own.

I chewed at my bottom lip, considering.

I'm not a pilot like you, Sarax, and I'll never be a soldier. But this, I can do.

"Okay," I said. "I'm ready to fly. As long as you don't tell me not to panic. It's annoying."

He laughed and patted my shoulder before stepping back.

"Just like we practiced," he said, indicating the carship with a broad sweep of his arm. "I've pre-booted and systems checked the car, so all you have to do is find the nearest asteroid with the sensors, input a course, and calculate our angle of ascent. I'll be double-checking your numbers, but honestly, you're a better mathematician than I am. So, panic all you like."

I smiled, just a little.

I'm listening, I said to the precog. *I'll get us home safe.*

//PANIC,// it warned.

Yeah, yeah.

• • •

I loved driving.

I loved the roll of the flatlands underneath my tires. I loved challenging the inertia of the mountain roads. I loved the feeling of oneness with the vehicle surrounding me, as though it was my own arm or leg.

But even more, I loved flight.

I had to grin through my terror as I gunned the accelerator and picked up speed. If anyone waiting in the spaceport looked out the window toward the training field and its single runway, they would have seen a trail of dust floating in my wake like a snaking dragon, the tiny student carship at its head, wings extended.

Holding my breath, I tugged the joysticks slightly toward me, so that the carship knew I intended to fly. The math I had entered into the computer would do the rest of the work of launching us up, up, until we ditched the atmosphere entirely and flung ourselves onto our intended trajectory.

Theoretically. I had only ever flown in atmo until now.

"Breathe, Mx. Janssen," Mr. Indigo said. "You're doing just

fine."

And for a few, shining, quiet moments, we were. My stomach swooped as we lifted off the ground, as our wings carried us into the sky before they retracted in preparation for spaceflight. We punched through a layer of thin, hazy clouds. The pink of the sky thinned into purple, then into nothingness.

As the "weightless" indicator light flicked on, I let out a whoop of joy.

That was when the alarm klaxon sounded.

//*DOOM AND MAYHEM,*// reminded the precog, unhelpfully.

I let go of the joysticks.

"I didn't do it!"

"Hands on the controls, Mx. Janssen," Mr. Indigo scolded, though absently, as he sat up from his usual slouch to squint at the numbers blaring across the viewer. "Those aren't local coordinates."

I gripped the joysticks a little too tightly as his fingers flicked across the viewer — a flat, invisible holographic sheet which lay between us and the windshield.

"*Course correction rejected,*" chirped the autopilot. "*Proceeding to N 036644783 by W 6459828 by D .0001.*"

"North by west by *down?*" I exclaimed. "The driver's manual said never to leave the elliptic disc!"

"It looks like we've been hacked," said Mr. Indigo in a tone which aimed for casual but missed the mark by light-years. He killed the alarm klaxon. The silence lay heavy across my nose and mouth. Or perhaps that was the precog.

"Who would hack *us?*" I asked.

No sensible being would have anticipated the carjacking of a piece of space-trash carship like ours, but although I was stiff with fear, I was unsurprised.

//*YES. ALL-ENCOMPASSING FEAR,*// the precog encouraged, as though I was only just now cottoning on.

Stars, please don't be the Tau-Ceti, I thought.

"I think it's the Tau-Ceti who escaped from Neptune this morning," I said.

"The who who *what*?" Mr. Indigo asked sharply.

It did not bode well for our chances that it was this information, rather than any foreknowledge of my precog or the carjacking itself, which caused a shift toward the panicked in Mr. Indigo's tone.

"You should really listen to the Ceres morning radio," I said. "If only for the asteroid charts."

"That woman's voice just annoys me," Mr. Indigo muttered. "She's so — *cheery*. A Tau-Ceti, huh? I wonder — but no."

He didn't elaborate. As we watched in silence, the carship bypassed merging onto an established solar-highway, forsaking space which was re-charted around the clock for an unknown course.

"I *told* you we were doomed," I whispered.

Mr. Indigo zoomed the coordinate map out to system view. "Looks like we're headed somewhere in the vicinity of Neptune. Good call, Mx. Janssen."

//*THE SEA IS TRECHEROUS*,// sing-songed the precog. //*SAILORS BEWARE.*//

We're not on *the sea*, I thought, annoyed. But the words struck a familiar chord in me.

"Mr. Indigo?" I said.

"Yes, Mx. Janssen?"

"I feel I should inform you that, as a half-Gliesean, my precognitive abilities aren't as refined as — as Sarax's were."

Mr. Indigo patted my knee, forgetful of its lack of sensation.

"Remember, I have every confidence in you, Quasix. I don't just mean driving."

"Even though I—" I cut myself off.

I didn't talk about my first precog. About my failure.

Mr. Indigo turned to face me, then, as fully as his grav-harness would allow.

"Quasix. I know this ain't no stunt-boat, and I'm no soldier, not anymore. But anything you're able to tell me will help me to get us home safe."

My immediate thought was, *That's my job*, but that was ridiculous. Mr. Indigo was the adult, and he *was* the soldier — the sailor — familiar with these waters.

Not. The. Sea, warred with, *you know what happens when you don't just roll with it. The sea, or the precog*, and with, *just let Mr. Indigo handle it — you're practically psy-null anyway*.

Releasing my fears in a too-quick rush, I blurted, "I know that you know that I let those miners die because everyone knows—"

"Quasix!" Mr. Indigo breaks in, shocked. "You were only a child—"

I barreled right over him. "—but I know now what I didn't know then. At least I think I do, no one ever taught me, but there's some amount of knowingness Glieseans are supposed to have and I *am* Gliesean, I *am*, if only halfway, and I think I know what I know, and—"

Mr. Indigo grabbed me by both my shoulders. "'Zix. Kiddo. Breathe."

I broke off, gasping.

Weakly, I said the words which filled my bones, even if they made no sense.

"It's a battle between pirates. No nations. No flags. Just cannons and the open sea."

Mr. Indigo blinked at me, uncomprehending.

I sniffled a little. He patted my head, feather and all. I was not reassured.

"Okay, 'Zix. Okay."

• • •

We flew. And flew. And flew.

I wished I had eaten more at breakfast. The entire jar of blackberry jam, for example.

• • •

Eventually Mr. Indigo unbuckled his grav-harness. He used the handholds on the walls, ceiling, and occasionally, floor, to swing himself through the no-grav, swimming laps around the cramped confines of the carship.

I watched this for an indeterminate amount of time, lazily, before rousing myself to join him.

• • •

Mr. Indigo slept. I didn't.

• • •

The proximity klaxon sounded. Both of us happened to be strapped back into our seats, at the time. Our heads snapped up to the viewer.

"Is that—?" I started.

"A ship graveyard," Mr. Indigo answered grimly. "No. Freaking. Way."

"What way?"

"Quasix, I know I promised not to tell you not to panic. But I know who hacked us, and I need you to try not to panic."

Before I could process this, the intercom buzzed to life.

"*A bit slow on the uptake, aren't you, Maurry? I hope you're not growing old on me. How tedious.*"

Mr. Indigo closed his eyes. He sighed, belly-deep. When he opened his eyes, they were filled with a worlds-weariness I had never seen before. And he was far from the only ex-soldier on Nausikka.

"Hello, Em," he said. "It's been awhile."

"*Indeed,*" the intercom voice agreed. Rather, it almost *purred,* like an unholy union between a cat and some ancient monster of the deep, deep sea. Smooth. Casual. Dangerous.

But rather than growing more frenetic, the precog stayed steady. Still skull-piercing in volume, but unbothered by the voice. *Interesting.*

The voice continued, "*When you get to my position, hitch up. Then I'll tell you what you need to know.*"

The intercom buzzed off into static.

Dreading the answer, I asked, "Who was that?"

"That," said Mr. Indigo, "was the most famous traitor in the history of the Tau-Ceti Empire, held as a war criminal by the Sol Interplanetary Confederacy at the Neptune Detention Center — until now, apparently."

At my blank look, he sighed, and added, "That was Em3nla the Scourge."

I flinched. My arm feathers, from flight to down, stood on end.

Every schoolchild in the Sol system knew of Em3nla the Scourge. Children watched old war-reels in fascination and disgust, learning of the atrocities committed by the Tau-Ceti Empire against the descendants of Earth and our allies in the Co-Way — the Coalition of the Free Peoples of the Milky Way.

Well, my class *started* the war-reel. But when the dry-voiced narrator reached the Attrition, and the destruction of Luna, we'd had to pause the film so that I could be escorted, sobbing, from the room, and sit in the nurse's office until Mother could come for me.

I was born on Luna. It was one of the soldiers under Em3nla's command who mutilated me as an infant. Sometimes I still imagined the soldier keeping my tiny, preserved feet in a box on Tau-Ceti, bringing them out for guests as a prized trophy of war.

I was one of the lucky ones. I lost my lower legs to infection, but I survived.

I didn't realize that I had succumbed to panic, but then Mr.

Indigo was unbuckling his grav-harness, kneeling in front of me
and gripping my shoulders with firm, steady hands. "You're okay,
'Zix, you're okay," he said, his voice like gravel and sanctuary.
"She's not going to hurt you. She went rogue, remember? I know
her. Your parents did, too. We flew together, her and Sarax and
me. She flew for our side, before the end, before the Outer Planets
took her in for trial. She's not going to hurt us."

I calmed as much as I was able. Then I pulled away and, not
meeting his eyes, said, "And yet, we are still in mortal peril."

"I don't doubt it," he said kindly.

//DOOM,// agreed the precog, petulantly.

During my panic attack, the carship had dipped below the
elliptic disc. We decelerated, then came to a stop amidst the twisted wreckages of tiny stunt fliers, of flagships as big as Nausikka,
all reduced to space trash and shoved out of sight and out of mind
after the war's end. We sidled up close not to a wreck, but to a
shiny, well maintained, standard one-person escape pod.

"Ah, I get it," said Mr. Indigo. "Can't get very far in that thing."
And, into the intercom. "I suppose you'll be joining us, then?"

"That might be best," Em3nla answered.

Even as I shook my head frantically, my thoughts were calm:
Can't get very far in a carship, either. Need a proper spaceship to get out
of the Sol system. What's she planning?

"Well, Mx. Janssen," Mr. Indigo said, affecting brightness,
"we're still technically on your lesson time. So — ready to practice
a hitch-up?"

"Hitch-ups aren't on the driver's test," I said. "I haven't read
that part of the manual yet."

"I'll walk you through it."

He met my eyes for a long moment until I nodded reluctantly
and unbuckled my grav-harness.

We tugged ourselves through the no-grav, handhold to handhold, until we reached the carship's space-doors, which I had
never used. Mr. Indigo was actually serious about me doing the

bulk of the work of the hitch-up: He talked me through deploying the cables and using the carship's pinchers to clip them to the escape pod's hitch. He only took over for the final few meters of towing the pod in so that our outer doors matched theirs, then had me push the button that formed a seal between us.

"I had better get my license for this," I muttered.

"Can't tell ya 'til the lesson's over," Mr. Indigo teased.

When the "Seal Successful" light blinked on, we pushed ourselves backward toward the ceiling and grabbed onto the handholds.

"You're good in no-grav," Mr. Indigo said, but he wasn't looking at me. He watched the space doors. To my bewilderment, he tugged on his shirt hem to straighten it, even though it hadn't been ironed in a decade, and took off his baseball cap.

I developed a sudden suspicion which was not assuaged by the precog's declaration of //*ALL BECOME LOST TO MAYHEM.*//

The doors opened. The figure of my childhood nightmares squidged into the carship like a queen entering her domain. Each of her eight limbs was tied into loops with soft yet piano-wire strong rope, to prevent their full extension. Still, her limbs rolled powerfully, tentacles popping imperiously on metal.

She was both more and less terrifying than I had imagined her — more, because a person's *aura* is difficult to imagine, and hers screamed *terror, blood, death.* But her aura wasn't what froze me in place, gape-jawed and more astonished than frightened.

Even my half-Earthian eyes could see that Em3nla the Scourge, mutilator and murderer of children, was heavily pregnant. If Tau-Ceti eggs bore any similarity to Gliesean ones, she could lay within the hour.

"Maurice Indigo," she greeted.

"Em," said Mr. Indigo shortly, jamming his cap back on his head. "What in the Six Sister Stars are you doing?"

Both of them ignored me, which suited me fine. I had to concentrate now on keeping my feathers from flaring as the precog's pulse quickened, zinging along my tendons and ligaments, filling the space between muscle and bone.

Six sisters, two sets of three, 3:33, I thought, somewhat hysterically. *No small things.*

"I could ask you the same," sniffed Em3nla, her cephalopodous scowl mirroring his mammalian one uncannily. "Living on a backward asteroid, flying only with *driving students.*"

I flinched. Her eyes flicked toward me momentarily, before dismissing me and refocusing on Mr. Indigo.

Mr. Indigo said, "We ain't all adrenaline junkies. So. How many?"

I thought he was asking, *How many eggs?* But then Em3nla sighed dramatically, and asked loftily, "Aren't you going to inquire after my health?"

An edge of hysteria crept into my thoughts. *Can he not tell?*

"Em-Threen-La," gritted Mr. Indigo.

She took her time settling herself onto the passengers' bench seat — which sat against the wall at right-angles from the copilot's seat — arranging her limbs with great care. Her suckers kept her in place without a grav-harness.

Mr. Indigo gave a frustrated huff, but followed suit, pulling himself forward and into the driver's seat.

I stayed where I was. I did not want to take copilot, preferring to keep Mr. Indigo between myself and Em3nla.

Finally, she answered, "Only three. No need to panic."

//YES PANIC. NEED. PANIC//

I blurted, "Three of what?"

Without missing a beat, she answered, "Why, assassins, dear. Nothing Maurry hasn't handled. Or does he not regale his students with war stories?"

Oh. Three. THREE. Assassins. Is that all? I thought, definitely hysterical.

"Do *not* tease Quasix, Em3nla, not about the war," Mr. Indigo said sharply. "They're Sarax's child."

"Yes, I know," said Em3nla. "With Creeletta Janssen."

My eyes widened. Mr. Indigo had said that my parents had known her, but to hear it from her own mouth was...

"Y-you. You knew my parents?" I whispered.

She didn't answer. Instead, she looked me up and down in a way that left me feeling exposed, like she was a med-scanner searching for imperfections. Her gaze lingered first on the stretch of prosthetic visible between the hem of my coveralls and my boots, then on the feather tucked into my hair.

She extended a tentacle. Mr. Indigo barked a warning "*Em3nla!*" but she ignored him. I held very, very still as she reached around the back of my head to touch not the feather, but the cloth which tied back my hair.

"I helped weave this," she murmured. "Creeletta *insisted* on a marriage cloth, but she was hopeless with a loom." She met my eyes. "There are no small things."

I shuddered. I did not return the adage, the words sticking in my throat.

She retracted her tentacle, her tone shifting back to sternness as she said to Mr. Indigo, "Well, by protecting me, you also protect Sarax and Creeletta's child."

"The child that *you* endangered!" Mr. Indigo snapped.

I was unclear whether he referred to the carjacking, the war, or both, but whatever the case, Em3nla did *not* take kindly to his accusation. She inflated menacingly.

"You would do well not to lecture *me* about endangering the family members of Creeletta Janssen, *Captain*."

At first I was terrified, watching tiny, scrappy Mr. Indigo launch a retort at a rapidly angering *Em3nla the Scourge* — the being who had indirectly cost me my legs, the moon I was born on, and my parent's life.

Then, their exchange began to feel familiar.

Mr. Indigo: "Cold-hearted, manipulative cephalopod—"

Em3nla: "Narrow-minded, hard-headed vertebrate—"

They were bickering. *Bickering,* like jilted teenagers breaking up and getting back together weekly over sodas and slices of pie at the Martian diner.

I floated in no-grav and surreality, just watching.

Then the precog flared.

//WHY ARE YOU NOT PANICKING HARD ENOUGH?//

"Um. Excuse me?" I ventured.

Neither of them acknowledged me.

I checked the viewer. In the gap between the ship graveyard and the elliptic, something moved. Not close enough to set off the proximity alarm, but headed our way.

"Mr. Indigo?" I tried again.

"Just a min', Quasix," he said.

//NO MINUTES. NOW. GO GO GO.//

Then Mr. Indigo launched into a series of creative insults about Em3nla's methods of locomotion, which, as a person with artificial legs, left *me* a little offended.

At least Em3nla had the excuse of pregnancy hormones for *her* behavior: Mr. Indigo should know better.

I pulled myself into the copilot's seat, now confident that even moving between them wouldn't shake their focus from each other—

—*If she hadn't been in prison for over a decade, I'd say* he *was the secondary parent*—

—and buckled the grav-harness with trembling talons. Taking deep breaths to steady myself, I pulled up the carship's course trajectory log. The panic urged me on, but I knew that here, I had to slow, had to be thorough, if I didn't want to crash us straight into a planet.

Or, into the blip — no, *two* blips, now — approaching us on the screen which, according to Em3nla, were probably assassins.

The driver's manual didn't cover outmaneuvering assassins!

//DOOOOOOOOOOOOOOOOOOOOM.//

Unhooking the hitch was easier than hooking it, and could be done from the copilot controls once I had disengaged the driver's. With a little bit of creative math, I coaxed the carship's old, weak sensors into course-correcting for the debris of the ship graveyard. *You're good at math, you're good at math,* I chanted to myself. Then, ignoring traffic updates which scrolled across the bottom of the viewer from Neptune's primary news station, I switched to the Ceres news, and Del Gains' newest asteroid chart. I corrected our return course for asteroid drift, double and triple-checking my numbers.

You're good at math, and you're an Astrodite.

Then, praying that I hadn't forgotten any variables, I grabbed the copilot joysticks and pushed them forward, *hard.*

The precog quieted, although it didn't disappear.

//MAYHEM AND PANIC,// it said.

"Better than doom," I answered aloud.

The jolt of sudden acceleration *finally* caught Mr. Indigo's and Em3nla's attention.

Em3nla gaped at the view-screen data. "What did you *do,* child?"

After squinting at the screen, Mr. Indigo let out a huff of laughter. "Look at us, Em. Lettin' assassins close in while we fight. Definitely getting old."

"Speak for yourself," Em3nla said. But unless I was imagining things, the expression on her face as she looked at Mr. Indigo was… *fond.* Even *affectionate.*

I didn't think I was imagining things. I wondered how long a Tau-Ceti could hold an egg. Longer than a Gliesean? Over a decade?

"Good job, 'Zix," said Mr. Indigo, ruffling my hair. "Rules be damned, I'm telling you now — I'm definitely recommending you for licensure."

Em3nla snorted.

Ignoring her, Mr. Indigo pointed at a string of numbers on the viewer which floated between our little dot and the dots moving after us. "See there? Whatever speed they're capable of, they're not catchin' us until—"

"The belt," I said.

"And ain't no assassin's gettin' the best of us Astrodites on our home turf."

• • •

On the return journey, Mr. Indigo insisted that I sleep. I curled up in the copilot's chair.

I woke once to the quiet murmur of conversation. Mr. Indigo sat next to Em3nla on the bench seat. They were close enough to touch. As I watched, Em3nla extended a cautious limb tip to Mr. Indigo's cheek.

I closed my eyes again.

• • •

Mr. Indigo woke me as we began our deceleration.

"Best buckle in." He re-engaged the primary driver controls. "Now, as good a copilot as you are, I think I'll handle our tails, hmm?"

As he gripped the joysticks, something like a predator's grin lit up his whole face.

"Pay attention, Sarax's child," Em3nla said into my ear, making me jump. "You could learn something."

At first, nothing happened. Mr. Indigo praised my calculations, and let them take us to the edge of the asteroid belt. Then, he disengaged the autopilot.

"What—?" I started.

"Shh," Em3nla said. "Let the man fly."

And fly, he did. Mr. Indigo decelerated faster than I thought possible in an ancient carship, and *dropped*. My harness kept me in my seat, but I would have bruises on my chest in the morning.

Our closest tail, despite their surely state-of-the art vessel, was unable to brake before a tiny hunk of space rock, too small even for inhabitants, cut into its path.

The resulting explosion was *spectacular.*

"They didn't name him a 'stunt flier' for nothing," Em3nla said.

Then, less than a second before Mr. Indigo noticed the third assassin which had been waiting for us in the belt, the precog howled, *//DESTRUCTION. DOOM.//*

"No, don't!" I squeaked.

At my warning, Mr. Indigo actually *took his hands off of the controls.* Rather than dodging the third assassin entirely, we took their volley of laser fire on our rear-right land tire. Nothing fatal, nothing that would keep us from landing.

"A little more warning, next time, Quasix, would be nice," Mr. Indigo gritted out.

But I was too elated to take the criticism. I was floating, lighter than light, the precog nearly non-existent now, just a small hum running up and down my spine.

That was it, I thought — relieved, euphoric, overjoyed. *I did it.*

• • •

I wouldn't learn what "it" was until later, a span of time less than an Earth day but which felt like a lifetime, as I sat on the edge of a hospital bed with a newly hatched infant cradled in my arms. By the window, Mother would hold the second. The proud new father would cradle the third and gaze into their tiny face with awe. On the radio, Del Gains would say, *"Experts tell us that no inhabited asteroids were affected by laser fire, asteroid drift, or space debris. Thank the stars! More than a pinch of luck with us, and no life lost,"* and I would smile down at the baby, and I would *know,* and I would never tell a soul.

• • •

Mr. Indigo wove our clunky old carship among the asteroids, closer to them than I would ever dare, like it was a state-of-the-art fight-flyer.

As the second assassin got caught in its own companion's laser fire, I said to Em3nla, feeling bold, "I see why you picked him."

"Yes, he *is* good at what he does," she said. "It's why I planned my breakout as I did."

At my curious look, she elaborated. "It took months, but I... *obtained* a live feed to his instruction schedule, so I would know when he was space-borne. He's the only pilot I know that can escape not one, but *three* highly trained Tau-Ceti assassins." She glanced at me sidelong, eyes again on my parent's feather. "Had Sarax lived, they would have been another such pilot."

My chest ached, but I didn't look away.

"The war cost me many things."

"I know. Believe me, child of Sarax, I know what I am responsible for. I would stay imprisoned indefinitely, awaiting trial, if not for—"

She was interrupted by the explosion of the final assassin and Mr. Indigo's wild laugh.

"Not an adrenaline junkie, hmm?" Em3nla teased, a sly smile softening her whole face.

Mr. Indigo grinned at her, his own affection clear. "Just pleased at a job well done, ma'am."

And yet, my precog still buzzed. Lowly, and almost pleasantly, sure. But it had not disappeared entirely.

"Will the Empire send more assassins after you?" I asked.

"Oh, those weren't Imperial ships," Em3nla said smugly. "Personal grudge, you see."

Mr. Indigo interrupted, although the majority of his attention remained on navigation. "The Empire wants nothing to do with us scrappy little nobodies at the mo'." He glanced askance at us and grinned wolfishly. "Still licking its wounds, see."

"Not that they would disapprove if a freelancer took me out," Em3nla added. "But the window of opportunity to take advantage of the Outer Planets' confusion at my escape was small, and has now closed. It would not be wise for the Empire to further provoke the governments of this system."

Grin fading slightly, Mr. Indigo asked, "What's your game, Em? Why now?"

Em3nla's return grin was savage — quite in keeping with how I had always imagined the fearsome general.

"I'm sure I can find some trouble to cause. After leaving our children in your — well. Not *entirely* incapable hands."

"Our — *what?*" squawked Mr. Indigo.

Em3nla rolled her eyes, and said to me, "Humans. Or is it just men?"

"I wouldn't know," I said.

"Your *eggs*, Maurice," Em3nla said, her tone long-suffering. "I could only hide three, and only for so long, in the hope that I could deliver them safely in a system recovered from war."

Suddenly I understood. "You can't take them to Tau-Ceti. A traitor's children, they would—"

I broke off and looked down at the boots which encased replacement feet. Following my gaze, Em3nla nodded.

"Yes," she said. "Or worse."

"I don't—" said Mr. Indigo, dumbfounded.

Smirking, Em3nla replied, "Signal your local medical facility to prepare for an emergency landing. Our children will be born on your beloved asteroid. You will make a far better parent than I. Oh, don't look so panicked, dear. I'm sure Creeletta will give you a few pointers. She seems to have done well enough with Quasix, after all."

And then, Em3nla smiled sweetly at me. "You'll help out my Maurry, too, won't you, Quasix?"

My hair and feathers stood on end as my precog resurfaced:
//NOW IS THE TIME TO PANIC.//

L. ROSE REED *writes queer, modern fairytales. Her writings reflect her upbringing on classic rock, sci-fi/fantasy of every variety, and Colorado's unique magic. She currently lives in Aurora with two siblings-of-choice, three cat-nephews, and a porch garden which she regards as a proud dragon does her hoard.*

The End of the Line

Andrew J Lucas

Mining Platform orbiting CYGNUS X-1
Apparent gravity @ Schwarzschild Radius: 10^6 Earth normal
Altitude above Schwarzschild Radius: 400 meters
Crew Complement: 345
2245 AD

"SECURE THAT REEL!" ALEX SCREAMED at the riggers scrambling to tie down the wire spool rattling violently in its cradle. The spool's support frame groaned as it struggled to pull free of its base, causing the entire bay to shudder in sympathy. A team of welders set to work on the base of the cradle, hurriedly setting up their plasma torches, but they were too late. The entire assembly pulled free, grinding its way across the bay until it caught up against the edge of the mining station's gantry. Beyond this protective wall was the well, a 30 foot hole in the bottom of the station, and beyond that the gaping Maw of the event horizon of the singularity.

Alex snapped the protective cover off the emergency release and hammered the red button beneath. Explosive bolts locking the gimbal assembly blasted the reel free of its mooring and the reel pulled free of its frame and snaked over the gantry, catching at the edge in a shower of sparks. The reel skittered and bucked around the edge of the Maw, bouncing and spinning as the titanium thread it held spun off the casing and whipped into the empty space beyond. Where the atom thin thread touched the

gantry it cut deeply, ripping huge chunks out of the station's superstructure. After a second or two of this abuse the reel rebounded upward, pulling the entire spool assembly over the Maw's gap
and out of the station.

A few seconds later the structure hit CYGNUS X-1's event horizon. The singularity flared across its entire surface as the reel,
spool, and thread wrapped around the spool evaporated into the
hungry black hole.

Armoured doors slammed shut on the well's aperture, closing
off the view of the black hole — not that there was anything to see
now that the spool assembly had disappeared, taking with it a billion credits worth of monoatomic filament.

"Damn it!" Alex watched the status display on his control
panel slowly fade from eye searing crimson to a steady green. The
fiscal report for the station would be in the red for months. But
that was a concern for head office. He was more concerned for his
wildcatters who were stumbling to their feet on the smelting floor
below. He activated the communication circuit, patching himself
into the radio channel of the shift's environmental suits.

"Everyone okay down there?"

"Barely!" Keith, the assembly floor manager shouted back.

Alex's most trusted co-worker, Keith never let him get away
with anything. If Alex made a mistake, Keith wouldn't hesitate to
call him on it. It was part of what drew Alex to Keith. Working on
a mining station on the edge of nowhere attracted some pretty
rough individuals. Keith was no different. It had taken a few
months for Alex to realize that there was much more to Keith than
just a gruff assembly floor wrangler. Breaking though Keith's
rough exterior to find the true man beneath had taken the better
part of a year, but was well worth the effort.

"What the hell are you doing up there?" Keith wasn't one to
mince words. "You trying to kill us all?"

"Not unless I have to, Keith."

"Smart ass. You'd have a hard time finding a bunkmate who

would put up with your shit."

That brought a couple of guffaws from the roustabouts working the assembly floor. But Keith's attempt at levity had fallen short of breaking the tension and fear the team was feeling.

"All right, All right. Everyone report in."

The team responded one after the other, various states of anger, frustration and relief evident in their voices. Alex knew they were fine. Their suit monitors were all displaying active, if elevated, vital signs. If any of them had been pulled over the Maw and into the singularity there would be no vital signs to detect. Well, that wasn't entirely true; when an object passed beyond the event horizon it didn't cease to exist, we just stopped being able to detect it from this side of the event horizon. Beyond the event horizon, the object dropped towards the singularity, stretching in the grips of unimaginable tidal forces, spaghetified into a stream of matter before being absorbed into the black hole itself.

The journey was instantaneous from our point of reference, but the object was accelerating at relativistic speeds. The journey was both instantaneous and infinitely long. Time would stand still for anything dropped into the black hole, a terrifying fate, but one that Alex and the corporation made bank on.

A shrill horn blared from Alex's console and, while tempted to, he knew better than to ignore a call from the command centre.

"Smelting bay."

"What the hell is going on down there!" screamed a voice from the other end of the line. Maxwell, of course; he would be on duty. Bastard hated Alex and made every effort to make his life difficult. He would make sure that an accident like this would be laid squarely at Alex's doorstep.

"It's under control."

"Like it is. I've got indicators deep in the red up here."

"We've had an accident. It's contained. We — I have it under control."

"The entire Goddamn C Spool assembly is missing! You call

that under control?"

"I'll have a damage assessment within the hour. Smelter out."

"Don't you dare…"

Alex closed the connection. Normally such an action would result in a formal reprimand, but that really wasn't a concern, not when his career had already disappeared down the Maw as surely as Spool Assembly C had.

Alex shrugged into his environmental suit and headed into the smelting bay.

The smelting bay was home to some of mankind's most sophisticated equipment and uniquely situated to take advantage of a few of the fundamental qualities of the universe. CYGNUS X-1 was an intermediate sized black hole orbiting a largely unremarkable blue giant star six thousand light years from Earth. It was just the right size for enterprising men to manipulate the physical laws of the singularity and reality itself to their advantage. Station personnel rarely called the singularity by its full designation, preferring to call it simply the Maw.

It was dangerous nerve-wracking work, but men had always found opportunity within the jaws of calamity. From herding mastodons at spear point during the Pleistocene to a 20th century North Atlantic oil platform, or a 22nd century Kieper Belt farmer launching frozen comets back to Mars for processing, mankind still rode the edge of disaster in search of resources. When an opportunity arose and technology allowed, mankind naturally set up shop harnessing the immense power of the stars. It didn't matter if they were brightly burning like Earth's own or the collapsed husk of a star like CYGNUS X-1.

Alex walked across the smelting bay to survey each of the unique and complex pieces of equipment it contained. Any damage to the machines would set the station's quota back weeks, months, even years. The Quantum Entangler showed scarring on the surface where the monoatomic thread had cut into it — deep and ugly but fortunately it hadn't penetrated into the machine's shell or damaged the delicate mechanism. Still it would need recalibrating to ensure that it was still able to create a quantum link between individual atoms: delicate work and vital to the function of the smelter.

The Entangler took advantage of a phenomena called quantum entanglement, in which two atoms would reflect whatever happened to the other no matter the distance between the two. And that wasn't even the most esoteric piece of equipment on the station: that distinction belonged to the dark matter anchors. Dark matter permeated the entire universe. It was everywhere but was perversely unaffected by normal matter, energy, and most importantly — gravity. The anchors shielded the station and held it and its occupants safe from the ravenous singularity it orbited.

The smelting bay held four massive assembly spool units and the quantum entanglement unit, which fed titanium ingots into the black hole while the spools wound the ingots in their own hopper into indestructible threads. The quantumly entangled metal miraculously lengthened into a monatomic wire, which was then wound onto the massive reel. The tricky part of the process was that both entangled ingots had to be held in close proximity to the event horizon of the black hole. This required the use of sophisticated robotic arms, winches, and minute adjustments, as the units skimmed just above the Maw. One error, one slip of the arm and the result could be catastrophic.

He moved on to Spool B and stopped to examine a hopper filled with ingots of titanium imported from Earth. These ingots were waiting to be entangled atom to atom with identical ingots attached to Spool A. The assembly was an incredibly sensitive and delicate mechanism that used a robotic arm to feed microscopic slices of ingots into the Maw, where the immense gravitational force would stretch them into an atom-thin strand.

As the atom stream became nigh indestructible their sister atoms — entangled prior to being dipped into the Maw — mirrored their state at a quantum level. An ingot fed to the Maw from

Spool Assembly B became identical in nature and state to a second quantum entangled ingot in Spool Assembly C. It was unnerving to watch an otherwise unremarkable ingot of titanium spontaneously transform into a thread of indestructible wire, but Alex and his team had become used to the sight. The thread was then wound onto a reel for transport back to Earth where it would be woven into structures such as the Earth-to-Orbit elevator or the keels of the fleet — at least if it hadn't been sucked into the Maw.

Alex ran a hand along the armoured lip of the Smelting Assembly. Huge gouges scored the metal where the thread had cut into it as it snaked across it into the black hole and massive chunks of the gantry were missing, allowing Alex to see the empty darkness of the singularity beyond. It was sheer luck none of the workers had been killed. The thread had cut deep, its serrated edge sawing through the metal, carving off huge pie-shaped slivers. Most people believed the thread the station produced was stretched out to a single atom's thickness and rendered indestructible by the combination of the singularity's gravity and the quantum entanglement of the paired atoms, but such was not the case.

For the most part the thread was indestructible and a single squashed atom in diameter — but occasionally an atom which retained its original nature, not stretched and certainly not indestructible. Somehow one in a thousand atoms resisted the entanglement and maintained its original nature even though its paired atom descended through the Maw's event horizon. The engineers believed it to be a processing error with the entanglement, but the smelting teams believed otherwise. At a quantum level the atoms were identical, entangled so closely that what happened to one was mirrored by the other — except when it wasn't.

It was a conundrum that kept physicists up at night: Somehow the entanglement was not reflecting the effects of the singularity, which meant that the atoms falling into the Maw were unaffected by the singularity. Somehow the laws of quantum physics were being resisted by the two identical atoms and both retained their attachment to the universe as we knew and experienced it. They retained their intrinsic nature in spite of the destructive forces surrounding one of them.

Theologians sought truth from the phenomenon, believing that the essence of some things were unalterable, that they are protected by some ineffable force — God, perhaps. Alex didn't know about that, but he believed some things were meant to be.

The practical effect of the phenomena was that the indestructible thread was slightly bumpy where two atoms sat side by side, one compressed and locked in time, the other as ordinary as any of the other trillions and trillions of like atoms in the universe.

The bumpy thread had acted like a serrated band saw carving into the gantry. Here and there Alex saw the frayed ends of similar threads dangling about ripped gantry, evidence of Spool Assembly C's passage. All spacefaring structures were woven from the thread that Alex's station and others like it produced, but as evidenced by the damage, these structures were not invincible. Alex pulled one of the threads and was gratified to feel the tension. The structure was stable, the weave solid and unlikely to unravel. He looked closely at the thread, itself a rope-like weave of monoatomic strands impossible to see with the naked eye, but as a thin braid it was the building block of all modern technology.

Even with pieces missing, the gantry was solid beneath his palm, which was comforting but Alex knew the gantry though strong was little more than stage dressing compared to the station's real protective systems. It might stop the loose objects from slipping out of the smelting bay and down into the Maw itself, but it was the dark matter anchors beneath the station that negated the immense gravity of the black hole. If anything happened to them, it wouldn't take long for the singularity to consume the mining station and everyone aboard.

A light shudder vibrated through the gantry, setting the threadbare edge of the cut section quivering.

Something was wrong.

Alex rushed to a nearby equipment locker and began snapping an array of equipment to his suit. A welding/repair unit went on his belt, a diagnostic gauntlet slipped tight over his right forearm. Finally he stepped into a harness and tested the attached wire and reel assembly — his only protection from the Maw.

"Alex?" came a worried voice behind him.

Alex turned to face his shift foreman.

"Keith," he began, looking at his friend, trying to make out his face behind his mirrored, rad-shielded faceplate. He could make out, a hint of a furrowed brow, a thin line of pursed lips both radiating concern and perhaps a little bit of fear. Apparently he wasn't the only one to notice the thankfully still slight wobble in the station's attitude. "I have to."

"I know. I know."

Keith took the other end of the line and attached it to a grommet built into the lip of the gantry. He knew what Alex was about to do, how important it was and, more to the point, just how dangerous it was likely to be. Alex pulled on the line, satisfied by the slight elastic give then firm tension. He looked back and met his foreman's concerned gaze.

Keith had slid back his suit's partially mirrored radiation and glare shield. Alex noticed that Keith's eyes were wet, but the set of his jaw reflected grudging acceptance of the situation. Alex knew that look well, he'd seen it at every meeting he'd had to deliver unpalatable news to the shift. It inevitably preceded a verbal free-for-all, and Alex was preparing for just that when Keith smiled. It was a tense smile, filled with all the emotion he was struggling to hold back. He reached silently, squeezing Alex's forearm, and then closed his faceplate again, sealing off his emotions.

"Be safe."

Alex held his own emotions in check as he clambered over the gantry and, using his safety line, rappelled down to the armoured doors sealing the station from the Maw below. His onboard monitoring system warned him that his heart rate was elevating, but the sound of his own blood pounding in his ears made that obvious. He steadied himself, breathing deeply again and again until his breathing and heart slowed to something resembling normal.

Then the world fell away and the Maw was suddenly beneath him.

The Maw had long since consumed almost every object within reach of its ravenous gravitational field except for the smelting station and of course its sister star which was too far away to consume but not far enough to avoid the grip of the Maw's gravitational field. The station was situated forty five degrees off of the Maw's axis of rotation, allowing it to avoid being ripped apart by the massive streamers of plasma the Maw was sucking away from its sister star and into the plane of its accretion disk. Were the station to slip off of its stationary position a scant dozen kilometers above the Maw it would shredded by gases moving at near the speed of light or baked by radiation.

Of course either fate was nothing compared to what would happen if the station slipped in its orbit and impacted the black hole physically, which was why it was vital Alex examined the underside of the station immediately.

There was enough light from the Maw's companion sun and its own spiralling accretion disk that Alex could clearly see the underside of the station. His eye were drawn to the four massive bulges which housed the dark matter anchors. A ragged line of ripped and shredded armoured plating scored the surface of one of the anchors, revealing the delicate mechanism within.

"How does it look?" came Keith's voice over Alex's helmet radio, his voice thick with tension.

"It's bad Alex, very bad." A sickening drop punctuated Alex's words as his safety line suddenly slackened, dropping him a few feet before stopping his unexpected fall.

"Can you repair it?"

Alex considered the question. From his angle below the station he could see directly into the guts of the damaged anchor, where the spool assembly had slammed into the armoured bulge and where the superstructure had given way, allowing shrapnel to make its way into the delicate machinery, shredding one of-a-kind components as it did. As Alex watched, a small shower of components dropped out of the anchor slowly falling towards him in a thin cascade of spinning, sparkling metal.

He reached out a gauntleted hand, passing it through the flow of shredded machinery. The stream parted easily, but continued unabated on its path towards the Maw. A few meters below where Alex dangled, the stream disappeared abruptly, accelerating nearly instantaneously to the singularity waiting patiently below.

The bubble of protection the dark matter anchors provided should have extended for kilometers, but it was now only a few meters below him. As he watched, the point where the stream of debris ended began to shorten. The bubble was shrinking. At this rate it would reach his position in minutes if not sooner.

"Keith! You have to evacuate the station."

"On it!"

Alex could hear a klaxon cut into the radio transmission, and above him armoured doors began retracting to expose the station's intersystem life rafts. He knew the evac drills inside and out. It would only take 3-4 minutes to evacuate the entire station. Would there be enough time, that was the question. He looked beneath him at the disappearing stream of mechanical debris. There was maybe half a metre between his feet and the end of the stream.

"Okay, we've begun. Get up here! I'll hold the last raft for you."

"No. You go, there's no time."

"Alex." Alex could hear the panic in his foreman's voice as clearly as the alarms in the background. "You can make it."

The end of the stream was just below his feet now and he could feel a subtle but distinct tug where his own safety line was being tugged at by the Maw, pulled past the shrinking bubble of dark matter which was negating the gravitational pull of the black hole. Tugged, then ripped into a stream of atoms to spend eternity falling towards the surface of an object that they would never reach, locked in time from the rest of the universe. It wouldn't be long before the edge of the bubble would be licking the soles of his feet.

"No, Keith. I can't." He knew Keith understood. Time and tide were forces neither of them could resist, nor outrun. "Go."

"Alex."

Alex cut the radio circuit. There was nothing more to say, they'd known each other for years and were far more than co-workers, they were friends, lovers. Alex released the clasp on his safety line and fell into the embrace of the singularity. His last thoughts on the cusp of the event horizon — two souls as entwined as theirs, would one protect and preserve the other?

"Let's find out."

• • •

2545

Keith looked out the view screen, marveling at the spectacle laid out before him. CYGNUS X-1 was still ravenously consuming any and all matter which came close, its broad accretion disk throwing light and radiation into the dark — a glowing buzz saw, cutting across the body of the black hole. Deadly but beautiful. Above and below the disk dozens of mining stations floated, just out of reach of the gas plume streaming away from the Maw's companion, like strings of pearls scattered across the darkness. Since the accident, many things had changed for Keith, but the greed of the corporations harvesting atoms from CYGNUS X-1 remained one of the few constants.

The number of mining facilities ringing the singularity had grown significantly since Keith had retired. Leaving had been bittersweet, but the galactic economy had shifted, and the stations he and Alex had worked had more in common with a twentieth century wildcat rig than these sterile, automated platforms.

One of the less important changes since Alex's accident.

Keith turned to the control panel of the interstellar excursion craft. The ship was a compact little vessel, just the right size for himself and a few companions. It pretty much ran itself, but his experience on the wilder edges of the galaxy had made Keith cautious. Especially here on the cusp of the singularity which had taken Alex.

Keith hadn't dwelt on what had happened those many years ago. He'd long since come to terms with what occurred both to Alex and to himself. He knew Alex hadn't felt any pain when he passed across the event horizon and into the embrace of the singularity. In many ways he hadn't yet passed across the Schwarzchild Radius and was still passing across it even though to the universe Keith was still a part of, he had vanished in an instant. An instant that Alex had spent the last three hundred years traversing.

Thinking about the quantum effects which gripped Alex always made his head hurt even after these many decades. Decades which had passed for Keith while the first second of Alex's journey to the core of the black hole had yet to pass. Time had stopped for Alex and the more unusual paradoxes of quantum theory necessitated that Alex would never impact, so intense was the time dilation.

For Keith's part, his life had ended along with Alex's. Their relationship was such that even apart, their thoughts had dwelt with the other, and Keith regretted each and every day that he'd been unable to avert the tragedy. But as much as he missed Alex, he had continued, he'd found employment on a second mining platform, years later becoming captain, then director and finally chairman of the corporation's board. He missed Alex each and every day, the days merging to weeks, then years, then decades, his hurt and love for Alex remaining as strong as that day.

As strong as he imagined Alex's love was for him — unchanging beyond the event horizon.

But time had advanced and Keith realized little by little, measure by measure, that he'd changed. His link to Alex was still strong years later. Years beyond, his health was unchanging, locked in, strong, fit, and not a single grey hair had turned, nor had his middle aged paunch set in, or the arthritis and heart disease which plagued his family. While the graduating class of 2237 sought out hip replacements and rejuvenation therapy, Keith was building his stock portfolio and perfecting his squash game. Mandatory retirement age came and went, and Keith simply changed profession.

Again and again.

His mind was a sharp as it had been that day so long ago when Alex had left, as was the hurt and loss. He had learnt to live with the loss and the hurt, each day the same, the absence unchanging, the hole in his heart as black and endless as the singularity which had taken Alex into its embrace, never to return him.

Once a year Keith visited CYGNUS X-1 and paid his respects.

Keith waved an arm through the ship's holographic control display, opening a small airlock just beyond the ship's control room, and propelling a small package into space. A stubby golden cylinder turned and spun into the void, rocketing into the black hole as gravity caught hold of it beyond the dark matter field of the ship. Within the ship, Keith held an identical cylinder and popped its hermetic seal. Foam bubbled out of the beer as he raised to the view screen saluting his lost, missed friend and soul mate.

He toyed with the idea, as he did every year, of simply cutting the dark matter drive and dropping beyond the event horizon and joining Alex on his dive through eternity. Perhaps one day he would, but until then he intended to see how long this magical entanglement would last. He was betting it would last as long as Alex and his love for each other lasted, no matter the distance, no matter the obstacles.

Keith took one final look at the black void which was CYGNUS X-1. It held something near to Keith and though it would never release him, Keith had never felt closer to Alex. It was a strange, yet comforting thought as Keith piloted his ship away from the black hole. He would be back here again next year, and the year after that, until their love waned, or the unique effects of their entanglement disappeared, or CYGNUS X-1 did.

• • •

Alex tumbled as the black hole pulled him past the event horizon with a grip stronger that anything still existing in the universe. Perhaps the only thing stronger was whatever hypothetical force had restrained the big bang which created the universe. The stars winked out slowly, very slowly and Alex's body felt numb as if he'd slept poorly and was waking. His mind was a haze of sensation and memory as his neurons struggled to push electrical pulses through his body.

His body was held tightly by the gravity surrounding him, penetrating him. The tidal forces of the singularity stripped his atoms into a spaghetified stream just as it had every other object passing across the event horizon. It stretched his body just as it stretched time itself. There was no pain, no fear; as the individual pinpricks of distant stars faded and went out, Alex still could see and feel.

He should have been compressed out of existence the moment he crossed the event horizon, smeared across its surface, ripped apart at a quantum level. A tickling sensation like water running down his body after a shower began in his scalp, passing from his head to his toes. He couldn't move, but his senses seemed independent of any flesh and blood. His focus moved, following the tingling. He watched his space suit, clothing and jewelry evaporate from his body and wash downward towards the black hole as a wave of undifferentiated atoms.

Then his body evaporated, layer by layer. Skin, organs, blood and bone all trickled away, until there was nothing left. He stared after the receding thread of atoms — his body. He felt no loss, he was beyond all that. Then there was nothing left except the blackness about him, his senses and his memories. He saw images, memories of his life, his childhood and the potential of his childhood. Every possibility of his life existed here, in his memories — and in this void falling between reality and the crushing singularity. In this instant between falling to his death and being ripped apart, he existed as mere potential, a mirage of life and life to be.

The moment lasted and stretched, the blackness and void playing tricks on Alex's consciousness. He saw the life of the universe he'd once existed within, an active participant, subject to its laws and rules — but no more. He'd been set aside, a toy discarded and done with, hidden within the shadows of a child's bedroom. The universe passed like a raging river before his eyes, aged and died and was reborn, massive, ponderous and overwhelming in scope. Alex's senses rebelled at the images, the sensations, his mind was everywhere, experiencing the entire universe as it died and was reborn. His grasp of time beyond this void failed him. He tried to anchor his thoughts, to find something, a single thing to hold onto to keep his sanity.

He focused his consciousness and found Keith.

In every universe marching from violent bright birth to the endless cold or crushing heat of their death, there was Keith. He felt his presence in each universe, a pinprick in the fabric of reality, existing for only a moment before extinguishing. In the next and the next he sought out that spark, anchoring his consciousness to his friend, his lover, his soulmate. Alex focused his thoughts to needle-like acuity, picking out the one singular being whose spirit he recognized as intimately as his own. Alex lived for a time in the instance of Keith's miniscule lifespan, drinking in the sensation of living again through Keith.

It was a strange sensation, being one with Keith, and Alex clung to it, dragging his lover's soul through the eons, before letting go only to find and grasp him in the next universe's incarnation. Again and again he held onto Keith as they both fell through eternity and deeper into the black hole. Life and the universe ended again and again. Each time Alex dragged Keith closer to the universe's end and rebirth, held without holding, dragged without touching, but always there — always.

Then it was over.

Alex's long fall through eternity had ended, his fall through countless realities, endless possibilities of universes, an infinity of potential. Within each, Alex had found his soulmate and clasped unchanging to him tight. Together they fell, separated by only one dimension of the myriad which made up the fabric of reality. The singularity stretched this fabric, stretched and compressed it until Alex finally impacted against the singularity and punched through. His consciousness finally dissipated, merging with the fledgling universe contained within the singularity — and passed beyond.

He was surrounded and bound by heat and pressure and possibility. Alex searched within and about him for Keith's essence, but he was alone. He probed further, piercing the bubble of infinite heat and pressure that contained him, and the universe exploded into being about him. He sought Keith the way had before, and in the seconds of creation, at the beginning of time, in this newly founded universe, he found him.

ANDREW J LUCAS has contributed to books published by Fasa, Dream Pod Nine, White Wolf Games and Atlas Games among others. His creative output is often blunted by his day job and the enthusiasm of his daughter in distracting him, he does manage to produce a few projects each year. Recently he has successfully sold stories magazines to an-

thologies such as A Bleak New World, Tales of Unseen Terror and Slumbering Horrors, Game Fiction Vol II, Starward Tales *and* Within Stranger Aeons. *Also in various stages of production are comic series coming from Antarctic Press, Splotch Comics and the soon to launch Cornerstone Creative Studios.*

Escape

Shadow

━━━━Wilf

"YOU'RE A GHOST, right?"

The question hangs in the air like dust throughout the desolate remains of Titan. It hangs amongst the meteors floating throughout the ruined space station. I readjust my mask, momentarily hiding what little is visible of my face. "I'm from Yol."

Vug crawls below me, seemingly unaffected by the lack of gravity, just as its presence never affects me. With his large grey-brown body, it would have been easy to mistake him for just more rubble if that lumpy stone that makes up his head didn't constantly crack open to reveal a rowless mass of amethyst teeth, like the inside of a geode, every time he chomps down on the surrounding debris. Two long crystals sprout out of his back that flash a seizure warning's worth of colors. Almost immediately the translator tied to the crystals pipes up, "That means you're a ghost, right, Helka?"

"That's, uh, a matter of debate." I say, before flying up to collect more meteors. I tag each one with a small sticker and press a button on the grav-stick. Gravity instantly connects and they fall to the ground with a clamor.

"Watch it!"

I apologize quickly, hoping to put the whole thing behind me, but before I can even reascend to grab the next batch, Vug's crystals flash again. "I don't care what scientists are debatin'. Why debate when we have a real life living breathing Yolian here that ain't living or breathing."

"You don't breathe either," I point out gently.

"Of course I don't, what do ya think they're paying us for?" Vug says before biting into the next hunk of debris. "Sit on our asses and suffocate?"

"To revitalize an abandoned station?"

"I was bein' rhetorical. So how'd ya do it?"

"Do what?"

"It."

"What?"

"You know," Vug says looking up from his meteorite. At least I think he's looking up. I'm not actually sure if Quarrians even have eyes. I've always been too afraid to ask. "How'd ya come back from the dead?"

I tag another couple meteors, moving between them as slowly as possible. Vug's not aggressive; if I just tell him to stop asking he might comply. But if he did get angry, well, I wouldn't want a two-ton Quarrian on me. "I don't know. Scientists are still debating."

"What a load of—" Vug's crystals turn an ugly shade of red that his translators decide not to pick up. "Ya just wanna keep the secret of immortality ta yaself."

Immortality? He really thinks this is immortality? What a sick joke! Oh if Vug could know all about what it's like to be me. To be haunted by words. To have "lived" on that sorry excuse for a planet. If I told him any of that he would not envy this half-life.

I say nothing.

Vug flashes red again and crunches into the meteor. With each snap, the debris break into pebbles falling between his amethyst teeth. Even those pebbles he scoops up and chews again until nothing's left. That's why Phoenix Corp. loves him. "If you're such a specimen of study, then how'd ya escape the Galliance's welcome wagon and end up here?"

I smile and say, "Just a bit of luck." And desperate pleading.

Vug's crystals flash red. "You ain't gonna tell me anything, are ya?"

"Oh, leave Helka alone," comes a voice from high above. I look up to see a metal cylinder blowing a light stream out of their four bottom jets, in order to descend. The top has four more jets, currently all pointed to the sides, one of which is on to push their body horizontally closer. The cylinder has two long arms, one of which serves as a basic grasping claw. The other ends in a smaller blowtorch. The cylinder itself had a sound area, similar to Vug's translators, set below a camera lens that serves as the robot's eye.

"Hi, Viola," I say, happy for the interruption.

V.101A turns their bottom jets onto a low buzz to hover next to me. "Is this clod bothering you?"

"I was just asking a question," comes the half muttered sound of Vug's translators.

"Oh it's nothing. But what are you doing down here? I thought they had you on the last couple cracks."

"I just finished," says the robot. "I am currently 0.846 percent of my way through double checking to make sure the site is completely airtight, but so far it seems to hold up."

I nearly drop my grav-stick. "But that means—"

V.101A can't smile. They took this job to save up for an emoticon attachment, but so far no luck. Still their voice goes up an octave as they say, "The organics will be joining us soon."

"Great," says Vug's back as he's mid leg-deep in a meteorite, "Now they can chuck all these perfectly good rocks into space, and all for what? The sector's biggest casino?"

"They're not going to turn Titan into a casino," I say without realizing I'm speaking out loud. "It's going to be a colony, like the original builders used it for."

"That's improbable. There are not nearly enough floors or floor space for this to have been a colony." V.101A's flexible blow torch arm springs out of her side and creates a bubble of oxygen before lighting it. The tiny fire ball floats up, illuminating the recently sealed grey walls and hundreds of floating meteors and metal wreckage. Soon it becomes just a dot of light in an otherwise dark sky, until it extinguishes itself against the ceiling. The sky was once again starless. "Whoever the original builders were, they must've been gigantic."

"Or they were just full of as much hot air as you two." Vug looks up, amethyst smile radiating on his lumpy face.

V.101A sends another fireball at him. It doesn't hurt his exoskeleton at all but leads to another 0.1 clocks of whining how it almost hit his translators and how horrible that would've been.

Finally after another .02 clocks of groaning and silent work, Vug's crystals light up again, "You know it doesn't even matter who built Titan or what for. It's a hunk of space garbage now, owned by Phoenix Corp. And once they're done with it they're gonna sell it and all those relics we keep finding to the highest bidder for 20 times what they paid us to make it all pretty."

"Are you implying that you do not enjoy the benefits?" V.101A gestures her claw at one last bite left of what was once a meteorite.

"It's not that," Vug's back flashes as his head chews into it. "It's just the same with all those humanoids, ya know? They don't — Eww what the" — red flash — "is in my mouth?"

Vug spits out the meteor-chunk, grav-stick still intact. V.101A raises her arm to torch the half-dissolved mass but I get in her way. There's something shining inside the lougie. I run my thin fingers into the grey-brown gunk to pull out something glowing white — one of those flat rectangles. We've found some of these and ripped pieces of them before, usually with smudged half visible images on them. We're told to just chuck them out into space, but when I unfold this one I find a stunningly well preserved image of a female. She's not of any species I can name, but definitely humanoid. Her fur's white. Countless tails meander behind her and frame her fox-like head, caught mid-laugh. I turn the card and the image changes into text. V.101A's saying something about an ancient form of Galingo she can't decipher but to me it looks much clearer than any of those scratches The Galliance calls a writing system. It means Kahle. Her name is Kahle.

• • •

After the shift we report that the site is now airtight. The supervisor says that starting tomorrow we are to start assembling the airlock, and he will call the CEO and tell him to start sending ships over. He then finds that Vug was sneaking meteorites off the ship, so that the organics wouldn't throw them away. This leads to a rather long and awkward stop and search, considering that Vug's entire body is almost indistinguishable from a pile of boulders already. No one mentions the card I keep hidden between my forehead and my mask.

After that we return to our rooms. I float into the cramped white cubicle feeling more like a prisoner than an employee. V.101A's room is covered in photographs of other repair bots and news-splicings of her time back in the uprising. Vug's room is littered with crystals, vocal recordings of his family. He also keeps a stash of meteorites under the bed in case he gets hungry.

Mine's empty. I never had more than the Phoenix Corp. banner to liven the place up. At least until now. I take out the card and lean it against a lamp I never turn on. Light and dark are the same to my eyes. I take off my uniform but keep the mask on. I never take it off.

After that I sit on the bed and try not to think. I don't want to sleep. Most "natives" of the planet Yol do not dream as you dream. Their dreams are not collages of memories they've experienced, at least no memories of their time on Yol. Yolians dream of strange and exotic species on far off worlds with alien architecture. In their dreams they see the faces of people they've loved, people they've hated, and people whose features escape them in the dim sunless morning. Most Yolians aren't even able to remember their names or the names of the planets and species they see. Those that do find little commonality between each other's dreams. Each Yolian has their own individual world locked inside their heads. Worlds which may never have existed. Most Yolians try not to sleep. I dream not of worlds but of words. One word to be specific: Escape. This is the word that haunted me like the ghost that I fear I am. It chased me down the pseudo-cities. It pushed me towards and through the trials of the death cultists. It carried me on after my only friend faded. I had almost stopped believing it when my salvation fell from the sky.

Unwilling to let sleep torment me, I entertain myself with memories I at least know are real:

I wasn't sure just how long I could keep this up. The word, my mantra, the very thought that kept my sorry excuse for a body mobile rang in my head, again and again. "Escape, Escape, Escape." But it was weak now, like a desperate nagging from someone who knows their wish would never come true. I had traveled all across that miserable rock and seen it all. And what did it get? love and love lost. We only did this to find the world in Abelard's head, and now he's gone and I'm left with nothing but a word.

My body was more ethereal than it's ever been, and yet moving it felt like dragging a boulder along. I was coming apart, melting into puddle, just like Abelard before he faded. I collapsed on the ground. Even turning my head up to look at the stars one last time was all my body could muster.

The sun was cold and distant, hardly more than a star, and yet it had a new competitor in the sky. I squinted, wondering if the exhaustion was making me dizzy. There was a second sun in the sky. Not much more than a star itself, but definitely getting bigger. I thought back to the death cults, and the talk of the white light they were all running to. Was it running to me?

I laid against the dry Yolian rock and stared as the light became two, and then a long metal beast came into view behind the lights. It was the size of a building and it was coming right for me. I didn't move. It was mere luck when the thing landed a couple dozen metyards away.

Once again, I saw nothing but the old sky. The sound of a door opening broke the serenity. Thump. Thump. Thump. Something was hitting the ground and hitting it rapidly. Like the lights before, the sound too was growing closer. Three figures blocked my view of the stars. They looked nearly identical, all with two arms two legs, and a glass sphere instead of a mask around their heads. Inside were beaked faces, just like Abelard's mask. One reached down and pulled my arm.

"Its arms, are... attached to its head?" said one figure in a language I could swear I never heard before yet instantly understood.

"That's not the description we got," came another. "You sure we're on the right planet?"

"The description also called it a planet of ghosts," came a third, "but I doubt this thing's gonna throw furniture anytime soon."

"Who... are you?" I whispered, surprising myself by speaking their language.

All three figures screamed.

As they ran back out of sight I turned my eyes away from the stars to watch them flee to their ship. There was something written on the side of it.

Phoenix Corporation
Proud sponsor of the Galliance

I didn't know the word yet, but back then it meant escape.
Escape.
Escape!
ESCAPE!

I open my eyes. The clock flashes 12% at me. Still another five before I have to turn in for my next shift. I sigh and float off the bed. Instinctively I take the card from yesterday and look again. Kahle's smiling at me. Now that I've had time to clean it up, I can see all the little details. Her fur's not white but possesses all the colors of the rainbow if you tilted it just the right way. The tails especially flash blue and purple then green or all the colors of an aurora. Her arms are slender and in the perfect humanoid position. Her face curves towards a gently pointed muzzle.

I look up and find myself staring at an ugly rag in the mirror. I have no legs, just a mass of wispy purple tentacles the scientists who found me said were straight out of a pervert's fantasies. My torso is far too thin to be called a proper stomach or chest. I don't even have bones for my ugly purple skin to cling to; it just hangs there in the air like an old shirt. Maybe the stubs I have for shoulders are part of the clothes hanger. They don't do anything else — my thin arms come out of the side of my head. The only good thing about me is my mask. It's not even a real part of my body, but just something I woke up wearing. It has wispy sleeves for my arms, which feel like silk. The harsh lines of the canine skull cover my otherwise featureless face. Out of that boring purple orb, only my blue eyes shine through the mask.

I sigh, and decide now is as good a time as any to start trying to get that damn Phoenix Corp. uniform to stay on. 0.03 clocks and several knots in my sleeves later I am ready. The airlock system is complicated and while V.101A is not designed for it, she understands the system well enough and tells me what to do. Even with Vug's sabotages we still finish before the first ships start arriving.

They're huge, not nearly the size of Titan but big enough to dwarf our tiny airless vessel. The supervisor spends more and more time off ship, allowing us to raid the bar with paying swipes. Finally we get direct orders to install the air tanks. It is time.

The morning of, my crew and I stand ready at the entrance, in new uniforms the Supervisor gave us. Something about raising morale. Mine keeps falling off, Vug's already ripped his in three different places, and V.101A narrowly stopped their uniform from catching on fire. Fortunately they were allowed to keep the holes placed right where their camera eye is. I hold the forehead of my mask, feeling the edge of Kahle's info card still tucked away, as the shuttle doors we've finished repairing half a Luna ago open to the void beyond.

The Phoenix Corp. ships clamber around like hovering flies. Along with them are small pods, minuscule flecks upon the darkness descending like pollen to our open doors. They blow past us landing with a gentle thud, and open to reveal orange spacesuits, each one embroidered with a phoenix.

The suits come in all shapes and sizes. Some slither out of their pods, and then roll down the hall in their tube sock suits. Some hover, either on wings that glimmer under their force fields or jets that blow through the vacuum. Some crawl on any number between four to six to six hundred legs. But most simply raise themselves to their full bipedal heights and walk out. These bipeds move with the most grace, not caring if they step on the tentacles of others in this novel environment. They're meant to be here and the front of the makeshift hall is reserved for them.

One of these comes in a silver pod. His suit is not orange, but black with a glowing flame pattern radiating from it. His helmet is triangular, perhaps concealing a canine face. Where the Phoenix Corp. emblem was supposed to be was instead a single name — Ka Hoh.

We lead Mr. Hoh through the landing bay, past the airlock, and out into the first floor where we've been stacking seats all morning. We lead him through the middle lane and around the giant tanks on either side of the stage, where he walks up a back staircase to shake hands with our supervisor. He then walks forward to the assembled mass and presses a button on the side of his suit collar.

"My friends." His voice radiates not from any speakers but from within the suits of nearly a thousand organics. Even from behind the stage I can hear his muffled words played over themselves hundreds of times. "We are gathered here at what may be the greatest site of untapped potential this quadrant has ever known!"

A roar of reluctant applause.

"When we discovered this site, this slumbering titan five Sols ago, no one was quite sure what to do with it. Many among the Galliance, the Archipal included, wanted to seize this vast wealth and all its resources and hoard them on Atama Prime for the state. They wanted to keep this place a relic, a floating grave and to watch how the dust falls from one cavern to the next, all to study who may or may not have built it.

"Well, I have something to say to them. The aliens who built this place are nothing but ghosts. They are gone, they've been dead for millions and millions of Sols. They may have died long before Sol even ignited. We owe nothing to the dead. This world is for the living now.

"I told the Archipal my concerns and with time I was able to persuade her to let me reinvigorate this ruin and give it back to the people. Not as a floating tomb, but as the new Titan-sized hub of life throughout the Galliance. But before we can have life, we need air, so I say let it rip." My supervisor pulls a crank and one of the tanks open up.

"Great," beeps Vug's translators on my right as his head chows down on one last meteorite he's saved. "Now my rocks taste all moist."

"Improbable," V.101A buzzes. "This air is too dry to dampen much of anything."

Hundreds of the employees take off their suits, Mr. Hoh included. When he turns to the side I get a glimpse of his profile. I'm not sure what I expected, perhaps Kahle herself to take off that helmet, or at least one of the beaked people Abelard told me about in his dreams. Hoh looks nothing like that. He has a muzzle, yes, though you could also call it a snout, the nose is so flat. Teeth reach to touch his bent whiskers. He has only one eye set on his face, and I wonder briefly if his species even has any depth perception.

"This is great," Hoh continues. "The majority can breathe freely. But some still are wearing their suits. Don't worry, I never forget about the little guy. I know not everyone breathes oxygen, and I'm here to provide a safe space for all you carbon breathers as well. So once again, let it rip."

The supervisor goes over to pull the other lever. I don't see him do it, of course. By now I'm much more interested in V.101A's and Vug's bickering. Something about robots not being able to taste anything. I don't know. But what happens next grabs my full attention.

Vug starts chewing the air, like he's going to spit out another fossil. There's some green thing between his jagged purple teeth. He closes and opens again and it just gets bigger. He closes it again but the green blob starts forcing its way out of his mouth before carving a new hole into his head. Vug's crystals turn red, right before his head explodes.

What Vug's translators refused to vocalize is instead picked up by nearly a thousand screaming organics. Everywhere, all around the bay, green balls form in mid-air. They cling and dig into the walls we spent so long fixing. They cling and dig into people's suits, and on their faces. No one slithers, no one hovers, no one crawls, and no one walks. The entire mob runs to the double doors as a single entity. But it's too late, they are sealed in airtight.

"Have these things been here the entire time?" I scream.

"Probable." V.101A says in her same monotone voice, though the words fly out much quicker than normal. "Such creatures couldn't escape detection in such a small container, though a couple scattered around an entire space station, could theoretically survive unnoticed for thousands of Sols undete—."

V.101A stops dead when they notices the green stain forming on their claw. They bring their other arm to burn it off, reshaping the claw in the process to something unusable. V.101A doens't scream but turns their faceless cylinder to look at me. Without a word we take off.

The doors may be sealed right now but we still built them. We know exactly where the emergency release button is. The mob is blocking the way to their only hope of salvation, but perhaps we could push our way through. We have to. It's our only chance. V.101A takes the lead but they're slowing down. So far they've managed to ignite all the blobs that tried to get in their jets but now one was cracking their camera screen, no matter how much they tried to wipe it away. They fall behind me and then I hear a deafening clap of thunder followed by nothing but a persistent ringing in my non-existent ears and the old voice.

I watch V.101A's body rain down in utter silence, the flaming metal burning the moss around me. What would their last emoticon have been?

I should've never left Yol. If I had only faded before the ship came at least I could've died in peace. Now I'm stuck in the middle of mayhem, feeling more alone and naked than I've ever been. Something's missing. Something's not in my peripheral vision. I touch my bare face and freeze. Dying is one thing, but losing my mask is so much worse.

I bring my sleeve up to hide by bare face while searching the ground beneath the trampling feet. Finally I find my mask lying nose down on the very edge of the room. During the explosion, Kahle's card had fallen out and landed next to my mask. Both face me. That's when I see it. The curvature of her muzzle, the bend of her brow. The blueprints are all there, carved right into my skull-shaped mask. My mask is her. The mask I came into this world wearing looks just like her. I feel my naked mouth smile.

I finally found it. I found the world within my head. At long last I've returned to the place I was supposed to be escaping!

I feel a tickling sensation and look down. The green stuff, I remember it now; we called it the moss. It's trying to wrap itself into my ethereal tentacles but just can't hold on. This is what it looked like? It was so much scarier as a microscopic plague, then again everything looked different when we were titans. I'm safe for now but soon it will jump high enough to find purchase on my arms and face. I can feel it digging in already.

I look at the doomed souls around me and pick one face out of the crowd. Hoh is on the ground some metyards away, the moss breaking into muzzle as his nearly consumed limbs spasm beyond his control. He's pushing himself forward with one good arm, slowly crawling to the door. He's trying to escape. He's already dead and he's trying to escape.

I laugh.

The moss digs into my neck but it doesn't even muffle my laughter. Farewell, Titan. I'm escaping for now, but it won't be long before we meet again.

██████ "SHADOW" WILF *studies religion, history, and creative writing at Ursinus College. He hopes to go on to grad school in Folklore studies. When not studying ancient faiths or drawing his friends' D&D characters,* ██████ *can be found performing alongside other members of Ursinus's "Bearly Funny Improv." This is his first official publication and he is quite grateful for the opportunity. He hopes you enjoy his story and challenges you to visualize or even draw his characters.*

Something Within Us Which Is Always Surprised by Change

Verity Reynolds

Editors' note: This piece is set in the Non-Compliant Space universe after the events in Verity Reynolds' novel Nantais. *Look for its sequel,* Nahara, *upcoming from Autonomous Press.*

RICHARD HAYEK WAS NO NAVIGATOR, but he knew how to get to Strict Observance. Or he had when Strict Observance was still there.

He blinked at the view from the *Iseya*'s forward windows at the choking cloud of dust and asteroid fragments filling the orbit once occupied by the system's third planet.

I should be surprised. Why am I not surprised?

He felt his right hand editing the call command before he registered what it meant: Beneath his numb stare, his brain had already interpreted the ping and sizzle of rock fragments against the shield to mean nobody on Strict Observance was going to answer him. Not now, not ever again.

"Benedict-1892, this is the *Iseya*," he heard himself say. "We had docking clearance at Strict Observance-40321. Please advise." He managed to avoid making *please advise* sound like *what the actual fuck?*

An answer seemed unlikely at this point. The entire system had a much larger problem than his docking time.

But the comm indicator flicked green, and a sardonic voice

with an Alashkani accent filled the tiny bridge. "Whatever business you had, consider it canceled."

"What happened?" Hayek asked.

A chuckle, or maybe a sneeze. "War, ambassador."

He didn't bother to correct the controller. The ship's credentialing system disguised his voice along with its access codes; there was no reason for anyone planetside to think he wasn't the Niralan ambassador and twenty reasons not to tip them off. Reasons like *not getting shot.*

"Any chance their diplomatic team was off-world?" he asked.

A pause followed this, long enough to make Hayek frown at the comm circuits. "Just one of them. Minor functionary scheduled for a vacation on Atalanta. Their ship got mangled in the attack, but they launched a shuttle. Got the hell out of here as fast as they could."

"Which direction?" Hayek asked.

This time the laughter was unmistakable. "Toward UGR space."

Hayek cut the comm link and adjusted the *Iseya's* heading. Normally, a diplomatic shuttle wouldn't pose a significant challenge to find: they could only travel at sublight speeds, and their communications signature was unmistakable. But "toward UGR space" covered significant ground, and the shuttle's comm array might not even be functional. Its pilot might even have taken it offline. Hayek would have, in their position.

Not for the first time on this mission, he wished he were the ambassador. Koa had a knack for pulling needles out of haystacks.

He set the system for a broad-range scan and wedged himself into the ship's galley to acquire a cup of coffee. The *Iseya*, like its predecessor the *Saya*, had been built by Niralan engineers to Niralan specifications. For humans, those specifications could be summed up in one word: *cramped.*

Hayek knew why. Personal space was a hindrance to Niralans, who needed physical contact for communication, emotional regulation, and gods knew what else. And their homeworld didn't produce sufficient nutrition for the average Niralan to reach anything like Hayek's own hulking stature.

Still, he was glad no one else had invited themselves along on this trip. The ship's dimensions were manageable as long as he didn't have to deal with another person in his space.

He returned to the bridge and a beeping Scan console. The ship's sensors had picked up an automated distress signal, and its signature was unmistakably human.

Hayek set the coffee cup down and adjusted his course.

The shuttle drifted, its exterior lights dark; only its beeping distress call and a faint power signature indicated it was more than mere space junk. Scan indicated a biosign inside, complex enough to be human.

It wasn't a diplomatic shuttle. But it was a human ship. And out here, its occupant would either drift until they died or until they were vaporized by a military ship looking for a little target practice.

Hayek disliked both options. He towed the ship into the cargo hold.

Let's see who we got, he thought as the cargo hold's interior doors slid open. He resisted the urge to draw his sidearm, but he let his hand drift over it, just in case.

The shuttle's occupant had managed to get one of the doors partway open and was wedging themselves through it as Hayek approached. He watched this sharply: two legs, an arm, definitely human.

Then the pilot's head emerged, and Hayek staggered directly into a pillar.

The pilot was Meredith Cattrell.

It had been ten years since her death, but Hayek still remembered Meredith: the mass of auburn curls like a living thing atop her head, the piercing grey-green eyes that spoke of an intense passion and a biting wit.

Except he couldn't be seeing her now. He also remembered Meredith Cattrell's corpse.

He shouldn't have remembered Meredith Cattrell at all.

"You're not Niralan," the pilot said, in Meredith Cattrell's voice.

He recovered the presence of mind to reply. "Richard Hayek. You are—?"

"Arenah Laurence," the pilot said. "Just 'Laurence' is fine."

Arenah Laurence. The name rang a bell. He'd been there to talk to a Devori diplomat, Arenah Talior. Had Talior had a human spouse? Hayek's knowledge on the man was limited; Nahara hadn't even seen fit to include a photo in the scant report he had received.

He grasped the hand Laurence extended, shook it, his head screaming all the while: *what the fuck are you doing?*

"What are you doing out here?" Laurence asked. "More to the point, how did you find me?"

"It's a long story," Hayek said. "I'm looking for a member of the Devori diplomatic corps, an Arenah Talior."

"My husband," Laurence said. "He died in the attack."

"I'm sorry to hear that," Hayek said.

Laurence shrugged. "It hasn't really hit me yet. I was lucky to get out of there in one piece. What did you need him for?"

Hayek weighed his options. Laurence might be his best source of information. Laurence might be a massive security risk. Either way, he wasn't about to comm back to headquarters for advice this close to UGR space.

"Let's grab a drink," he said, "and I'll fill you in."

As Laurence occupied the bathroom, Hayek filled a second cup of coffee. On a whim, he added two sugars. He wondered how Laurence would respond.

Despite the risk, he found himself wishing he could talk to headquarters. The desire rebounded as he tried to push it away. It was futile, on several grounds. One, he didn't know where Dar was. Headquarters did, but he'd only blow her cover by attempting to contact her. Two, unlike Hayek, Dar did not remember Meredith Cattrell at all, despite the fact that, unlike Hayek, she should have.

Three, Dar was not speaking to him at the moment.

The absurdity of it made him want to laugh, or hit something. While Hayek couldn't have explained the science behind his current situation, he understood the gist: physical intimacy with Niralans tended to give humans the ability to read their emotional states. Somehow, Hayek had also picked up Dar's memories of her late wife.

Dar, who had been married to Meredith for over thirty years, didn't remember the woman at all. Hayek, who had met Meredith exactly twice (*once as a corpse*), couldn't forget her.

Laurence emerged from the bathroom. Hayek would have liked to know whether the diplomat's spouse was Meredith's sibling or perhaps a clone, but the question was too rude to ask.

"You did your homework," Laurence said as Hayek handed them the coffee cup.

"I — yes." Easier than the truth: *I have your ex-wife's memories of you. All thirty years of them. By the way, she doesn't even remember your name.*

"So," Laurence said, perching on one of the chairs in the dining space just outside the galley, "what business did you have with my late husband?"

That, at least, was a question Hayek was prepared to answer. He passed Laurence his omnipad. "We're looking for this man."

Laurence glanced at the omnipad for only a second before handing it back. "So is most of registered space."

He held the omnipad up. "Look again. That's not Aqharan Bereth."

Laurence leaned forward, frowning slightly. "A clone? Or — How old is this image?"

"It was taken last week," Hayek said.

"Definitely not Bereth, then. His son? Grandson?"

"We're not certain. That is, we're not sure how he reproduces, exactly — there's no record of him going about it in the way Reveni normally do." He impressed himself by saying this with a straight face. "But his UGR registry lists two heirs, and this is the other one."

"I can't say I've seen him," Laurence said. "Or his parent, for that matter."

Hayek frowned. "You can't say you've seen him because you haven't seen him, or because you have but you can't tell me that?"

"You *have* spent time with Niralans."

He laid his omnipad on the table between them. "So have you, by the sound of it," he said, knowing he was pushing boundaries and not caring.

Whatever hope he'd kindled with the comment turned to dread on the rebound as Laurence replied, "I met the previous ambassador once, early in my marriage to Talior. We did not speak the same language."

"Unsurprising," Hayek said, knowing full well he meant *disappointing.*

"Does this… person have a name?" Laurence asked, gesturing at the omnipad.

"His father calls him Jenereth," Hayek said, "but we've uncovered over two dozen aliases so far."

"Seems like he'd do something about the face."

Hayek hesitated. "There may be a reason he hasn't."

Laurence drained their coffee cup. Set it on the table. Leaned back in their chair. "And that's why you launched yourself into a war zone just to find my husband."

Something in the way they said this irked Hayek, made him think of one too many arguments over trivialities born of misaligned perspectives. "It didn't strike me as a humanitarian move to stuff refugees into the cargo hold of a Niralan ship," he said, "but if you want to head back for a fishing expedition, let's go."

Laurence looked taken aback for a moment, then laughed. Shrilly; too nervously. "That's not what I meant. Only that I doubt your sole reason for coming this far was to ask someone you've never met if they've seen someone else you've never met."

He wished he knew how to stay mad at Meredith. "We think he's behind the destruction of Solovor — and, now that I've seen it, of Strict Observance as well."

Laurence's eyes widened, and Hayek smiled internally. They weren't playing the game anymore; he'd managed to tell them something they didn't already know. He had the wild urge to call someone and report his victory.

"You can't be serious," Laurence said.

"It's a hypothesis."

"Solovor? Why would Aqharan Bereth's son destroy a UGR planet? It makes no sense."

"But asking your late husband did," Hayek said, "because he was there when it exploded, and he was at Strict Observance, too. And now here you are."

Laurence regarded Hayek too coolly for Hayek's comfort. "If you're accusing me—"

"—of living in the center of a series of unlikely coincidences, yes, I am," Hayek said. Few things had pissed Meredith off more than men speaking over her, and pissing her off worked better than surprising her when it came to the game. He remembered a night in a bar just outside the Interstellar Science officers' training school, a bar Hayek himself had never entered, and from which Meredith had been banned. A liter of sangria smashed on the tiles of a burbling fountain; Meredith's raised voice, then sudden silence as her fists spoke for her.

A surge of pride, not his, and the memory of wonder: Was this love?

He saw Laurence stiffen, saw the gray-green flash of their eyes, and knew he was on the right track.

Until they drew a deep breath, smiled, and said, "Well. I suppose that's fair." Their voice was bitter.

"I'm not accusing you of killing anyone," Hayek said. "Unless I should be."

Laurence looked pensive for a moment, then said: "Dalton."

"I'm sorry?"

"I know him as Brett Lancaster, Baron Dalton. Quite a lot of plastic surgery, makes him look almost human, but it's the same face under the added pigmentation and the eyelid work. And yes, he was on Solovor the evening before its demise. At a diplomatic function. He asked me to dance, and he made certain… insinuations about my gender."

"Like his ability to alter it with his genitals?" Hayek asked before he thought.

Fortunately, Laurence laughed. "You have spent *too long* among Niralans. Between us, I'd like to believe he died along with Solovor. But you're telling me that what happened on Strict Observance implies otherwise."

"It's possible," Hayek said.

Laurence paused. "Not to sound self-centered, but — do you think he was trying to kill my husband?"

The thought had not occurred to Hayek, though he couldn't say whether it had occurred to anyone who had sent him on this mission in the first place: Jiya never saw fit to give him the details and Dar, as he'd already been reminded once that day, was not talking to him at all.

Meredith would have taken a no as patronizing and a yes as a personal challenge. Hayek wasn't certain which option offered the better strategic advantage — assuming Laurence was Meredith. His head had doubts: Laurence possessed a calculating focus Meredith had lacked, and of course they didn't share a gender. But his heart told him they were more alike than different.

He decided to go with the truth. "I hadn't thought of it. But now that we're here, why would the UGR have a reason to kill you?"

Laurence smiled. "That's classified."

"I'm on your side, here."

Their laughter might have sounded genuine if Hayek didn't have thirty years of memories labeling it derisive. "A human, somehow entrusted with the Niralan ambassador's ship? You are on nobody's side, Mr. Hayek. You are *target practice.*"

Knowing it was true didn't make it hurt less.

"I can tell you this," Laurence said, sobering. "After I rejected Dalton's 'offer,' he excused himself from the festivities. I thought I'd merely punctured his ego, but his parting words.... He said, 'Normally I'd warn you to watch out for me. Instead I warn you to watch out for *us.*"

Hayek frowned. "Us?"

"Right? I have no idea who he means."

Hayek thought about this. "His father is the obvious choice, but even the UGR admits they don't know where he is. His sister disappeared before the war even began. Who is he working for?"

"I don't know," Laurence said. "But something tells me this isn't the mission you expected."

"I expected Strict Observance to exist, for one," Hayek said with the lilt of a joke. *And not to be plagued by memories of my ex-wife's ex-wife.*

The comm system beeped.

"That'll be Benedict's control network," Hayek said. "I assume you'll want to find your own people as soon as you can."

Laurence tapped their wrist against his omnipad, which chimed. "There's my info," she said. "I'll let you know if something comes up. Stay in touch."

Hayek turned his attention to navcom, scowling slightly. Meredith hated offers to "stay in touch."

In her hotel room on Benedict, Meredith Cattrell activated the omnipad she's purchased a few hours earlier and opened a secure datashell.

My love—

I've written this letter every night for ten years, knowing I can never send it, knowing I'll never stop writing it.

I owe you an explanation, and an apology.

I hurt you, and I'm so sorry. I never expect you to forgive me.

My love, I've never entirely been who you thought I was. For our entire marriage, I worked for — and reported to — an agency I can't name, tasked with maintaining order on a scale larger than you or I can or ought to comprehend.

They approached me after that night at Dominic's. That boy I knocked into the fountain turned out to be one of their best agents. Given their mission, I didn't feel as if I could say no.

I never asked you for a divorce because I wanted to leave you. I asked because I was ordered to sever all ties here and to tell no one why. All I could do was give you a reason to hate me in the hope that you'd find it easier to say goodbye.

I've never stopped thinking about you. Wishing you were here to give me advice, to share some perspective. To help me remember who I was. Who I am.

I hope you're happy, my love. I hope you're at peace. I hope you found someone who makes you feel as strong and safe and self-assured as you always made me feel, as your memory still does even when your presence can't.

I'll write this letter every night until I die or until we're together again.

Dar, I love you.

—Merri.

S. VERITY REYNOLDS is 30-50 feral hogs in a writer suit. The author of the Non-Compliant Space series, she blogs under a stolen identity at danialexis.net.

Hermitage

Bipul Banerjee

When emotions wither in winter
It is time to hibernate
Resonating disturbances of urban chaos
Mundane discourses of a mechanical life
Trade mill run of unending lusts
Churn whirlpools of expectations
Hurts
Hates
Miseries profound
Camouflaged desires presenting
Masked intentions
Fatigue of deliveries
Debility of burn outs
Fling me to a hermitage
Where my battered soul
Seeks asylum
A place to meditate
A spot to rejuvenate
To arrest the cancerous growth
Of toxic thoughts
Burn out the layers of insomniac outbursts
Clean the grease of towered ambitions
Restore the sparkles
On dusty panes
I am here to stay

Stay for a while
I know this is not a place forever
But a terminal
Where the laboured passenger
Can alight
Offload grumpy baggages
And move on
To yet another journey
That shall consume
The flame of spirituality
Lit for a while ....

BIPUL BANERJEE, *popularly known as "Dusk" in literary circles, is an Indian poet featured among 100 emerging poets of Asia. His poetry has been published in numerous international books and e-books, and he has been recognized as a featured artist by* PoetrySoup.com *(2016-17), St. Charles Artsfest gallery (Chicago, 2018), the* 13Alphabet *Magazine (2017-18), and was recognized as author of the year by* Story Mirror *(2018). He also has five research articles and two book chapters to his name.*

Sans Weight

Rosalind Wulf

MY MOTHER SMILED with cold, glistening teeth. Everyone told her she had such a pretty smile. When I smiled, just like she did, everyone thought it was scary.

She wrapped me and my brothers up in her lap when we were young. She would coo and sing to us. I didn't always know what to do when she did. Sometimes I just cried. Sometimes she cried too.

Sometimes, when my father would get off shift, she'd already be asleep.

I learned when I was older that she wasn't really drinking medicine out of those flasks.

Always too tired to really engage with me, father would set me up with a book. I learned before long that if I sat there laughing at the funny earth animals in the books for long enough, he would fall asleep. That's when I'd take the viewscreen from his belt, power it up, and delve into my first love. Oh, engineering schematics, where would I be without you?

I'd rock back and forth with the viewscreen before me, picture books cast to the side in a messy pile, and learn how the world that I lived in worked. By the time I was seven, I knew how our home ship propelled itself through space. In my opinion, I knew more about the warp drive than some ensigns.

I knew so much about the intricacies of my ship, but everyone aboard still wondered about me. The ship's physician would run test after test on me, but always came to the same cryptic conclusion.

"This is strange." He muttered under his mouse-like mustache.

My mother clutched me close, her fingers like an eagle's talons around the flesh of my arms. "Strange? What is it?"

"Well, that's the thing," he said, petting his mustache. "We don't really have a word for it anymore. I mean, we do. It's just been so long since we've recognized a case."

My mother clawed into my arm deeper, and I squirmed. "A case? A case of what?"

"Autism Spectrum Disorder."

Maybe I was just broken in certain aspects, like the doctor would go on to imply. Maybe I could have improved my social skills if I tried. I never really found out. I wasn't about to set myself up to fail by trying to socialize with people — people who probably didn't want to like me, and definitely didn't know the difference between the warp core and a warp conduit!

Sure, as we aged, they learned. But by the time that those 16-year-olds caught up with the 8-year-old me of the past, I was light years ahead of them again. And while it still didn't matter whether I went to my classes in uniform or my underwear — the ignoring and avoiding didn't change at all — some folks had actually noticed me.

I was on the zero-gravity deck, pulling loops through loops and yarn over hook as I honed my skills at crochet-sans-weight, when the entrance tunnel opened.

Before me floated the chief engineer. I tried to stand to a salute, but the nature of zero-gravity meant that I somersaulted my respect instead.

"At ease, Arla," Chief Engineer Tajiri said with a chuckle. He was so gregarious and charming. I envied him.

"Ah, yes, um, hello, yes—"

"At ease. As in, calm down. I'm not the Captain, you know." Tajiri shook his head, but smiled.

"But you're Chief Engineer of our great ship, and I am such a big—"

"Yes, I know. I read your paper on me. The one you wrote for the project on careers in the Galactic Fleet."

My face warmed from a blush, and I began winding the yarn from my project wildly around my fingers. "Oh, I'm sorry, I—"

"Let me cut to the chase. We've been watching your progress in school, as well as your extracurriculars."

"Extra—"

"We can tell that it's not your father downloading schematics to his viewscreen."

The blush drained from my cheeks. "I'm not — ah! I swear, it's just—"

"You're studying, we get it. That's why I'm here."

I blinked.

"You know, I was a lot like you. Very much so. I spent more time in my room, staring out at the stars, than anybody I knew." He bit his lip, looking to the near wall above him. "Didn't know many people, granted. Yeah, we're alike. And now I'm Chief Engineer aboard here. Do you catch my drift?"

I blinked again. I stared at him, and then slowly shook my head side to side.

"Oh, yeah, we're alike all right," he laughed. "Guess I can't do subtext with you. What would you say to shadowing me at work for a few days? Maybe a week? You could see what the job of Chief Engineer is like."

I stared at him again, this time in disbelief.

"Look, Arla. You've got some great knowledge under your belt, thanks to your ... extracurriculars. You clearly have an eye for detail, and you definitely have a passion. This could be a future for you, and I'd be honored to help you get to that future." He reached out in the zero gravity, and with some effort, grasped my shoulder.

I felt his hand's warmth through my uniform. "I — no, I mean, yes, I'd be honored. I'd be honored!"

He smiled, crow's feet wrinkling by his eyes. "Great. I've already asked for approval from your teachers. Starting Monday, report to Engineering at 0800. We'll see how the week goes, and take it from there."

As abruptly as he appeared, his form disappeared into the exit tunnel. I stared at that exact spot where he had been floating.

Shaking my head vigorously, I smiled. I flapped my hands and kicked out my legs, an impromptu dance of amazed excitement. Yarn flew in every direction, intermingling with my thoughts.

I reported to Engineering that Monday.

As it would happen, I reported to Engineering again, shortly after graduating at 18. I was a Night Shift Engineer. Months later, I was on day shift. After another year, I was put in charge of day shift.

I was watching the controls and screens like a hawk near the end of my shift one day, when a warm hand rested on my shoulder. I felt the gentle heat of another human radiate into my bones, but the comfort was cut short when I remembered that there was only one crew member willing to touch me.

I sputtered and nearly toppled backwards in my chair, my knuckles white as I gripped the console for stability. "Chief!"

"I've got news."

My eyes went wide. "What? What happened?"

"I'm stepping down as chief engineer. It'll be just as soon as you're ready to take over."

"You! You can't, you're — you're you, and… wait! Me? Who?"

"Ah. Never change, Arla. What do you say?"

"Me? Really? Well I can't possibly—"

Tajiri chuckled. "Of course you can't possibly, because you can definitely."

"No, no, I'm just—" broken. Wracked with social deficits. Never going to amount to anything. Never—

"Just the woman who can lead engineering. I've seen you

study. You haven't stopped for a day since I first noticed you."
Tajiri knelt down so that we were eye-level with each other. "Look,
if you've got one downside, it's that you're not confident in what
you know. You know this stuff! You know the ins and outs of this
system better than anyone, save for maybe the designers."

"Well, maybe. But confidence—" my mind wandered back to
my childhood. That was one of those traits, the ones I was forever
barred from. "Confidence is important in a leadership role."

"And you can be confident, Arla. You can demand respect
from your crew. I know you can. Hell, you're respected by the
crewmembers on your shift now."

I stared blankly. "No, they hardly speak to me. Unless they
need orders or have a question about something, we never talk."

"They're not your friends, no. But they do respect you. Heck,
doesn't that say something? They can't figure out how to chit-chat
with you, but they know damn well that they need to listen to
what you say."

I stared at my feet for a moment, letting myself absorb Tajiri's
words.

He kneeled there for a moment, before smiling and putting his
gentle hand on my shoulder again. "I know it's hard to believe in
yourself, sometimes. I've known about you since you were a little
girl, and — well. I know what you've gone through, let's say. So
— really. You don't have to believe in yourself to do this job. If it
helps, just believe me." He winked.

I blinked.

"Right. You can think about this for a while. There's no
need—"

"I'll do it."

For the first time since we properly met, I had startled him. He
straightened his collar and smiled. "That's the attitude." He
looked down, chuckling. "I knew you had it in you."

From the moment I made the agreement, up through Tajiri
stepping down and my first footsteps as Chief Engineer, I lived in

a fog.

When I finally stepped past the threshold into engineering and knew that it was my domain, the fog cleared. My heart fluttered alongside my fingertips, and it felt like I was in the zero-gravity chamber as my toes tapped the floor. The crew watched me descend towards the warp core's glow as a changed woman. You could pilot a ship through their wide eyes.

I had seen the warp core plenty of times, but now I felt like it saw me, like we saw each other. I considered that perhaps I did have a friend in this universe. As my hand glided along the edge of the control panel, I considered Tajiri's kind, crow's-feet-nested eyes.

I then believed that I had two friends.

Tajiri was correct, of course. I did not need friends to become Chief Engineer, nor would I gain any from the extra pips on my uniform. When I gave orders, they were followed swiftly and carefully, but the only respite I felt from the chill of the engineering room came from the warm glow of the warp core.

"Are you still at work, Chief?" Tajiri's voice echoed against the metal walls.

"Yeah."

"You know, this ship allows for leisure time."

"I know." I held my head in my hands. "The AI always wins at holosports, though."

"You can set them to easy, you know."

"I do."

Tajiri sighed, sitting down next to me. His dark hair had become so peppered with gray in the time that I'd known him. "Still not figured out the socializing thing, then?"

"I can't do it. I just can't." I turned to face him directly but averted my gaze for my own comfort. "Now more than ever, I'm not a candidate for friend. I'm their supervisor. I'm their chief."

"If you weren't off limits before, you are now, eh?"

"And I certainly was off limits then."

Tajiri furrowed his brow. "I know you crochet, yes?"

"Sans-weight, yeah."

"There's a few folks on board who do as well. You might have some common ground there."

I bit my lip. "They like to talk while they work. I prefer silence to gossip about the crew."

Tajiri stuck his thumbs in his belt, sighing. "Well. I guess I can't help you there. Ah, I'll be missing you."

"Missing me? Why?" I looked him in the eye.

"I'm retired. I'm not needed here," he said, "so I'm leaving tomorrow. Going to spend some time on Earth, maybe vacation around the galaxy some—"

"You're leaving?" I felt tears well in my eyes, but I fought them back.

"I wish I had a parting gift for you. I really enjoyed watching you grow. I considered myself your mentor, in a sense."

"I should have a gift for you. That's the custom."

"You've been a gift, yourself. You've let me know that this ship, her core, and her crew are in good hands. Don't worry about some purchased token."

"Tajiri—"

"I've got to go, now. Need to pack. Would you do me the honors of seeing me over the threshold, one last time?"

I wordlessly escorted him to the exit. He stood and looked at me.

"Well?" I whispered.

"I can't just walk away from a conversation with a high ranking officer."

"Right."

Tajiri's eyes twinkled. "Right."

"Dismissed."

Tajiri nodded and turned, walking down the corridor.

Tajiri did have a gift for me. His gift was dominion over the warp core, yes, but it was also that precious feeling of belonging somewhere. While he was on the ship, I was not alone.

The warp core also had a gift for me. A special one, shared between friends.

It came in the form of alarms whistling through my ears at 0300. It came in the form of a red line illuminating along the floor, begging me to follow it from my bed to the escape pods.

I ran the other way. I ran to the one friend I had on the ship. I skidded through the corridors, running counter-current to the sea of people trying to get off the ship, people desperately fleeing their lifelong home. My eyes were set forward, and yet, I swear I saw Tajiri in my vision, urging me on.

Crossing the threshold to engineering, I did not bounce on light feet. I scrambled past my station, right up to the warp core. I could see that slight change in its glow. The hissing grated at my ears. This shouldn't have been possible. It was supposed to last so much longer.

"Old friend, you—" I put my hand on the core's container, but yanked it back as the touch seared my flesh. A warm touch gone beyond.

I knew this warp core. I knew her birth, and I knew her long life. My lifetime of studying the core taught me how to solve the worst.

Then there was this.

Tears trickled down my face as I slowly crept my hand towards the core, stopping just before the heat became too much to bear. What was I without it? I'd been Chief Engineer of this ship for a few weeks at this point. What did I have without this core?

Tajiri, of course. I could count him as a friend. But he wasn't on board.

As the warp core ruptured, I told myself that he would understand.

I closed my eyes and awaited death. Perhaps the fact that I had a chance to react should have indicated something was amiss, but I opened my eyes shortly after. I looked at my hand before me. I suppose my hand wasn't there, actually, because all I could see was an outer glow. I turned my hand, examining it against the starry backdrop of the universe I called home.

"Am I dead?" I spoke soundlessly. Nobody knew what dead looked like, no. But at the same time, nobody knew what direct contact with a warp core breach did, either.

Color began to fill into the void of space. Before long, I stood — for some value of standing — in what appeared to be a city street on Earth. It had to be the past. The sun was too clear in a blue sky that was too clean. If breathing were possible, I would have liked to taste real, unfiltered air. Alas, seemed like the state I was in wouldn't allow this.

I looked around. People were marching through this city street. They approached me, they passed through me, they engulfed me. I listened to their chanting.

"Ho ho! Hey hey!" A woman with a megaphone cheered.

A man in a wheelchair rolled by, calling in unison with the crowd, "Autism is A-Okay!"

This structure of communication was interesting, but—

Autism?

My childhood, the doctor, the diagnosis he couldn't really give—

Autism?

Watching the scene, a ghost of the future, dead in the past. I watched how they moved, how they walked and rolled, how they gestured and smiled.

"Two, four, six, eight—"

I looked at my glowing limbs.

"Eradication is just hate!"

I watched the marcher's hands, their flaps and twirls. The clumsy gait that I found in myself, I also saw in some of their footsteps.

These were my people.

These were my people, fighting so that they could persevere

into my generation.

I suppose they did. I had been there, after all.

"Don't tell me you died, died with—"

Stars replaced the scene, blackness filling in the rest, but the darkness soon poured out again to show the gray rooms I was familiar with. Was I back already? Back on the ship?

No. It was my time, but this was not my ship. This was an older model. I could tell by the shape of the room — loving schematics had its uses — that this ship must have been about half a century older than mine, roughly.

This room was decorated in a way that made me believe it belonged to a young boy, and shortly after I arrived, a young boy stomped through the doorway.

"Come back!" An older woman's voice called, before being cut off by the door closing.

The boy sat on the bed, slumped over with his head in his hands. I heard him sniffling. His knees bobbed up and down as he cried.

The door opened, and a woman entered with delicate foot-steps.

"It's okay. It's okay, dear."

Choking out words, the boy replied, "But — the doctor—"

The woman hugged him. "It's okay. She said nothing was wrong."

"She said she didn't know what it was! She said it wasn't a thing anymore!"

Sighing, the woman stood up. "Well, you know, I think it doesn't really matter. You're a great kid, no matter what."

The boy shuddered, tears streaming down his face. "You just — don't — you don't get it."

Setting her lips in a firm line, the woman nodded. "I know. Okay, I'll give you some space, hmm?" She paused, waiting for a response she didn't get. "Alright. Good night, Nikko."

The woman left the room.

Nikko stared through the window in his room. "I just want to be something," he mumbled, "because everything else on this ship has a name for what it does." He idly opened a viewscreen, flipping through the display. "I'm just a broken part."

I eyed the name label on the viewscreen.

Nikko Tajiri.

I felt like I could cry. I probably couldn't cry. I probably couldn't do anything.

I stepped up to young Tajiri. In my ethereal state, I recalled the warmth of his hand on my shoulder.

Placing my hand on his shoulder, I smiled. I wondered, had he been able to see me, if he would have seen crow's feet crinkling by my eyes.

"You're not broken," I whispered, "and you're not alone."

I knew he couldn't hear me. I supposed it didn't matter.

I heard myself.

I felt false tears trickling down a cheek no longer there. They felt warm, somehow.

"Someday, you'll know that."

Pulling my hand away, I noticed his silence, and wondered if he really was entirely oblivious to my presence.

I smiled once more, before everything began to fade out, stars included. "Believe me."

I did.

ROSALIND WULF *is an author, artist, and possible changeling. She loves the fantastic, scientific and otherwise. Her hobbies include being Autistic, though she also dabbles in mental illness, and she enjoys writing on both.*

Letter to my Younger Dad

B. Allen

DADDY,

Our last conversation was an argument.

It was Tuesday, January 11, 1983, you wanted my opinion on the band Toto, and I told you I had never heard of them. You were insistent I had because they were big enough to warrant Grammy nominations, even though you hadn't heard of them either. But the voting members of the Recording Academy don't consult fifteen year olds with a disdain of Top 40 radio or their forty-four year old fathers, so Toto got nominated for Grammys in multiple categories. I interjected that if I had to pick an album that warranted a Grammy award for popular music, it would have been Joe Jackson's *Night and Day*, and you agreed. In normal times, this conversation would have been funny. It would have been another data point in the long timeline of us against the world moments. Instead, your voice got louder and sharper, and I raised my voice to match. We were agreeing, yet we were yelling at each other.

In the moment, it hurt that you could jump down my throat over something so petty. I didn't know then that it had been weeks since you stopped taking the medications you needed to survive. When it takes so much effort just to exist, it's difficult not to break when things as inconsequential as small talk don't play out as expected.

My last words to you were, "I'm not going to stand here and fight when we're both saying the same thing." I wanted to lash out. I felt my face flush and my ears burn with anger and resentment. Without you to protect me, I made so many compromises in order to survive the three years before you entered rehab. Now you had fifty weeks of sobriety, and I was living at home full time again. Part of me wanted you to understand everything I'd been through. Another part prayed you would never find out. But on your last day, I chose to walk away from that meaningless argument because repairing our connection meant more to me. While it's not a warm, happy memory, it's also not an ugly moment I regret. For that, I'm proud.

I know that feeling that you can never be enough. The shame of not living up to the lofty expectations set upon you. When your brother ended his life three years prior by stopping his meds, and no one dared call it suicide, the unthinkable turned into the feasible. The feasible turned into the only option. Then it was simply a matter of enduring the pain, playing out the clock so that your death could be plausibly attributed to the life insurance policy's definition of natural causes.

I understand the pull to just be done. Even now, with all the joy my life holds, it calls to me more often than not. The option to be done with constant physical pain, to never face failure again, is warm and seductive. It feels like safety. At times, only the knowledge of how my life played out with you gone has kept me tethered to this plane.

You needed someone like the person I became to teach you how to survive as the person you were. There's so much you don't know, and I can't go back and tell you.

I'm not going to be okay.

I know you had a plan. Your death was supposed to provide me with a solid future. But at fifteen, I am not loved and valued by anyone but you. Not only will the money not buy me security, I won't even see the money. There will be no college degree. Instead, there will be surgeries against my will, attempts to have me institutionalized, and a parent who views me as nothing but a burden.

You loved and trusted with an overwhelming intensity, but you miscalculated. That's not your fault. I'm not angry.

You are not a failure.

I know the family formula for success has been hold yourself to a higher standard than everyone else, but the formula is flawed. It results in a string of accomplishments that feel like failures. It sets you above the people you're fighting for, disconnected.

The pressure to be consistently extraordinary will crush you.

Afford yourself the same compassion you usually reserve for others.

Lowering expectations is not only acceptable, it's wise. There is a vast expanse between perfect and worthless. You don't need to be in the spotlight, particularly when the attention yields only exhaustion. You can lead from the middle. Let people work with you. Hold each other up.

This world is not built for people like us.

People say things they don't mean and mean things they don't say. You consistently held people to their stated ethics, and more often than not, they let you down. I wish you could have surrounded yourself with people who understood that the problem wasn't your naivety, but others' hypocrisy.

You were worth more alive than dead.

Tens of thousands in medical debt, the maxed out credit cards, the second and third mortgages, the leaking roof, the rotted dry-wall, the collapsed ceiling, all of that was fixed after you died. Mom got the house of her dreams. I got a car because I no longer had you to drive me home from school. I got a trust fund to pay for any university I chose, although I never saw a penny. Even if I had received the money as you intended, I would rather have had my father.

Independence is a fiction.

By the time I truly found my stride, I was only a couple years younger than you were when you died, and it only happened because I found someone who loved me as I am. Before that, I spent decades wanting to be more, do more, but I could not break out of survival mode all by myself. Humans need humans. That's not a weakness. That's how we're designed.

I miss you every day. We are as alike as you suspected. You have been my role model, my inspiration, and my cautionary tale.

I love you,
Bird

P. S. — You really would have hated Toto

Programmed to be a mid twentieth century housewife with a second wave feminist veneer, B. ALLEN gleefully disappoints. Since the 1980's, in venues ranging from indie weeklies to the Huffington Post, Allen has been writing highly personal stories of disability's intersection with poverty, feminism, queer culture, and abuse. Keyword searches to find B. include: autistic, chronic illness, intersex, parenting, transgender, and queer.

Time Traveling Blues 2: A Sestina
A Critique of Andrew M. Reichart's Time Traveling Blues

Andrew M. Reichart

This is a tale of the Summoner,
A tale of time traveling blues:
The sorrows of striving to change the world,
Trying not to believe in cursed destiny,
Striving (badly) to do right by Beth,
Trying and failing to guess the ways of fate.

Perilous are the ways of fate,
At least so insists the Summoner
Endlessly, to himself, to whoever will listen, mostly Beth,
Shoving her into her own singular Blues:
The sorrows of loving a man who believes in cursed destiny,
Stuck trying and failing to change the world.

What does this even mean, "change the world"?
The courage to strangle fate,
To conceive our own destiny?
Is it true we are each our own summoner,
Subject to blame for our own blues?
If you want a real answer, ask Beth.

Wouldn't this have gone so differently were Beth
The one trying to change the world?
Would we even have these time traveling blues?
Without his high-strung fear of fate,

How better might she have served as summoner,
Without his fever dream of cursed destiny?

But surely in a parallel cursed destiny
That timeline's freaker-outer's Beth:
Mad with dread at being the Summoner,
Desperate with hope to change the world,
Twisting in the face of her own fate,
Every bit as critical hit by Blues.

One might wonder if there's any escape from blues.
Whether or not there's such a curse as destiny,
Regardless of the factualness of fate.
Whether you or me or Max or Beth
Could ever hope to truly change the world,
No matter how godlike the Summoner.

Or perhaps there is no need for Summoner
To Change the world.
Better ask Beth.

ANDREW M. REICHART is managing editor of Argawarga Press, an imprint of Autonomous Press dedicated to genre fiction. He is co-author, with Nick Walker, of the epistolary science fiction novel Insurgent Otherworld *and the* Weird Luck *webcomic. He has also written four genre-blurring novels,* Wallflower Assassin, *available in an illustrated edition from Argawarga Press, and the* City *of the* Watcher *trilogy, which will be re-released in a single illustrated volume in 2020. For his day job Andrew helps run a small utopian tech firm, and he is also an activist with a grassroots abolitionist project. He lives in California with his wife and a couple of dogs.*

Made in the USA
Middletown, DE
15 February 2020